COMING UNGLUED

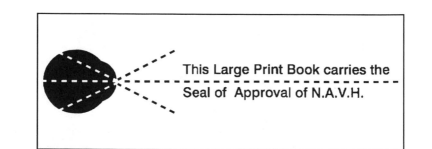

This Large Print Book carries the
Seal of Approval of N.A.V.H.

SISTERS, INK, BOOK 2

COMING UNGLUED

A SISTERS, INK NOVEL

REBECA SEITZ

THORNDIKE PRESS
A part of Gale, Cengage Learning

GALE
CENGAGE Learning

Detroit • New York • San Francisco • New Haven, Conn • Waterville, Maine • London

GALE
CENGAGE Learning

LIBRARY OF CONGRESS CATALOGING-IN-PUBLICATION DATA

Seitz, Rebeca
    Coming unglued : a sisters, ink novel / by Rebeca Seitz. — Large print ed.
       p. cm. — (Thorndike Press large print Christian fiction)
    Originally published: Nashville : B&H Pub., 2008.
    ISBN-13: 978-1-4104-1519-6 (alk. paper)
    ISBN-10: 1-4104-1519-8 (alk. paper)
    1. Scrapbook journaling—Fiction. 2. Large type books. I. Title.
PS3553.O225C66 2009
813'.54—dc22
                              2009000795

Published in 2009 by arrangement with Riggings International Rights Services, Inc.

Printed in the United States of America
1 2 3 4 5 6 7 13 12 11 10 09

For my husband, Charlie, who prays me through life's difficulties and calls down God's peace into our life. I love you.

ACKNOWLEDGMENTS

Writing a story about betrayal and forgiveness is an extremely difficult and exhausting undertaking. Through conversations with friends and family members while writing this book, I learned just how prevalent betrayal is in our culture — and how destructive it can be. I also saw, though, the power of forgiveness to break a cycle of betrayal and bring beauty where sorrow stood.

For that lesson, I am grateful and renewed.

And, so, I'd like to thank each of you who had a hand in helping me write this story — from the technical aspects to the emotional portions. My sincere gratitude goes to:

Karen Ball, an editor who cares enough to invest herself in these stories and grow me as a writer. I love God's presence in your life, Karen, and how you let the rest of us see the ways He works in you. You're a teacher without equal. I am incredibly honored to call you sister and friend.

John and Marinilda Leatherman, a couple who embody God's living love in a marriage. Mari, you have been there for me through deep betrayal and heart-wrenching loss over the years. You held my hand while I cried, and you laughed with me to stave off lunacy. And you cared enough to share your own losses with me, to let me see the hurting side of you. That day years ago when I begged God to bring me a best friend, I could never have imagined the blessing that is you. Thank you for your steadfast presence in my life and the gift of your friendship.

The doctor in Vanderbilt's burn unit who wishes to remain nameless — thank you for sharing details of your experiences with burn victims. The work you do saves lives and I appreciate your time and willingness to tell me about it.

Mother, you've been such an amazing cheerleader with this series (once you got through the first fifteen pages — ha!). Thanks for telling everyone about me — well, about the better part of me. We'll keep the rest of me just between us.

Daddy, I remember so much of the wisdom you shared when betrayal entered my life. You held my hand, you told me it would pass, and you kept me looking toward the Ultimate Prize while things fell apart. I pray my kids never need me in that way, but if they do, I want to be like you.

Christie, shoot, I don't know where to start. I wouldn't even be a scrapbooker if it weren't for you! I'm still getting over the fact that you read my books at all when you've got forty-thousand other things on your plate, needing your attention. Of course, we both know you're just checking to be sure I didn't reveal too much of you, right? Ha ha! Thanks for sticking by my side, sister, even when I'm bull-headed, opinionated, and obnoxious. (Hey, those other two days of the year are great, though!)

And for all of you who have lived through betrayal, know that you are not alone. There are millions of us. You will get through this. It is not the end of you or your story. It is a chapter. Close that page and choose to begin the next. From one who stands pages and pages from that dark time, know that your story can become a fairy tale. You need only talk to the One, Jesus Christ, who crafts your path. He loves you, more than any earthly man ever can or will. And He provides.

ONE

"I mean it, Harry," Kendra Sinclair let a bit of her fright and frustration leak into her tone.

Harry's chuckle mocked. "You know you don't. Come on, everybody has to eat."

"Like I said, I've already eaten." *And I don't need this kind of complication right now, even if I want it.*

"Dessert, then, Kendra. You don't want to end the day without dessert, do you?"

Yes, she did. No, she didn't. Well, yeah, she did. She *should.* The sigh was out before she could stop it.

"I heard that. I'll be there in fifteen minutes."

"But —"

"See you soon."

Kendra slammed the phone down and stared at it, waiting for it to jump up and bite her. It might as well have, for all the craziness it had brought her life in the past

11

two months.

Okay, *six* months.

But there was that two-month lull, so really, four months altogether.

"Imparticular man," she muttered, pacing away from the phone and back. Her purple toenails gave a nice contrast as her feet sank into plush carpet the color of a pure snow-drift. "Kendra Sinclair, you are not a con-niving woman. What has gotten into you?"

She plopped down onto the overstuffed couch the saleslady had called "polar bear" and pulled Miss Kitty onto her lap. Strok-ing the cat's fur, she stared across the room. Tufts of fur fell onto the sofa, blending into the fabric.

"Where's Oprah when you need her?"

The cat purred its approval of Kendra's long fingernails and sank down further into its mistress's lap.

"Probably on some beach with Stedman, laughing at the rest of us who haven't got-ten it all figured out just yet. Right, Miss Kitty?"

The motoring purr increased in volume, and Kendra smiled.

The phone rang, and she jerked so hard Miss Kitty toppled to the floor.

"Oh, sorry!" Kendra tossed the apology to Miss Kitty and jerked up the handset.

"Hello?"

"Hey, how's Stars Hill's finest lady tonight?" Darin's smooth voice hummed over the line. Kendra's heart did a double take, frantically downshifting from the previous call. She straightened on the couch, then felt stupid when she realized he couldn't possibly see how out of sorts she was through the phone line.

"Oh, I'm good. Good. Yeah, really good. How are you?"

"Wow, that's three goods in the first five seconds. Something wrong?"

She propped her elbow on the arm of the couch and rested her jaw in her palm. Other women lowered their gazes and offered demure smiles when they were out of control. But Kendra? She stammered and fell all over herself with streams of words. "No, no, nothing's wrong. Just sitting here talking to Miss Kitty."

"Lucky cat."

Kendra chuckled, feeling her heart rate settle back into the normal range even while her skin heated at the sound. "Tell *her* that. I knocked her off my lap when the phone rang."

"And she hasn't clawed your eyes out yet?"

"Declawed, remember?"

"Oh, right. Anyway, I know it's last

13

minute, but I was wondering if you'd had dinner yet."

"Oh, um, no. Well, yes, but that was a couple of hours ago. I mean, not that I need to eat anymore today. Gotta watch my waistline and all —"

His chuckle stopped her mid-sentence. "I'll be over in about fifteen minutes. See you soon."

She heard the click of the phone and stared at it. Not five minutes ago a different man had said the same words. Her silk caftan swirled as she jumped up and fled to the bedroom, praying the first caller hadn't been serious and was just leading her on.

Which in her heart of hearts she knew wouldn't be out of character for him at all.

Two

"Coming! I'm coming!"

Kendra stuffed a red bangle bracelet on her wrist, layering it with other bracelets of varying red and orange hues. She made it to the front door and stared through the peephole.

Thank heavens, it was Darin. She pulled open the door and smiled. "Hey, you."

"Hey, yourself." The hallway light beamed off his bald head, and his dark chocolate eyes danced with mischief. "Sorry again about being so last minute."

"No worries. I was just sitting here, you know."

He quirked an eyebrow. "I can't seem to imagine you 'just sitting' anywhere, but I'm glad you could come all the same."

She stepped out into the hallway and turned to lock the door. Stars Hill might be a small town, but a single girl living alone could never be too careful.

"Hey, I sit every now and then. A girl's got to stop long enough to get some inspiration."

"You have a new project in the works?"

She scrunched her nose as they made their way down the stairs of the grand old Southern home that had been converted into apartments. "Not really. I'm trying to finish the painting for Tandy and Clay's wedding, but I'm blocked."

Darin reached in front of her and pushed open the massive mahogany door. He followed her onto a wide, wrap-around porch and held her elbow as they walked down the steps. "I'm sure you'll come up with something. You always do, right?"

She grinned, praying the desperation that rode at her side nearly every waking moment stayed hidden behind her eyes. "Yeah, I always do."

He opened the door of his Barracuda, and she slid onto the leather seat, inhaling the spicy yet soapy clean scent that was Darin. His car reflected his personality so well.

What did such a man see in her? And how was it possible they were still dating after four months?

"You know," she said as he got in the driver's side, "I'll have to thank my sister for making me go on that blind date."

16

"You mean you haven't yet?" Darin started the car, and she watched his long fingers on the keys, remembering how deftly they maneuvered the strings on the bass guitar he played. His cobalt-blue shirt pulled against a well-defined bicep when he shifted into reverse.

She shook her head to clear it and sat back. "Nope. The only thing Tandy wants to talk about these days is her wedding. It's all 'bridesmaid's dress this' and 'white lily that.' I'm telling you, if I don't wring her neck before she gets to the altar, it'll be a miracle."

"They sure did get engaged fast." Darin shifted again and pulled out into the street. "Four months? Man, that's quick."

"Not really. They've known each other since junior high. I can't believe it took Clay four months to pop the question. I thought for sure he'd do it the week she moved back to Stars Hill and started Sisters, Ink."

"Pop the question without a ring? You really think Tandy would have been okay with that?"

"The woman moved the entirety of her earthly possessions for the man. I mean, she's back in Stars Hill because he lives here now. I don't think she'd let the absence of a diamond change her mind about him."

"Hmm. Maybe not, but he knew the proposal had to be worthy of the woman. And that meant a diamond." Replication-antique streetlights illuminated the planes of his face when he shot her a smile and turned onto Lindell, the main street of Stars Hill. "It takes time to have a custom ring designed and made. I thought the guy was going to have a coronary before they got the thing finished." He pulled the Barracuda into a parallel spot and stepped out. "Speaking of which, is Clay's okay with you?"

Kendra looked out the window at the navy and yellow Clay's Diner sign hanging beneath a matching awning. If Clay was in there, chances were high that Tandy was nearby. Her sister rarely left Clay's side for long these days. Normally, Kendra welcomed a chance to see her sister. But now . . .

What if Tandy sensed Kendra's stress? And what if she asked Kendra about . . . ? Then again, Tandy's wedding focus seemed to have dimmed her sister radar like morning sunshine on the moon.

She turned back and caught Darin watching her, brow creased. She reached up and smoothed a line, ignoring the small voice inside mocking her, telling her she didn't have a right to such a wonderful man, that he deserved better than a conniving woman.

"Sure, this is fine."

"You positive?" The line deepened as he wrapped long fingers around her hand and kissed the back of it. "We can go somewhere else if you're not up for family tonight."

"Darin, you are *way* too good to me."

"Yeah, just remember we're still in the courting phase. I'm *supposed* to be too good to you right now."

"Courting?" She laughed. "Has anybody used that word since *Happy Days* went off the air?"

"Your dad used it just last Sunday when he was talking about Zelda."

Best to ignore that. Daddy was perfectly within his rights to date. He was, after all, a widower. It wasn't his fault that — even ten years after their mother's death — none of the sisters could completely reconcile the image of Daddy with anyone other than Momma.

"Last I checked, mister, I wasn't over fifty with red, spiky hair."

Darin unbuckled his seat belt and grinned at her, wiggling his eyebrows. "I don't know. Dating a redhead might be kinda fun."

She yanked her hand from his and watched him get out, then walk around the front of the car to her door. "You are *so* not funny."

He pulled her out of the car and circled his arms around her waist in a loose hug. "Funny, no. Wild about you," he dipped his head and wiggled his eyebrows again, "yeah."

His kiss felt soft and gentle, as undemanding as the man giving it. Kendra kissed him back, still unsure what he saw in her or why he stayed around. Maybe no one had given him the skinny on her yet. Hard to believe since they lived in Stars Hill where 98 percent of the population could give both the *Reader's Digest* Condensed *and* Deluxe Expanded Editions of every one of the four Sinclair daughters' life histories.

She tried to push thoughts of her own worth away and focus on the magic of his lips on hers, but images of her childhood haunted her like ghosts on a Louisiana bayou. She felt his hand on her neck and the wisps of history curled along with his fingers. Why couldn't she just let go and kiss him?

Darin ended the kiss and stepped back, keeping his arms around her waist. "Is everything all right with you? You seem, I don't know, preoccupied."

Kendra smiled and put her hands on his

chest. "I'm fine. Just tired. Worried about getting this painting done in time for the wedding." She nodded toward the huge plate-glass window of Clay's. "I'm pretty sure Tandy will kill me if I don't get it done."

Clay placed a quick kiss on her forehead, then turned them toward the door. "You'll figure it out. I've got faith in you."

Kendra pulled out of his arms and moved toward the diner. Maybe she should run up to Barnes & Noble in Nashville for a book on forgetting your childhood. Weren't book-shelves full of self-help titles like that these days?

"Hey, Earth to Kendra."

She blinked and saw a yellow pencil wag-gling in front of her face. Her eyes followed the fingers holding it up a freckled arm to her sister's concerned face. "Hey, yourself, Tandy."

Her eyes narrowed. "You okay? You were in another world there."

"Yeah, yeah, I'm fine." Kendra slid into a booth. "Low blood sugar or something."

"Then you came to the right place." Tandy tapped her pencil on an order pad. "Your choices are cheeseburger, cheeseburger, and cheeseburger."

"Clay order too much hamburger again?"

Tandy's eyes sparkled. "Yeah, I think he's

21

more focused on finding the perfect honey-moon spot than rechecking his food orders."

"Darin says he's gone wedding crazy."

"I did nothing of the sort," Darin defended. "I would never betray a buddy like that."

"Relax, hot shot," Tandy patted his arm, "he'll never hear it from me."

"Of course not, because there's nothing to hear." Darin slid back out of the booth and walked toward the kitchen in the back. "You ladies do your girl thing; I'm going to check on my man Clay. The one who —" he raised his voice — "is *not* so wedding crazy!"

Kendra and Tandy chuckled as Tandy sat in the spot Darin had vacated. "So, seriously, you okay?"

"Couldn't be better." Kendra waved away Tandy's concern. "Just need to get some food in me so my brain can kick back into gear. Not the cheeseburger, of course. Did he manage to throw some veggie burgers on the order form?"

Tandy smiled. "Yeah. He knows you'd have his head if he forgot your precious health food." Tandy looked at her for a long second, and Kendra busied herself with the menu. *Don't ask . . . don't ask . . .*

"Kendra Sinclair, you know every single

thing on that menu, and you're studying it like it's got directions to a pot of gold. Now, spill."

She'd spill just as soon as she fit into jeans from high school. "Nothing to spill, Sis."

"You're keeping something from me? *Me?* It's gotta be something big."

"It's nothing." *Nothing that anybody in this town needs to know.* "Let it go. I'm just tired and cranky because I'm hungry and some overzealous sister of mine is sitting there grilling me instead of a veggie burger." Kendra looked back at the menu.

"See, that's even more proof something's up. You know I don't cook, and here you are telling me to go grill you a burger like I would even know how to turn a grill on, much less produce something that isn't either mooing or doing an imitation of shoe leather."

Kendra kept her head down but raised her eyes to meet Tandy's hard gaze. "Okay, it's something. But I ain't about to blab my business all over town." She took in the full diner and turned back to Tandy. "So how about we continue this conversation later tonight? When you can also explain why you're in here taking orders instead of down the street working in our office."

Tandy pointed a finger at Kendra, then

stood up. "Now we're talking. One burger, cooked by Stars Hill's greatest grill man, coming right up." Tandy sashayed toward the back and hollered, "Clay! Kendra's hungry!"

Kendra shook her mahogany, spiral curls and heaved a sigh. Her reprieve was up. Tandy should have caught on before now, given that Kendra's world had been haywire for months. With the two-month lull, of course. But then Tandy *was* in the middle of planning a wedding worthy of Stars Hill's finest.

Kendra twirled a curl around her finger and gazed out the window. Across the street Zelda and Daddy walked beneath a streetlight, arm in arm, heads bent low. Kendra tried to ignore the twinge in her heart, but after nearly eleven years without Momma, it really was time for Daddy to show interest in another woman. Hadn't she told Tandy that very thing? To let Daddy be a man, not just her daddy?

"Might want to take some of your own advice there," she mumbled and pushed the menu aside.

"Talking to yourself again?" Darin slid back into his seat, putting a Diet Dr. Pepper in front of her and swigging his own Mountain Dew.

24

"It's the only way I know I'll get an intelligent response."

"Hey, I think I do pretty well for you."

"*Pretty well* and *sure thing* aren't the same, though, are they?" *Rein it in, girl. That came out a little harsh.*

"I guess not." He reached across the table and took her hand. "Though I think another four months might put me in the sure thing category."

She looked at their joined hands, his tanned from the summer sun and hers a few shades darker. It made for a beautiful blend of color, one that would be easy to create with oils. She cocked her head and viewed the tableau.

He squeezed her hand. "I think I've lost you to the art world again."

She looked up and smiled. "Occupational hazard."

"So I'm learning. Do you always see the world through an artist's eyes?"

She shrugged. "Most of the time, yeah. It's hard not to. I mean, look around." She gazed out over the booths populated by Stars Hill citizenry dressed in every color of the rainbow. "See how Emma's red dress pulls your eye over to her corner of the room? And how that makes you notice the orange stripes in Emmy's jumper? Look at

25

how those colors animate them, sitting beside that picture of a lime-green Granny Smith."

"Hmm, can't say I even noticed that until now."

"Textures are just as cool." She shifted in her seat, warming to the topic. "Look over there at the rice on Gina's plate, with its rounded edges and steam. It's perfect next to that golden piece of chicken, which mirrors the rounded edges but has a shape all its own." She pursed her lips. "But it could have been put on a better plate."

Darin laughed and leaned over the table. "Kendra Sinclair, you are one *amazing* woman."

She pulled her hand away and began fiddling with the straw paper. "Oh, I don't know about that."

"Stop fishing for compliments."

"I'm not! I don't think I'm much better than anybody else in here." She slumped, looking out across the tables of happy people. "Probably worse than a lot of them."

He sat up straight. "You're kidding me, right?"

"No, I'm not." Exhaustion and misery tempered her tone. "How many of them spent years in foster care? How many of them had parents who cared so little they

26

gave up rights to their own offspring?" *Shut up already. Nobody likes a sob story.* A big gulp of Diet Dr. Pepper washed the rest of her words back down her throat.

"Is this what's been bugging you lately? That you were adopted?" He reached for her hand again, but she put it in her lap.

"Yes. No." She sighed. "Not really."

"Then what? Because you haven't been acting like the confident, sassy woman I met four months ago."

"Thanks, those are words every woman wants to hear."

"I thought women valued honesty."

"About everybody else, sure. Even about yourself, fine. But about us, personally? No. Feel free to tell me I look skinny in everything I ever put on and that my makeup is perfect and my hair is flawless. I promise to believe you."

"Uh-uh." He wagged a finger at her. "You're not ducking this conversation with a joke. Why are you worried about your childhood all of a sudden?"

"I'm not. I told you, not really."

"Which isn't the same as no. And I seem to recall a yes thrown in there as well."

She slumped. "It's the low blood sugar. I'm hungry, and I think Tandy must have distracted Clay because it's been forever since she went back there."

"Nice try, but no go. You want to table this conversation for later? Fine. I'm free all night."

"Can't. I'm meeting Tandy."

"Okay, then right now is good for me, too." He sat back in the booth and crossed his arms.

Big, thick arms that were made for hugs and end in those long fingers.

"Kendra? Come on, honey, out with it. I think it's about time we did the whole childhood talk anyway."

And run you off? I don't think so.

Tandy appeared in the corner of her eye, and Kendra took in a grateful breath. "We'll talk about it later. Right now —" she nodded toward her sister who approached the table with two plates piled high with cheeseburgers and fries — "I think we're going to eat." *Saved by a burger.*

Darin turned in his seat, then looked back at her. "Fine with me. I've always loved a nice walk after a big dinner, and the park is only a block away."

Tandy's arrival saved Kendra from replying. "Two burgers, medium well, with enough fries to make anyone think twice about a bathing suit." She sat the plates on the table. "Knock yourselves out."

28

"You know, it's probably bad for business to remind folks what this food does to the waistline."

Tandy winked and turned away. "Good thing it's not my business." With that, she headed back to the kitchen.

"She makes a good point." Kendra reached for the salt and latched on to any conversation topic that would keep them away from the previous issue. "What is she doing over here slinging burgers?"

"My guess is she's helping her future husband with the dinner rush."

"Hmm." She chomped down on a fry. "I guess. But Sisters, Ink is still a new business, and we need to be working on it more than we are."

"It's seven o'clock at night, Kendra. I think the business will still be there in the morning."

"Yeah, but it'd be a *better* business if one of us was still there tonight." Which made one wonder why *she* hadn't just gone to their new offices to work instead of telling Darin she'd go out for this impromptu dinner.

"Well, I for one am glad you decided to have dinner with me rather than slaving over a computer the rest of the night."

"Get outta my head." The man always

seemed to be reading her thoughts.

He grinned and swiped a French fry through ketchup. "I kinda like it in there. Gives me a whole new perspective on the world. Take this French fry, for instance." He held the fry aloft and cocked his head. "See how the red of the ketchup contrasts with the pale of the potato?"

She balled up her napkin and threw it at him, laughing. "Oh, hush your mouth."

He put the fry in his mouth and looked her in the eye. "That's better. Your smile is too beautiful to hide for long."

Her smile. It always got her into trouble. From before she even knew the power it possessed, this smile of hers was always leading the way down a dark corridor. And she tripped along after it every time, even when she'd learned her steps could only lead to disaster.

Just like they'd done six months ago when they led her to Harrison's table.

THREE

"Daddy!"

Tandy tripped over Kendra as they fell through the heavy oak door of the farmhouse where they, Joy, and Meg had shared their childhood, "I'm home! And Ken's with me!" A torrent of rain beat the ground outside, washing clean the barn and fields. "And there's a good chance we're gonna need Noah's ark before the night's over!"

The bottom had fallen out of the sky just after Kendra ducked into Tandy's car from the diner. Thank goodness she'd avoided the walk with Darin. In the park the only shelter was the old caboose, and Kendra knew what happened to girls who ducked into the caboose with a boy.

Tandy and Kendra walked toward the back stairs, shaking their hands and hair. Water droplets left little dark spots on the worn hardwood. Cooper came barreling down the stairs, woofing, his big basset paws sliding on the hardwood.

"Hey, Cooper." Tandy knelt and kissed the basset bump on the top of his head. "Did you hold the fort down while Momma was gone?"

Cooper woofed again and wagged his tail. He turned a soulful gaze to Kendra.

"Oh, no, mister. Don't give *me* those puppy dog eyes. I've got no treats for the likes of you."

Tandy rose and walked on into the living room. Kendra followed.

They saw the note propped on the mantel at the same time.

"I've got it." Tandy went over and plucked the note from its place. " 'Tandy,' " she read aloud, " 'Zelda and I are catching a late dinner. Be home later. Call if you need me. Love, Daddy.' "

"He sure is spending a lot of time with her." Kendra walked around the sofa and dropped into it, holding out her arms to take stock of the rain's effect on her clothes. They didn't seem to be much worse for the wear.

Tandy pushed back her precipitation-soaked waves of red hair and crumpled into Momma's old recliner. "I know. I don't want to say anything, but I think he's getting serious about her." Cooper settled at her feet and rested his big head on his front paws.

"Serious how?" Kendra pulled her feet up under her on the sofa and snuggled in. She began to remove her clunky bracelets, wiping each one dry on the hem of her shirt.

"Serious enough to see her nearly every night."

She stopped wiping. "What? Why haven't you said something before now?"

"What am I going to say?"

"I don't know. How about, 'Girls, I think Daddy's getting serious about Zelda. Do we want to do anything about that?'"

"It's not our place to do anything about it, Ken."

Kendra harrumphed and resumed the removal of her bangles. "You sound like Meg."

"Thanks."

"I didn't mean it as a compliment."

"I know you didn't. But Meg's sounding an awful lot like Momma these days, so I'm going to take it as a good thing."

"I think it's having three kids at home. She's got the Momma voice down pat."

"Speaking of which, have you talked to Joy lately?" Tandy pulled a lever on the side of the chair to release the footstool just as a boom of thunder sounded outside. Glass

33

rattled in the old windowpanes.

"How is that a 'speaking of which'?"

Tandy shrugged. "We're talking about kids. Joy and Scott are trying to get pregnant. It's a speaking of which."

"That's a stretch."

"I like to make sure I'm pushing myself every now and then. Have you talked to her?"

"Not really. Saw her last week at the salon, but we haven't talked since."

"Speaking of which, what's up with you?"

"No way is *that* a 'speaking of which.' "

"You haven't talked to a sister in a week. Meg told me this morning *she* hasn't heard from you in over a week. You're avoiding us. Speaking of which . . ." Tandy tapped her fingers on the armrest as rain left wavy sheets on the windows.

Kendra pulled in a deep breath. "Okay, it's a speaking of which."

"Thank you, now tell me what's going on with you."

"Wouldn't you rather talk wedding plans? How are the dresses coming?"

"The dresses can wait. Come on, Ken, we don't hide things. I know something's up with you, and it's freaking me out that you won't tell me what, so spill."

"Maybe I'm not ready to talk about it."

34

"So there *is* an 'it,' right?"

"Yeah, there's an 'it.' "

"Well, that's something."

"Actually, that's *it.*"

"Very funny. Is *it* anything I can help with?"

Kendra fiddled with her bracelets while God performed a lightning show on the other side of the panes. She could sic Tandy on Harrison; he'd never know what hit him. But then if she let Tandy know about Harrison, there was no coming back. It was one of those decisions in life that only offered the ability to continue down the path, not retrace your steps and figure out another direction.

"No, I don't think you can help."

"Are you going to get hurt? Because if *it* will hurt you, then you should know that I'm against it."

Kendra studied the wave patterns on the windows. "Remember when we drove up to Gatlinburg that summer in high school?"

"Before my freshman year? Yeah, I remember. You got mad because I kept having to stop to use the bathroom."

"Well, if you hadn't been drinking a giant lemonade, then we would have gotten to the campsite a whole lot faster."

"Ah, but the journey wouldn't have been

quite as sweet."

"Touché."

"Why'd you mention it?"

"Remember the indoor skydiving place?"

"How could I forget? I was so scared I just about peed in my pants when we got in that crazy cylinder and fell forward to a rotating propeller where the only thing separating us from its whirring blades was a crisscrossed mesh of wire. We must have been out of our minds."

"Ah, but remember the freedom once all that wind from the propeller had pushed you in the air?" Kendra began putting her dried bracelets back on.

"Yeah." Tandy's voice took on a dreamy quality. "It was like magic, being weightless and floating like that, able to direct my movement with a simple lifting of the arm."

"It *was* magical, wasn't it? Worth the scared part?"

"Yeah, definitely worth the scared part."

"And later, when you turned your arm too high, fell against the side of the cylinder, and sprained your ankle, was it worth that, too?"

"Yeah, it was."

"That's what I thought." Kendra nodded and considered the lessening rain. "Sometimes you have to take the pain to have the experience."

"Unless you can get the experience without the pain."

"I can't. Just as surely as the ground outside wouldn't be wet unless the clouds opened up."

"Are you sure the experience is worth the pain?"

"If I could figure that out, I'd know which direction to go."

"Then tell me the experience, and I'll tell you what it's worth."

"Sorry, sis, no can do. This is one I've got to figure out on my own. At least for now."

Silence fell on them like a quilt fresh from the washing machine, its wet heaviness a small price to pay for the clean scent.

The clock on the mantel — selected by Kendra for Momma and Daddy's fifteenth wedding anniversary and paid for only after all the sisters had pooled their allowances *and* raked leaves for several neighbors — ticked as regularly as stitching. Kendra took the sound into her being, waiting until the rhythm of her heart matched the rhythm of time. The two steady beats were off by a hairsbreadth, just enough to cause a lengthening difference.

Maybe I should try joining the pattern of the rain instead. I'm a walking storm.

"Hey, Ken?"

"Yeah, T?"

"If *it* makes you look so sad, are you sure you shouldn't run the other way?"

FOUR

A tinkling bell sounded as Kendra walked through the back door of Sisters, Ink the next morning. Last night's sleepless hours had etched new lines on her face that the bathroom mirror hadn't been slow to reveal an hour ago. The best escape was work, so Kendra threw on some makeup and made her way down to Lindell Street.

If I keep this up, my face can double as elephant skin in another couple of months.

It was early, barely seven, too early for any of the sisters to be up and in the office. Besides, Meg and Joy didn't spend nearly as many hours here as Tandy and she. They'd said from the beginning that they wanted to be partners, just not as active as Tandy and her in the business. Which worked out perfectly.

Kendra dropped her turquoise leather satchel on the hardwood floor by her desk, its beading and tassels making a pleasing *plop.* Hands on hips, Kendra turned around the room and took stock of their little operation.

Morning light poured through the front window and bounced off every available surface, suffusing the room with its cheerful illumination. The office was coming along nicely. Four months into starting Sisters, Ink, a company committed to networking scrapbookers at the local level, they had roughly a thousand members and growing. The freshly painted pale yellow walls served as proof of the profit they'd sunk back into the business. It hadn't been a huge investment, and Joy'd been right about the effect of the bright color on their work ethic and product. Working in a bright room made for a much nicer, easier day.

They'd made smart use of the small space leased from the next door tenant, Emmy of Emmy's Attic. It wasn't big, about a thousand square feet, but it housed her desk and Tandy's with enough space left over in the back for shipping supplies and some merchandise bearing the Sisters, Ink logo.

Satisfied that the business was on track for success, Kendra dropped her hands and sat down in the bright red swivel chair at her desk. Finding a red desk chair wasn't the easiest endeavor, but Joy's point about color hadn't been taken lightly.

Kendra opened her laptop and waited for it to power up. In a few minutes she had her inbox open and watched the screen as e-mails from women wanting to become Sisters, Ink members poured in. Her lithe fingers, strong from years of sculpting and painting, flew over the keyboard as she created a member ID for each woman, processed her small membership fee payment, and e-mailed a welcome to the new member.

She smiled at the thought of these women finding other ladies with whom they could scrapbook. Romance was great, but who could make it through life without girlfriends?

Hearing the creak of the back door, Kendra turned to greet the visitor.

"Joy!"

"Kendra! Hey, you're here!"

Kendra got up and met her sister near the door. "Here, let me help you." She took a box from Joy's overloaded arms and set it on Tandy's nearby desk. "What are you doing here so early?"

"I could ask the same of you, my long-lost sister. Why are you not answering your phone?"

"I am."

"Then why are you screening my calls?"

"Oh, please. I'm not screening your calls." *Anymore, since it's not working.* "I've just been busy with Tandy's wedding painting and haven't had a chance to talk."

"You can't speak to your sister and paint at the same time? Isn't that the purpose behind these little headsets?" Joy pointed to the Bluetooth device on her right ear. On a person as tiny as Joy, the earpiece looked gargantuan. It's dark plastic stood in stark contrast to her pale Asian skin.

"I think they make those so we'll all look like Trekkies." Kendra held up her hand in the signature Vulcan salute. "Live long and prosper and all that jazz."

"I'll believe that when they're able to beam me up. A matter-relocation device would have come in handy with these boxes."

Kendra pulled the flaps free on one of the boxes. "Yeah, what'd you bring?"

"Simply a few more items to make our humble offices a bit more businesslike yet warmly inviting."

Kendra chuckled. "You are such a Martha Stewart wannabe."

"I wouldn't make fun if I were you. Martha Stewart seems to have done well."

"If you overlook one small stint in jail."

Joy turned her delicate head and sniffed. "You know we do not speak of the Incarceration."

Kendra stifled a giggle at Joy's proper manner and well-modulated tones. One trip to the Tennessee Performing Arts Center in Nashville when she was in the fifth grade, and Joy's tomboy behavior vanished forever. For weeks after the theatre trip, the entire family had endured Joy's repeating, "The rain in Spain stays mainly in the plain." They all thought she'd never give it up; and, indeed, it took Momma telling Joy that a proper lady is always aware of the effect of her presence on those around her to put a stop to the "rain in Spain" line. Joy was changed, forever, though. Her love of all things etiquette-related never waned.

Kendra pulled out a desk organizer. Of course Joy would want to put everything at the Sisters, Ink offices in order.

"Oh, hand me that." Joy took the organizer and walked over to Tandy's desk. "I was in here over the weekend and dared to open a drawer of this desk. I'm telling you, I have no idea how that law firm put up with Tandy's horrendous office hygiene for so long."

"What horrendous office hygiene?" Kendra sidled over to the desk to see what had

Joy's nose so out of joint.

"This!" Joy pulled open the middle desk drawer, and Kendra leaned over to take stock. Various pens and pencils rolled among rubber bands, half a roll of breath mints, and a postage stamp. "Can you believe she gets anything accomplished with this sort of clutter literally under her fingertips?"

Joy pulled all the mess out of the drawer and inserted the organizer.

"You know, Joy, I'm not too sure Tandy's going to appreciate your efforts here."

"Sure she will." Joy's little fingers worked quickly; and Kendra watched, fascinated, as each bin filled with items of like accord. "She may be a bit miffed at first, and that's all right. But after a little while she'll see that this allows her to be much more efficient."

Joy dropped a last rubber band in with its siblings and shut the drawer. "There! All set." She turned to the front window of the office space. "Now, for this display window."

"Okay, whoa, sister." Kendra stepped in front of The One Who Will Not Have Mess. "What happened to playing a near-silent role in Sisters, Ink?"

Joy blinked. "This *is* a silent role. I'm not telling you how to run the business, just making certain the office looks presentable for any visitors."

"You just rearranged someone's desk drawer. I don't think Tandy's going to see that as silent."

"I told you already," Joy walked by Kendra and continued on to the front window, "she'll see reason eventually. She was an attorney. They love reason, don't they?"

Kendra opened her mouth to argue, then realized Joy made a good point. She regrouped and followed in Joy's perfectly pressed wake to the window. "But designing our window is something we all should discuss, don't you think?"

"What's there to discuss? If it mattered to either of you what the window looks like, you'd have done it already. It's been four months. People are beginning to wonder how serious we are about Sisters, Ink."

Kendra's hackles rose. "People are talking?"

Joy shrugged her thin shoulders, and Kendra noticed in passing how artistic the gesture was on her tiny sister. "Not much, but the talk is starting. I was in Emmy's and overheard a couple of comments about there needing to be a display in this window. I thought it would be easiest to take care of it myself rather than adding something to your to-do list or Tandy's. We all know she has enough to handle with the planning of the wedding."

Once again, a valid point. Her sister was becoming downright logical. "Okay, fine. At least let me help you with it. What kind of display did you have in mind?"

"I pulled some things out of the attic that I used in the conservatory last year. Remember the red and gold zinnias?"

"Ooh, I loved those!"

"I thought so. If we put those in the cut crystal vases, we can set up a little autumn scene. I was thinking an antique bicycle to add some height, and then some scrapbook layouts about going back to school, raking the leaves, that sort of thing."

"Hey, I like that!"

"Don't sound so surprised, Artsy One. I spend all day matching hair color to skin tone. Putting a few flowers together in a vase isn't much different, right?"

"I guess not. So what can I do to help?"

"You may get those boxes and bring them up here, then tell me why we haven't talked in a week." Joy turned back to the window and climbed up onto the platform designed for displays. On hands and knees she crawled to the far corners. "And bring back some window cleaner and those antibacterial wipes. This display is filthy."

Ignoring the reference to her weeklong silence, Kendra turned and made a beeline for the boxes. Perhaps if she dawdled, Joy would take the hint and let it go. She slowed her pace and cast about for a topic of conversation.

"Come on, sister, dear." Even Joy's raised voice managed to sound cultured. "I haven't got the entire day for this."

So much for dawdling. Kendra hefted a box and, swiping the window cleaner and wipes from a deep drawer of her desk, trudged back to the front of the store. "How's Scott these days?" She set the box down and handed Joy the cleaning agents and a pair of pink latex gloves. Leave it to Joy to own designer cleaning gloves.

A faint frown line formed at Joy's mouth. "He's doing well. Working more than he probably should be, given that we're not exactly spring chickens. But that's the way it is with real estate, he says. Follow the boom or suffer the consequences."

"He's still selling a lot of property?"

"Oh, yes. The Nashville people love the land in and around Stars Hill. Scott makes certain to drive them down Lindell, where they inevitably fall in love with the idea of living in a town the size of Mayberry."

"Huh." Kendra grunted. "If he keeps selling all the outlying property, we're not going to stay the size of Mayberry much longer."

"I wouldn't worry about that." Joy swatted at a corner cobweb. "These people aren't home long enough even to meet the townspeople, much less come to a town meeting and really invest their lives in the area. They spend all their time at the office or off on business trips."

"Then why move here at all?"

Joy pulled a wipe from the container and cleaned the molding around the window. "I asked Scott that very thing. He said they're in love with the *idea* of living a simple life but not enough that they'd give up what the city life has to offer."

"Wow, that's cynical."

Joy tossed her head. "It's not cynical if it's true, correct?"

"I don't know. Guess not."

"For instance, I could say you're a procrastinator but only because you're seeking to ensure I forget the question I asked previously, which means you don't love or trust me enough to share your life with me. All of which would be true, not cynical."

"Um, ouch."

Joy stopped cleaning and raised her striking blue eyes to Kendra. "I worry, Kendra. It isn't in your nature to be so elusive. And when I finally do run into you, I find you at work at the crack of dawn. Is something wrong with Darin? Are you two still doing well?"

"We're fine, Joy. Great, even. I just have some things on my mind." *Like how I can get out of town for a few days.*

"I understand. Is there anything I can do to help?"

"If there were, I would have called you."

"Perhaps there is something I can do, but you would prefer not to have to ask?"

Kendra shook her head. "No, really, I just need to think about things for a little while."

"You've always done this, you know." Joy went back to scrubbing.

Kendra crossed her arms. "Done what?"

"Retreated into yourself."

"Seriously?"

Joy nodded, and the light bounced off her shiny black bob. "I remember once when we were in school a boy said something to you about your hair — it was right after that awful cut you got — and you didn't talk to any of us for two whole days. Just sat up in your room, doing and thinking Lord knows what, for two entire days. I kept wanting to go see about you, but Momma said you

49

needed time to think it through."

"I barely even remember that."

"She said you were smart enough to know your beauty didn't come from a haircut but from within." Joy finished scrubbing a difficult spot, then sat back on her heels. "There, I think that about does it." She blew her bangs out of her eyes and looked up. "Did a boy say something about your hair again?"

Kendra stared, not sure if she was more surprised by Joy's insight or by the fact that she hadn't seen it coming.

"Maybe something along those lines."

Joy removed her gloves, tossed them in the box, and then began unpacking the box and arranging items in the window. She nodded ever so slightly. "I thought it might be. It's all right if you don't want to speak about it. Just wanted to remind you your beauty doesn't come from a haircut."

Kendra watched Joy move products this way and that, sit back to review, then lean forward to move something to a better location. She waited, but Joy didn't seem inclined to add any further wisdom, and there *was* an inbox full of membership requests waiting.

"I guess I should get back to work."

Joy didn't even look up. "Go right ahead.

Don't let me stop you." She reached out to tug a zinnia, and Kendra turned away. "Hey, Kendra?"

Kendra glanced back. "Yeah?"

"I love you."

Kendra grinned, and the tightness in her chest loosened. "Back at ya, Martha Wannabe."

"Don't mock The Martha!"

Kendra laughed and walked back to her desk. As she plopped into her red seat, the phone rang. "Sisters, Ink."

"Hello, I'm looking for some female companionship, and I understand your company can help me find it." Kendra's heart stopped at the familiar voice. Harrison was calling her *here?*

"I'm sorry, sir —" she played along, twisting the phone cord in her fingers — "we're a company that networks scrapbooking women. I believe you've misunderstood our mission."

"Well, then, I beg your forgiveness and ask that you allow me to make it up to you." The smile in his voice was unmistakable, and gooseflesh rose on her arms.

She shivered. "Oh, no apology necessary. I'm curious, though, how you knew to call us?"

His deep-throated chuckle went straight

51

to her spine, and she stiffened in her seat. "I'm in Stars Hill." Her breath caught in her throat. *What?* "Saw you through the window. Is that Joy you were talking with?"

Naturally he had never met the sisters. Kendra forced breath out of her lungs and looked around. If she could stay on her toes long enough, he never would.

"Yes . . . what brings you to our fair city?" She cast a furtive glance up to the window, but Joy didn't show any sign of listening to the conversation. Still, there was no need to take chances.

"Since I'm only familiar with one thing in it, I believe you might be able to deduce the reason for my visit."

Okay, he'd made the hour-long drive from Nashville just to see her. Giddiness bubbled up inside her, but she tamped it down as fast as it rose. The complications that could result *should* outweigh the giddiness. "I'd hate to presume such."

"Oh, please do. Can you get away?"

This was an awful idea. If she were smart, she'd tell him to go away. Put a stop to this thing before it got even more out of hand. She glanced out the window for encouragement — and saw him standing across the street.

Harrison Hawkings.

All six feet, curly blonde hair, and green eyes of him was standing on Lindell Street. *Her* Lindell Street. In full view of everybody. Staring at the Sisters, Ink offices, one hand casually stuffed in the pocket of what she knew to be Tommy Bahama linen pants, holding a cell phone to his ear.

"Oh my gosh! Is that you?" *Keep your voice down.* A thousand horses' hooves couldn't match the pounding of her heart.

"In the flesh. And it's some mighty lonely flesh. Are you coming to keep it company or not?"

There went the goosebumps again.

"Where's your car?" *Hush your mouth! You're supposed to be telling him to go away.*

He turned and started walking.

See, he's going away. She tried not to notice how well Tommy Bahama clothes fit his frame.

"It's this way, by a park."

She sighed. If she got into his car at the park, half the town would see, and all the sisters would be calling her before lunchtime to get details on the unknown hunk. "I can't meet you there." *I don't need to be meeting you anywhere, ever again.*

"Too public?"

"Roger that." Kendra racked her brain for an anonymous place they could meet, but

53

the pressure of getting him off Lindell before anyone could see him and ask questions overrode her ability to think on her feet. And, oh yeah, she was trying *not* to meet him.

"You still there?"

"I'm here. Just thinking."

"Relax, doll. Nobody knows me, and they certainly don't know I'm here for you. I doubt anyone even noticed me."

He was here *for her.*

"Trust me. They noticed you." Her fingers drummed on the desk, letting the good and bad characters in her mind duke it out.

"How about we meet at the exit before Stars Hill? I don't remember any gas stations there, so no people would be around."

"Good idea." *So not a good idea.* "I'll be there in about fifteen minutes." *Who needs good ideas?*

"I'll be counting the seconds."

She waited for the click that signaled he'd hung up, then replaced the handset and stared at it. Harrison Hawkings was here. And she was going to see him in fifteen minutes. Why hadn't she just told him to go away?

Because you're you, a small, nasty voice whispered in her mind. *This is who you are.*

Maybe. Maybe not. She snatched her

54

purse from the floor and headed to the back door. She'd meet Harrison and tell him in person that they had to end things. It wouldn't be polite to do this over the phone.

Yeah, right.

She ignored the voice, hollered a "Be back in a little while" to Joy, and went out the back door, studiously ignoring the haste of her own steps.

FIVE

Joy watched Kendra's little RAV4 turn off of Lindell onto University Drive and closed her eyes.

Oh, Ken . . .

The signs were all present. Kendra's secrecy, elusiveness, and now last-minute meetings. It all pointed to the old pattern: Kendra was having self-esteem issues again. Someone must have made a comment or looked at her in a manner similar to that of her birth mother's boyfriends. Customarily, a look or word was all Kendra needed to retreat into her cracked shell of a childhood.

Touching the Bluetooth headset at her ear, Joy said, "Call Tandy mobile," and waited for her cell phone to interpret the command.

Sometimes Kendra pulled herself back from the abyss, and the sisters would be relieved of the responsibility to intervene. But the handsome stranger outside talking on his cell might have something to do with Kendra's hurried exit. And if that was the case, then Kendra was in need of sister help.

"Tandy Sinclair."

"Kendra's in trouble." Joy craned her neck but saw no sign of either the stranger or Kendra's vehicle.

"I know. I told you last night, she was at the diner with Darin — shoot, hang on a second." Joy listened to Tandy shushing Cooper. The basset hound's bark sounded like a cannon report in a closed room. "Anyway, she was in the diner but might as well have been on the moon for all the interaction I got."

"No, I mean, I *know* she's in trouble."

"Why? What happened?"

"I got to the SI offices this morning, and she was already here."

"How early?"

"Before eight."

"No."

"Yes. Sitting at her desk, working."

"Okay, that's not like her, but I'm not sure it means she's deep enough for us to intervene."

"And did I mention the hot stranger she just dashed out of here to meet?"

"You may have forgotten that tidbit." Joy

57

heard the frown in Tandy's voice. "How hot?"

"The flowers were bending their heads in adoration as he passed."

"Oh my word. You're right. She's in trouble. Are you sure she left to meet him?"

"I suppose it could be a coincidence, but he stood out there staring at the store, talking on his cell at the same time that Kendra got a call. Just after he hung up, she left."

"You haven't seen him since?"

"No."

Tandy's sigh was loud over the phone wire. "What set her off? She hasn't had an episode like this in, well, I guess I don't know the last time."

"You were still in Florida. It's been nearly two years. I thought maybe that was the last of them."

"Wait, I remember that. Meg called to put me on alert to come home, but then she said you and she handled it."

"Not exactly. The guy was employed as a truck driver, so he was only here for a few days. When he left, she came back to her senses."

"Maybe the hot stranger is another truck driver."

"Putting aside the fact that we shouldn't be all right with *any* inappropriate man, I'm fairly certain that truck drivers do not walk around Stars Hill wearing the latest Tommy Bahamas and a Sig Sauer watch."

"You saw his *watch?*"

"I think you've lost focus."

"Remind me to put more thought into my wardrobe when I'm around you."

"Your wardrobe is fine. I would have told you if anything was amiss. Although you could spend a bit more time on your nails."

"I'm starting a business. My nails are the least of my worries."

"You might reconsider that when your wedding day arrives. It will be here before you know it."

"How did we go from Kendra having a meltdown to my nails needing attention?"

"We're just good like that."

"Very funny. Okay, I feel a scrapping night coming on."

"You call Meg. I'll be at the house around six tonight. I'll need to make arrangements for Scott's dinner."

"I can't believe you still cook that man multicourse meals."

"He puts in a long, hard day. And I like cooking. What's there to disbelieve?"

"You're weird."

"I love you, too. Call Meg."

"Will do. See ya tonight."

"Bye." Joy touched the button on her earpiece and took stock of the display window. Bright orange and red zinnias sprouted from a Tiffany vase that she'd placed in the corner. Scrapbooking layouts were at varying heights, their numerous patterns and colors lending a crazy, party feel to the look. Joy bobbed her head and crept down out of the window. Much better.

She packed leftover odds and ends back into the boxes, then hauled them out to her car. At least one thing in life was going according to plan — unlike her desire to have started a family a year ago. What was taking so long? Other women got pregnant the month they started trying, but not her. Here they were, twelve months into trying, and still the stick stayed stubbornly white every single month. It wasn't fair. Her own sisters were proof of women's ability to get pregnant even when they weren't trying. Even when the last thing in the world they needed or wanted was a baby.

What kind of God lets that happen, then doesn't give a baby to the ones who desperately want one?

Joy shook her head. Good heavens, she was standing stock still in the parking lot. With a sigh she got into the car.

"Honey," she could hear Scott's sweet, reassuring voice in her mind, "you've got to stop worrying. Worrying only makes this harder."

He was right. She knew he was. The doctor told them that stress would make conceiving more difficult, but how was she supposed to *not* worry? What woman in her right mind would look at twelve months of failure and not experience at least a twinge of doubt?

The time to see a fertility specialist had arrived. Scott wouldn't be happy, and he'd buck at her decision, but he'd eventually go. He'd do whatever it took to make her happy.

And right now only a baby could do that.

Tandy lay on the bed she'd had since being adopted by Marian and Jack, staring at the ceiling and petting Cooper's big basset head. Cooper snored softly, lost in a doggie dreamland where he probably chased cats and birds and won.

Kendra was off somewhere, right now, with a strange man. What if they were in an accident? What if she and whoever this guy was ran their car off a bridge or were hit by an out-of-control semi? Would anyone know to call Daddy? Or a sister? What was Kendra *thinking?*

Tandy punched the speed dial on her

phone and held it to her ear.

"Hello?"

"Hey, Meg, it's Tandy."

"What's wrong?"

"Four words. I said four whole words."

"Yeah, four words dripping in sadness. What's wrong? Did Clay do something? Did Kendra do something?"

"Looks like she's falling further than we thought." Tandy conveyed what Joy had seen at the office.

"That sounds bad."

"Mm-hmm. Can you be here at six? I'm calling a scrapping night."

"Yep. Have you called Kendra yet?"

"No. You think she'd answer? If Joy's right, then she's with that man right now."

"All the more reason to call. Interrupt whatever might be going on and give her a dose of reality."

"Good point. Okay, I'll call her now. See you tonight."

"See ya."

Tandy punched the End button to ensure the call had disconnected, then dialed the shortcut number for Kendra. Joy was right: Her nails looked bad.

She rolled her eyes — *Now is not the time to think of your manicure* — and held the phone up to her ear.

"Kendra Sinclair."

"Hey, Ken, it's me."

"Hey, me. What's wrong? You sound down."

Because you're probably sitting there with a strange man whose morals are lower than a slug. "A little. I'm calling a scrapping night. Can you be here around six?"

"I'm not sure. Let me check my book."

Tandy heard muffled voices. Her book. Right. More like Kendra was checking with her mystery man to see if their little date, or whatever it was, would be over by six.

"I should be able to make that."

Oh, goodie. You'll be done with loser boy by then. "Great."

"Something wrong with the wedding?"

"No, no, nothing like that. I must be tired or catching your low blood sugar."

"Right. Well, see you tonight."

Kendra snapped her phone closed and turned her head. She'd caught a glimpse of herself in the visor mirror and liked the contrast of her dark spirals on the light-tan headrest. From the look on his face, Harrison enjoyed the view as well.

She stifled a grin. His eyes were always on her, cataloging her every move. Her self-awareness heightened with each passing second.

He quirked an eyebrow. "Which sister was that?"

"Tandy."

"Ah, the redhead, right?"

Kendra nodded. So nice to be known, to know that he listened when she talked about her family.

"So what's a scrapping night, and tell me again why it's important that you be there instead of with me?"

The air between them crackled at his reference to the night. Memories of intimate conversations shared beneath a star-studded sky made her breath quicken. "Only dire emergencies — think death or disfigurement — are grounds for missing a scrapping night."

"You have to go every time somebody wants to scrap?"

"No, no, of course not. Just when someone calls a scrapping night. When a sister says, 'I'm calling a scrapping night,' it means she needs to talk about a problem or get something off her chest."

"Oh, kind of like calling an intervention or something."

"A little like that, yeah."

"Hmm."

The silence grew as they stared at each other. So much possibility in the air, a plethora of opportunity to fail or fly. Harrison was fire. Hadn't she learned long ago that playing with that was dangerous? But Kendra wasn't dumb. She knew the inevitable burn was coming; she just didn't care.

Or maybe I deserve a little burn every now and then.

Nerves snaked their way along her spine as she stared out the windshield. The field before her, awash with high waves of cornstalks, held such beauty. A majestic oak rose in its midst, almost lording itself over the crop. Parked here, on a slight rise, she could make out the undulation of earth, see the incremental rise and fall of the plants as the gentle breeze made their golden tassels sway, as if the stalks were breathing in the moisture-heavy air around them.

"Let everything that has breath praise the Lord."

Momma's voice! Kendra's heart skipped.

"If we're silent, Kendra, even the rocks will cry out with their praise for the Lord."

Momma had loved how Kendra saw the world with an artist's eye. She'd point out the presence of a Creator as they drove down the two-lane highway to home or walked down Lindell together smelling pot-

65

ted petunias.

Momma. Such a good woman.

Good but gone.

Kendra looked across the field again, this time seeing only rows of plants. The magic of art had gone.

"Your face is breathtaking."

She turned her head at Harrison's husky whisper. "What?" *Say it again.*

"I know it sounds like a line, but it's true. When you look out there," he pointed toward the landscape, "you go to another place, and your face takes my breath."

Her heart filled with his words. Words that conveyed how special she was. But he must not know her need for him. Men didn't like to be needed, only wanted. Sylvia's boyfriends had illustrated that lesson time and time again. The second Sylvia's gaze turned from adoration to need, Kendra began counting the days until they woke up alone again.

She'd never minded when her birth mother's boyfriends left. It was easier that way; she breathed better with the knowledge that her nights would be uninterrupted and her days filled with silence. But Sylvia would always find another man, a new person to confirm what her mirror showed less and less of as each day's hard living etched itself on her face. Sylvia was born with beauty but had squandered it with bad living.

"Did I say something wrong?" Harrison's hand brushed her face, and Kendra realized a tear had snaked its way down her cheek.

She ducked her head and didn't meet his gaze. Adoration. Not need. "No, no. Just —" she thought fast — "overwhelmed by the beauty of the surroundings."

"Hmm, me too." He took his hand away, and she tried not to miss it. This thing between them was thick, a pull of something that she couldn't quite place. Maybe God.

No, that can't be right. Her gaze snaked over to the simple gold band on Harrison's finger, and her stomach went cold. *No, not God.*

Yet this felt so right. So very, very right. How could something that felt this right be wrong? She pushed the feeling away, stuffing it in a corner of her heart with all the other feelings she wasn't ready to analyze, and turned to Harrison.

"How was your drive down? I can't believe you came all the way to Stars Hill." *For me.*

He shrugged. "It's just an hour."

She tried to keep the disappointment from her face. Did he say that so she'd know she wasn't that important? Or because he was trying to hide how into her he was?

"Still, you've never made it before. Did something happen?"

"I was sitting at my desk, listening to that radio station on iTunes I told you about. Remember? The jazz one?"

She smiled.

"And that Al Green song came on."

Butterflies floated in her stomach as she remembered the night at B. B. King's blues club in Nashville when she sang for him. She hadn't *known* she was singing for him, but as soon as their eyes met, she knew. Their shared pain drew them together more powerfully than any narcotic and just as addictive. In his eyes lay the truth of the words she sang. *How can you mend a broken heart? How can you stop the rain from falling down?*

The more she sang, the farther forward he had leaned in his seat and the stronger their bond became until, by the end of the song, it seemed only natural to put the microphone back in its stand, walk across the room, and sit down at his table.

"Six months since you sang that song, doll," his fingertips were soft across her face, "and threw my world for a loop."

"This is crazy, Harry. We both know how dumb this is."

"And yet I'm still coming after you, chasing you down the highway to Small Town,

USA, just to get a few more minutes of conversation."

"Does she know where you are?"

Pain filled his eyes but went away so quickly she wasn't sure she'd seen it. "She thinks I'm still at work, I guess. That song came on, and I just couldn't sit there anymore. I had to come find you and see if I had made you something you aren't."

"And?"

"My mind can't do you justice." His fingers played with her curls, and she leaned into his hand. Their one kiss, three months ago the night she thought she'd ended this, was etched into her brain. A wrong kiss. Of course it was wrong, no matter how perfect it felt. And she wouldn't do that again. Couldn't do that again. The guilt had nearly been their undoing.

But sitting here, just talking . . . what could be wrong with that? Just words, simple words, between two souls that had gone out into the world and been hurt by it. Nobody getting hurt, nobody the wiser.

If only that had the ring of truth.

"Harry, what keeps you coming? I thought we decided to end these get-togethers before she found out."

He dropped his hand and sat back in the seat, studying her. "I can't stop, Kendra.

It's too soon to tell you words that I want to tell you. I've only known you a few months. Who can know a person well in a few months' time? It's too soon. I'm crazy for even thinking them. But when I'm with you, even when I'm not with you, I think them. And I can't get them out of my head. I can't get *this* out of my head. You." He shook his head. "It's just too soon, and I can't wrap my mind around it."

He seemed to be talking more to himself than to her, but still she drank in the words. "Too soon for what?"

"You know the answer to that."

Yes, she did. But maybe if he said it, they could talk the situation through. "I'm not sure I do."

The tortured look on his face faded into a lazy grin.

Do not kiss this man. You'll ruin the best conversation you've ever had in your life.

He leaned toward her, and the smell of his spicy aftershave wafted through the small space between them. Instinctively she drew in a deep lungful, needing to have some part of him. He stopped just short of her, their eyes barely two inches apart.

"I can't figure this out, Kendra. For the life of me, I can't get control. I see you, and I don't care that I'm married. I don't care about anything but looking at you, talking to you."

She put her hands on either side of his face and rubbed her thumb across the beginnings of a five o'clock shadow. Holding his face away from her own, she felt the tremble in her fingers and knew the intoxication he experienced. "I know," she breathed, "but you *are* married."

His eyes closed, the tortured look returning, and she hated herself for bringing it up. Then loved herself for being strong enough to do so. Then hated herself again because why should *she* take up for a woman who obviously wasn't taking care of her man? Then hated him for making her be the strong one.

Oh yeah. She was a mess.

His big hands came up to her shoulders and squeezed. "Oh, doll, where were you three years ago?" The anguish in his voice rang so real it hurt her. She'd give anything at this moment to turn back the hands of time. To find him before he ever met the woman he now called his wife.

Before you met such a wonderful man as Darin . . . single Darin . . .

Yes, but she didn't have the same bonds of matrimony with Darin that Harrison answered to.

He squeezed once more, and she felt it down to her toes. This was the electricity romance novels talked about. When one touch caused a sizzling throughout the body. That was what she and Harrison shared. She'd finally found it!

With a married man.

She swallowed hard. Yes, a married man. A man whose wife did everything wrong, granted, but who still shared his last name and his bed and his future.

That's about the kind of luck you deserve, Kendra.

If only . . .

What? Leave his wife? How pathetic is that? What about all those female empowerment books you read? How can you even consider treating another woman that way, causing her that kind of pain?

Kendra shrank back from the shame. What was wrong with her? What was she *doing?* If the roles were reversed and *her* man were sitting in a car with another woman, wouldn't she want the other woman to send him back home?

I'd take care of my man. He wouldn't need *another woman.*

Harrison leaned back in his seat, taking his warmth with him, and she shivered at the sudden chill.

"We've got to figure out a solution here." His ragged voice betrayed the struggle he still fought within. "I know if I keep meeting you like this, out here," he waved a hand at the expanse on the other side of the windshield, "where no one can see and we can do anything we want, then we're going to end up doing what we want. And, God knows, Kendra, we both want it too much to keep denying it. You feel that, right?"

Her breath caught in her throat.

He must have heard her swift intake because he turned to look at her. "The thing is, I don't think either of us is ready for what would come after."

Who cares?

She stamped the thought out. She was not her mother. She was not! "You're right. Coming out here is not smart." What a surreal sensation, saying the exact opposite of her desire. "We're both intelligent adults, though, and we can figure this out."

"I think an intelligent adult," his smile held chagrin, "would have walked away after the very first notes of that song."

"Well, I couldn't very well do that. I think they'd have noticed me clocking out before the song was through."

"Yeah, but they wouldn't have noticed me." His gaze dropped to her hand, and she felt his touch just as sure as if he'd actually grasped it.

"I would have noticed."

"Would you?"

A curl fell across her face as she nodded. He needed to know. "I would."

He stared at the curl. She held her breath. Would he right it? She hoped he would, prayed he wouldn't. Because one touch, just one very slight brush of his hand against her skin, and she'd be gone.

"Okay." He looked away. "Then we agree that we've got a rare thing here and we should be smart about it."

She blinked at the shift, telling herself to be grateful she'd avoided such a huge sin. "Right."

"I've got an idea."

"Let's hear it."

"I'm not an exhibitionist."

"Good for you. I am, but I'm not sure what that has to do with this conversation."

He squinted. "You're an exhibitionist?"

"Hello? I'm an artist! I make a living by putting my thoughts and feelings on display for the whole freaking world to see. You met me while I was pouring emotion through a microphone."

"Good point." He smiled at her, and his dimples just about did her in. "My idea might not be such a great one, then."

"We'll see. What is it?"

"I was thinking, if we limit our meetings to public places, then there's a really good chance that, though we're not going to stop *wanting* it, we won't be able to do anything about it."

She thought about that for a second. It was a good plan so long as they didn't meet anywhere that Stars Hill citizens would be. Then she could keep seeing him, maybe even eventually introduce him to the sisters as a friend. Maybe incorporate him so fully into her life that . . .

What? His wife will magically disappear? Fade into the background without a whimper?

"Hmm, where are we gonna meet that we won't run into folks we don't want to see?"

He shrugged. "Nashville's a big town. There are lots of places."

"True." She fiddled with her bracelets, thinking. "Okay, I think that's a good plan. Safety in numbers."

"Your exhibitionist tendencies not withstanding?"

"I'm not *that* kind of exhibitionist." She swatted him on the shoulder. "Dirty mind."

"When I'm with you, yeah."

Her pulse quickened again. Public places. Definitely. See? There was always a solution

75

when intelligent adults put their minds to work. No need for her to give up such fabulous conversation.

No need at all.

Six

Darin shut the fridge and tossed a can of Coke over to Clay. "You think she's seeing somebody else, man?"

Clay popped the top and guzzled caffeine, then swallowed. "Tandy's worried about her. That's all I know."

"Can't you get Tandy to tell you anything? Come on, help a brother out!" Darin jerked his head toward the living room, and Clay got up to follow him.

"You know I've got your back, Darin. I just don't think she knows what's going on." Clay picked up the remote from the coffee table and hit the button to turn on the big screen.

"Maybe not, but she's got a good idea or she wouldn't have called a scrapping night."

Clay shrugged. "I think the scrapping night might be so they can do some digging. You know, tag-team Kendra."

Darin shook his head and swigged his

Coke. "Man, am I glad I don't have a bunch of sisters."

Clay channel surfed. "Leave me to my own problems. I hear you."

They watched the television for a minute, then Darin said, "I think there's somebody else."

Clay looked over at him, eyebrows raised. "Seriously?"

"Yeah."

"Why?"

Darin studied the top of his Coke can. "I don't know. She seems distant sometimes. Like, I call her, and I can tell she'd rather be doing something else besides talking to me. It wasn't like that before, but it is now."

"Why don't you ask her?"

"So she can kick me to the curb?" Darin took a drink, then shook his head. "I don't think so. Long as I play dumb, I'm still in the game."

"Do you *want* in the game? I mean, you think she's cheating on you."

"Have you met this woman? I don't care who I've got to beat. I'm in."

Clay turned back to the television. "You've got it bad."

"Tell me about it."

Tandy watched through the kitchen window

as Joy made her way across the yard to the porch. At just before six on a warm August night, the glow of daylight was barely fading, warming Joy's pale skin and making her seem healthy and alive.

"Hey, T! I'm here!"

"In the kitchen!" Tandy pushed a small black button, and a light turned on inside the oven. *Mmm, that'll add an inch to the waistline. But who cares?*

"What are you making? Should we let the neighbors know the kitchen's about to blow up?"

"Very funny." Tandy turned from the oven to face her sister. "I'm making brownies. Thought we might need some chocolate courage."

"Excellent idea. She's not here yet?"

Tandy shook her head, reaching up and releasing the clasp that held her copper curls. She gathered the tendrils that had escaped, twisted them with what she'd released, then piled it all back on top of her head and secured the clasp. As soon as this wedding was over, she'd have Joy chop it all off. "Nope. I hope she shows up."

"She wouldn't miss a scrap night. You called it, right?"

"I did. But I think she was with him when I called. She talked to somebody before saying she'd come."

"She ran a *scrap night* by this man? This must be more serious than we thought."

"My sentiments exactly."

They turned at the sound of Meg's voice. She entered the kitchen and boosted herself onto the counter. "We've got about five minutes. Is there anything either of you hasn't told me?"

Tandy and Joy looked at each other and shrugged. "Nope." Tandy opened a drawer and pulled out an oven mitt. "I can't figure out when this started. She seemed fine when I moved home."

Meg pulled her legs up into an Indian-style position. "I think maybe before you came home for the visit back in May. She was getting a little distant then."

"Really?"

"Now that I think about it, you might be right, Meg." Joy took glasses down from the cupboard. "Until you came home, Tandy, Kendra spent quite a bit of time on the road to Nashville. I think she went there at least once each week." She pulled milk from the refrigerator and began filling the glasses.

Tandy pulled brownies from the oven and put them on a cooling rack. "And no one thought to tell me this before?"

Meg shrugged. "She seemed fine after you

came home. We hoped whatever it was had gone away."

"Well, it didn't." Tandy didn't even try to make her tone less grim. "So if you're right about the timing, this little relationship has had about six months to grow."

Joy straightened even more than her usual perfect posture. "That's a long time. I don't think any of her episodes has lasted longer than two months, three at the outside."

"No way has this been going on right under my nose." Tandy shook her head. "Ken and I have spent umpteen hours together planning the wedding. I'd *know* if something was up."

"Perhaps she ended it."

"And this is a new one? So fast?"

"Or it started back up."

Though Meg's offered explanation made more sense, it didn't make Tandy any happier than the alternative.

A car door slammed outside, and Tandy peered out the window. Kendra. She turned back to her sisters. "Guess we'll find out soon enough."

Kendra bounded up the porch steps, still riding the wave of emotion Harrison had stirred in her. The man had an amazing way with words. And the widening of his eyes, the shocked look he sometimes got when he spoke those fabulous words, let her know they were sincere. This *thing* between them, right or wrong, surprised them both.

Having a man to talk to — an intelligent man who knew hurt and talked about it with her — was such a gift. He was so honest and . . . *real.*

And married. Don't forget that, girl. Married.

She shook her head. Why keep bringing that up? It wasn't as if she were doing anything wrong. All they did was talk!

The tempting smell of baking chocolate coaxed her toward the kitchen.

"Hey, y'all." The air felt heavy with unspoken words, and she shot a look at Tandy. Nothing seemed amiss, but Tandy had been the one to call the scrap night, so she was probably the one with the problem. "What'd I miss?"

"Nothing yet." Meg hopped down from the counter. "We were waiting on the brownies to cool before we got into anything."

Despite the fabulous odor wafting from the tray of brownies, something definitely didn't smell right. They were all giving *her* looks of pity and curiosity.

You're just being paranoid. This is about Tandy.

"Let's just take 'em upstairs to cool and get some scrapping done."

"Great idea, Kendra." Joy put the oven mitt on and picked up the brownies. "Grab that tray of glasses, and we can all head upstairs."

Kendra did as directed, growing more disturbed by the second. Joy and Meg weren't looking at Tandy; they were looking at *her.*

She followed Joy out of the kitchen and up two flights of stairs to the converted attic that had been Momma's old scrapping studio.

The big square table Daddy made stood proudly in the center, their layouts still sitting atop it from where they'd quit scrapping last weekend. That was one of the best things about scrapping in Momma's studio — no need to clean up before next time. Just leave your pictures where you wanted and know that the next time you came up those steps everything would be just as you left it.

Comfort in the unchanging.

Kendra settled on her stool and took stock of the layout before her. Pictures of her and Tandy hanging upside down from the caboose in the park were cropped and layered on red cardstock. Background paper of orange and red polka dots made the green grass in the picture pop. She reached for a length of white ribbon and began finishing assembly of the layout, glancing every now and then at the Becky Higgins sketchbook that lay open to her left. It took a few minutes before she pulled out of her scrapping reverie enough to realize the sisters were shooting looks at each other.

"Okay," she put down her paper, "that's enough. Somebody say something." She walked over to the brownies and began cutting, knowing without being told that the chocolate was meant to be fortification for whatever lay ahead. "Tandy, you called the scrap night. What's up?"

Tandy cleared her throat. "Ken, look, you know we love you."

Nothing good starts that way.

"And it wouldn't be right if we thought you were going to get hurt and didn't do anything about it."

Kendra spun around, mini spatula still in hand. "Y'all think I'm going to get hurt? By who?"

"Whom." Joy's correction was quiet.

Kendra waved the spatula, dropping little bits of chocolate. "Who, whom, *whatever.* What's going on?"

Meg sat very still, hands crossed neatly

before her, the mother of concern. "Are you seeing anybody?"

"You know I am. Y'all have met Darin. I thought you liked him."

"We *do* like him." Tandy shifted on her stool, and Kendra's stomach clenched.

"It's the other man we're a little worried about."

They *knew.* Her heartbeat pounded, and she forced a smile. "What other man?" *Best not to blurt out an admission of guilt. Gotta find out how much they know first.*

"Oh, come on, Ken," Tandy pleaded. "Don't be coy. Joy saw him this morning on the sidewalk."

Stupid of him to come to Stars Hill like that. I knew someone would see. She placed brownies on napkins and laid them before each sister, letting the silence lengthen while she thought of a response.

"So Joy saw some man on the sidewalk, and I'm all of a sudden a cheater?" She pulled a brownie from the pan and went back to her stool. "Thanks so much for your belief in me, sisters."

"Kendra, you know we believe in you." Meg played with the corners of her brownie. "Just like you know you've got a history that demands we bring this up."

"Yeah, well, not all of us were adopted

near birth, Meg." *Whoa, cool it there.*

Meg stared at her. "I'm not talking about your childhood, Kendra. None of us would ever think less of you because of the stupid choices Sylvia made. How could you think I'd do that?" The clock on the wall steadily ticked off seconds as Meg looked down. Her voice, when it came, was quiet. "I'm talking about the various men that have paraded through your life."

"I'm over thirty years old, Meg. If a few men hadn't paraded through my life by now, I'd suggest you question my sexuality, not call me a cheater."

"Kendra, you know we only have your best interests at heart." Joy's soft voice calmed Kendra's rising panic. "If you say you're not seeing someone other than Darin, then we'll believe you. I'm afraid this is my fault. I saw a strange man this morning outside the office and thought that's why you left so quickly."

No more Stars Hill visits. "Why didn't you just ask me, Joy? You didn't have to call a scrapping night. Or — check that — call Tandy to call a scrapping night."

"We thought you might be heading down that path again." Tandy slid off her stool and went to get another brownie.

"What path?"

"You know, the one where you decide you only deserve a man who will mistreat you or take advantage of you, so you hook up with some lowlife."

"I do *not* have a pattern like that." Kendra popped a bite of brownie in her mouth to stem the flow of defensive words.

"Sure you do." Meg nodded. "You've had it ever since high school. Though I'll happily admit you haven't fallen into it for a couple of years now."

Kendra chewed on her chocolate. Did she have a pattern of choosing a horrible type of man? Sure, she'd had a lot of boyfriends over the years. It was to be expected, though, that she'd date a lot between high school and now. How else could a woman go about finding Mr. Right these days? At least she wasn't out barhopping every night, trolling the night clubs, on the prowl.

She swallowed. "I have no idea what you guys are talking about. So I date a lot." She shrugged. "Most healthy, red-blooded single females do."

Tandy came back to the table. "Normally, I'd back you on any man you want to date. But every now and then you seem to go off the edge and end up with somebody who leaves us wondering what in the world you're thinking."

Kendra started shaking her head before Tandy even finished. "You're wrong, girls. Just wrong. I've had my fair share of poor choices, but there's no pattern. You're making a mountain out of a molehill, and what's worse, we're wasting valuable scrapping time here."

Joy laid her hands, palms down, on the table. "In that case, I'd say we table this discussion for now and get to the scrapping."

Kendra tried not to show her relief. As hypersensitive as they seemed to be today, the sisters would jump on her in an instant if she looked like she'd dodged a bullet. "Great idea. Did anybody have a chance to pick up the new Uhu glue rollers at Emmy's yet?"

"Oh, shoot!" Joy said. "I knew I was forgetting something when I left there this morning. I was in such a tizzy thinking you'd left with that handsome stranger —"

Kendra raised a hand. "Okay, let's not go there again. I'll run by Emmy's tomorrow and get enough for all of us. I'm really, really sick of these that we're using." She reached out and snagged a glue roller from the tool turnabout in the center of the worktable. "But we can make do for one more day."

As her sisters focused on their layouts, Kendra kept watch out of the corner of her eye. Thank goodness. It looked as if they were mollified.

For now.

How much longer until one of them brought it up again, though? As she cropped a set of pictures from the Iris Festival parade a few months ago, she tried to come up with a solution. One that would keep her from having to admit her sisters were right. And that would keep her from having to cut off all ties to Harrison.

Not that she *shouldn't* cut ties to him. She should. Of course she should. But there was the conversation, the intense conversation about everything from politics to religion, personal feelings to future goals. Having Harrison to talk with was like having a living, breathing diary that listened and gave good feedback. Who could give that up? Besides, why did that have to be wrong?

It *didn't* have to be. They had a plan. Public places only.

Kendra rolled the glue runner down the back of a picture and fixed it to paper. Public places where the sisters wouldn't be, she amended. If seeing a strange man on the streets of Stars Hill had prompted a scrapping night, then there was no telling what seeing him a second time would do. Daddy might call hellfire and brimstone down on her head during his next sermon.

She pictured Daddy behind the pulpit at Grace Christian, vein bulging in his neck as he hammered home the consequences of adultery. He'd be right, but not about her. What she shared with Harry was friendship. A special friendship, yes, but just a friendship.

SEVEN

Kendra jumped at the sound of a drawer slamming and looked up.

"I can't *believe* she arranged my desk drawers!" Tandy ran a hand through her red waves. "How could you let her do this?"

Kendra went back to the computer screen in front of her. "Nobody *lets* Joy do anything, you know that. She was on an organizing spree."

"What happened to having a 'silent' partner?"

"She said this *was* silent." Kendra finished a welcome e-mail to another new member and hit Send, then turned to focus on Tandy. "You've gotta admit, it was a silent move."

"This is so not funny, Kendra. How would you feel if she came in here and started organizing your desk?"

"I think she knows better, which is why I

still know where my pens and rubber bands are."

"Huh." Tandy took another look in the newly organized drawer and slammed it again. "I've half a mind to call her up and find out what she was thinking."

"Oh, T, it's not as bad as all that. She put your stuff in order. If you hate it, dump it all out, and you'll have the mess back."

"Well, maybe it's not *so* bad."

Kendra grinned. "Good for you."

"Yeah, well, she should be happy I'm working on learning the fine art of compromise."

Kendra's eyebrows rose. "You? Compromise? What happened to the tough lawyer who wouldn't take anything less than an acquittal every time?"

"I think I left her back in Orlando." Tandy smiled. "She wasn't very good at planning a wedding."

"Uh-oh. Troubles in paradise?"

Tandy put her elbows on the desk and rested her chin in her hands. "Not trouble, exactly. It's just a whole lot harder than I thought it would be. I had no idea there were so many options out there for everything from dresses and flowers to colors and music and the time of day we have the wedding. And every single choice has ramifications. An evening wedding means I need a formal gown. A noontime wedding means a casual affair, so the dresses you guys wear have to have a shorter hemline or be made of a cotton or linen. A morning wedding is evidently unheard of anymore because no one can decide if it's a formal or casual time of day."

Kendra chuckled. "Somebody should tell the sun he needs a tux to usher in the new day."

Tandy's smile was halfhearted. "Yeah."

"What time does Clay want to get married?"

"That's just it. He's as opinion-less as a human being could be. Every time I tell him all the options for one particular decision, he shrugs and says, 'Whatever you want, babe.' And I want to throttle him. What I want is an opinion, for goodness' sake!"

"Okay, take a breath, Bridezilla." Kendra came around her desk and sat on the corner of Tandy's. "I think you should get married in the morning in early October. Mornings in October are beautiful, with all the trees in glorious color and the hint of winter in the air but not strong enough to leave anybody cold. You could have brunch afterward, which will keep your food costs down, and folks still have half the day ahead of them after you and Clay take off for your honeymoon."

"Morning, hmm?" Tandy closed her eyes, and Kendra fell silent, letting her sister picture a beautiful wedding morning full of autumn promise. It'd be tricky, planning a wedding for early October when they were already into August, but it could be done. And Daddy could always get the church for them if Tandy didn't want to get married outdoors.

A small smile began to grow on Tandy's face. "Morning. Yep, I think the first Saturday in October at nine in the morning."

"Perfect timing. Late enough for folks to sleep until seven, but early enough to be finished in time for brunch." Kendra walked back around to her desk. "And brunch will be easier on Daddy's wallet than dinner, so he'll be happy. Feel better?"

"You have no idea. Thanks, Ken."

Kendra shrugged. "What's a sister for?"

"A host of things, and you seem to do them all for me. Really, thanks."

"Enough with the gratitude. Call Clay and tell him you picked a date and time."

Tandy picked up the phone and dialed. Kendra's cell phone vibrated in the pocket of her capris, and she pulled it out to check the caller ID.

Darin.

"Kendra Sinclair."

"These arms of mine," Darin sang in a pretty good imitation of Otis Redding, *"they are lonely . . ."*

Kendra burst out laughing. "Darin, you freak! What do you want?"

Darin cut the act short. "I'm hoping you can do something about these lonely arms. They're really, really wanting to go dancing tomorrow night; but I had a long conversation with them, and they just refuse to bare their loneliness to the world."

"You are a complete freak. You know this, right?"

"It's been said."

"Good, as long as you're comfortable in your freakiness, then I guess the rest of us can accept you for who you are."

"Does that mean you'll go to Heartland with me tomorrow night? My arms would be eternally grateful for the presence of your alluring beauty."

"With arms like that, who needs romance novels?"

"I take it that's a yes?"

"Yes, it's a yes. Do you know if Daddy and Zelda are going to be there?"

"I don't. Clay might, though. Want me to ask him?"

95

"No, I'm sure they'll be there. They always are on Friday nights." She tried to take the bitterness out of her voice but failed.

"He's allowed to date, you know."

Kendra sighed. "I know. And I was fine with it when I thought he was just exploring something new and all. But Tandy says he's getting serious, and I don't think I'm cool with that."

"Would your dad stop seeing Zelda if you or one of the sisters didn't approve?"

"He would, but I'm not gonna get all up in his business like that."

"Probably a wise choice. How's the painting coming, by the way?"

"It's coming. I worked on it last night." *While I talked with another man. Should I tell you that?*

She closed her eyes. It was as though she were living two lives. One was the Kendra who talked with Harrison late into the night; the other, this Kendra who accepted dancing invitations from Darin. Was this what it felt like to lose your mind? To have multiple personalities?

"When can I see it?"

"The first Saturday in October. Tandy finally picked a date." No need to tell him that "working on it" meant staring at a blank canvas, struggling to figure out how

96

to paint a happy picture full of love when her own life was such a mess.

"She did? That's great. Wait, you mean you're not going to show me this until the rest of the world sees it?"

"I mean I don't know if it's going to be finished even a day before the wedding."

Darin's guffaw rang across the line, and she melted inside. This man was so *good*. Gorgeous, talented, interested. What was she doing messing around with Harrison? Stupid other Kendra.

"You'll finish it, Kendra."

"Oh, you think so?"

"I do."

"Guess I missed seeing your crystal ball the last time I was at your place."

"I brought it out of storage just for you."

"That's mighty sweet of you."

"Well, I'm a mighty sweet guy."

"So I've noticed."

"Have you now?"

"It's kinda hard to miss." She twirled a curl around her finger.

"Then I guess I'm doing this courting thing right."

"Seriously, you've got to quit using that word. You sound like you're stuck in 1950."

"From what my momma says, 1950 was a pretty good year."

"Be that as it may, I don't think I want to turn the clock back quite that far."

"What? You don't want to experience free love and bell bottoms?"

"I think that was the late sixties and early seventies. And, no, bell bottoms make me look like Dame Dumpy."

"Dame Dumpy?"

"You'd understand if you ever saw me in bell bottoms."

"An occurrence I can assume will not happen anytime in the near future?"

"Try existing future and you'll be getting close."

He laughed, and she was warmed again by the sound. This was crazy, going back and forth between Darin and Harrison.

So stop. Just accept your fate. You know Harrison is what you deserve. That he's all you can ever have in life. All your mother left you suitable for.

The snide inner voice left her cold.

She sat up straight and closed out of the program she'd been working in. Time to head home. "Anyway, I need to get out of here and get a little more work done on that painting."

"Are you trying to get rid of me, Kendra Sinclair?"

"Me? Never. Can't believe you'd think

such a thing."

"Mm-hmm. Never play poker, honey. I'll pick you up at seven?"

"I can just meet you there if it's easier."

"It might be easier, but no way am I running the chance of another man seeing you in the parking lot and snatching you up before I even get a dance."

"Hmm, guess I'll tell my other boyfriends to leave me alone until after the first dance, then."

At the sudden silence on the line, she frowned. Had she lost the connection? "Darin?"

"I'm here. Just wondering how much of that was a joke."

Her heartbeat slammed into overdrive, and she kicked herself for being so stupid. "What do you mean?"

"I know we haven't talked about it, so I don't have a right to expect you not to see other people, I guess."

She waited. Would he keep going or let the issue die?

He sighed. "How about we talk this over tomorrow?"

She slowly released the breath she'd been holding. "Okay. See you at seven."

She closed the cell and finished the shutdown procedures for her computer. "Hey, I think I'm going to head on home."

Tandy glanced at her. "Already? We've only been here a couple of hours."

"I know, but I've got this sister who wants a painting for her wedding present, and you wouldn't believe what she'd do to me if I didn't get it done in time."

"Sounds like an awful monster."

"She has her moments."

Tandy shot a rubber band at her, barely missing Kendra's arm.

"Hey!"

"You had it coming."

"Maybe so." Kendra slung her bag over her shoulder and headed for the back door. "All the same, I'll see you tomorrow night at Heartland, okay?"

"You going with Darin?"

"Who else would I be going with?" Kendra pushed out of the door before Tandy could answer and went to her RAV4, images of Harrison and Darin battling for preeminence in her mind.

She debated the whole way home, arguing the logic of having no contact with a man who sported a gold band on a finger, even if all they did was talk. Even if his commitment to his vows might be wavering right now.

Or maybe because of that.

Reality demanded that she end things with Darin, though, not Harrison. Because Darin's goodness, his rightness, his smart choices in life dictated that he not end up with the likes of her. Harrison, on the other hand, could offer exactly what she deserved — the opportunity to be the other woman. How many marriages had Sylvia broken up? How many men had used Sylvia to prove to themselves what they already knew — that they weren't in love with their wives and weren't willing to do the work it took to be in love again?

The inevitability of the situation hit her as Kendra pulled into her driveway. How could she be expected to do anything other than what she was doing? That old saying, "The apple doesn't fall far from the tree," must exist for a reason, right?

Her feet hit the stairs like anvils as she trudged up to her door. The weight of her past, of a childhood she neither asked for nor relished, hit her anew. Letting Darin get involved with her, responding to him — that's what needed to stop. If she had a decent bone in her body, she'd set him free.

She unlocked her door and entered to find Miss Kitty lying on the back of the sofa. "Hey, Miss Thang." She went over and scratched a hello on the cat's head, then walked down the hallway to her painting studio. An empty canvas stood silent sentinel on its easel. She punched the button on her stereo system, and Kelly Clarkson's voice filled the room.

"The trouble with love is, it can tear you up inside . . ."

The mirrors lining half of one wall reflected back her sad smile. How could she be expected to paint a happy scene for a wedding gift when the mess of her own love life rivaled Jennifer Aniston's? Crossing the small room, she picked up a paintbrush and stared at it. Some artists believed the brush itself held a touch of magic and mystery, that it would speak if the right person wielded it.

She held it up to the canvas, barely allowing the clean bristles to touch the canvas. Closing her eyes, she let herself feel the beautiful tension that always rode the air when Harrison was in her presence. Her shoulders rose, and she sucked in her breath. Tossing her head, she watched the scene on the backs of her eyelids. It presented a lovely tableau, its essence broken only by the knowledge that this could never be right. He was *married.*

Which meant she couldn't have Darin because he was too right and she couldn't have Harrison because he was too wrong.

She opened her eyes to see that the paint-brush had stayed stubbornly still.

In a surge of defiance and anger, she threw it against the wall.

The opening violin strains of Al Green's "How Can You Mend a Broken Heart?" replaced Kelly Clarkson's voice, and Kendra clutched her stomach. Were there music gremlins hiding in her stereo, waiting to play just the right song to make her feel even worse?

Why couldn't she call things off with Harrison? How long could this go on? How many more days — weeks? — before Darin found out that he wasn't the only man in her life? He'd made it clear that they would be having "that" talk tomorrow at Heartland. And what would he say when she told him she thought they should keep seeing other people? Or could she tell him with a straight face that they should only see each other? No, not unless she meant it. But could she mean it? And if not, could she end things with him?

Maybe Harrison wouldn't call anymore. They hadn't spoken since his impromptu trip to Stars Hill earlier in the week. That didn't mean much, though. They'd gone months without speaking to each other —

months that had allowed her to move on and start seeing Darin — only to have Harrison call and pick things up right where they'd left off.

Well, not *exactly* where they'd left off. At least she had that; they would never share a kiss again. There was a line somewhere that couldn't be crossed. Together she and Harrison could find that line. They were close to figuring it out now. Meetings in public places. Conversation only. Okay. Not a sin against anybody. If his wife saw them talking, surely she couldn't get upset over her husband having a friendship. That would be stupid, right?

No more stupid, of course, then neglecting your husband to the point that he *could* sneak off for conversation with another woman, anyway.

Kendra lifted her head and looked herself in the eye on the wall mirror as Al Green sang, *"We could never see tomorrow. No one said a word about the sorrow."*

As the Reverend sang on, Kendra sank to the plush carpet and felt a part of her being ripped from its moorings. It had to, or she would drown in the moral abyss.

EIGHT

Tandy flipped a page in *Brides Magazine* and reached to dog-ear the page. The pale shimmer of gold silk on this dress would be perfect in the early morning light. Plus, the color would look great on Kendra's dark skin and against Meg's blonde hair. It might not be the absolute best color for Joy, though.

She cocked her head and considered the color again. What would Joy's pale skin look like swathed in pale gold? Hmm, either she'd look gorgeous or sick. Tandy reached for the office phone and called Joy's cell.

"Hello? This is Joy."

"Hey, Joy. It's Tandy."

"I cannot believe I haven't programmed the SI office line into my phone yet. Every time you call, it shows up as Unknown."

"Good, I get to take you by surprise."

"Only until I get the number in this phone, and I'm making a note right now on

105

my to-do list, so enjoy your last surprise phone call, sister."

"Oh, drat."

Joy's tinkling laugh sounded. "What's going on at the SI offices?"

"Not a whole lot. I'm getting out some new-member T-shirts and helping the club out in Los Angeles organize an all-night crop."

"That sounds fun."

"It is. I can't believe this is my day job now." Tandy looked around the cheery office and felt blessed all over again. "Listen, though, I'm calling about the bridesmaid dresses."

"Did you finally pick a style? A color? A date? A time? A theme?"

"Whoa, sister. Take a breath!"

"Sorry. You know me and weddings."

"I know, I know. You live for the happily-ever-after moment."

"You better believe it. Now, what is it about the dresses? I place my expertise at your service."

"Well, I picked a date. It's going to be the first Saturday in October at nine in the morning. I've decided to do semiformal, and now I'm picking colors. How do you look in pale gold?"

"Not as good as I look in pale blue."

"Eww, pale blue? You've got the nursery vibe happening again. Ooh, are you pregnant?"

"No, still nothing." Joy's voice lost its lilt, and Tandy frowned at the phone. "We're trying. Actually, we're trying like crazy."

"Yuck. Yuck. Too much information."

"Tandy, we're married. We're allowed to try to get pregnant."

"Yep, and I'm allowed to live in blissful ignorance and continue believing that all of your children will be delivered the same way Meg's were: by the stork."

"So long as you're happy, then."

"Thanks. It's good of you to know what's important."

"You know, sometimes I wonder about you."

"Only sometimes?"

"All right, nearly every moment of every day. Though I'll admit my concern has been somewhat lessened since our dear Clay put that lovely diamond on your finger."

Tandy held up her hand and admired the glint of light off of her engagement ring. "It *is* something, isn't it?"

"A one-of-a-kind, designed-by-the-groom-himself ring? Yes, I'd say that's something."

"Which is why I've got to do well in planning this wedding. So back to pale gold.

Not your color, hmm?"

"To be honest, I'm not certain what that will look like on me. But if it's the color you love, then it's the color I'll wear."

"Aww, you're the bestest sister ever."

"Be sure you call Meg and Kendra with that news."

"Will do. Bye, sis."

"Bye."

Tandy hung up the phone and considered the magazine again, tilting her head and nibbling her lower lip. The color really would look great in morning light. And at least two of the three sisters would be pretty in it.

She tore the page from the magazine and added it to a manila folder labeled "Wedding."

She continued to flip through the magazine, tearing out pages of various wedding accoutrements. Within about half an hour, she had a pretty good idea of what kind of cake she wanted (rolled fondant with simple pearls on top, five-tier), which dress would best fit the type of ceremony she'd chosen (evening pearl instead of stark white and clean lines, no sequins or butt bows for her), and which tuxes the guys should wear (ivory all the way, no tails, elegant yet informal enough for morning).

There were still tons of decisions to make, like what food they would serve, what music would play at which times in the ceremony, how many invitations to send out, picking out an invitation, registering at which stores in Nashville, and a host of other possibilities.

Tandy pushed off from the desk and swung her chair in a circle, then turned her head to take in the image of Cooper sprawled beside her. "Coop, this wedding stuff takes forever to plan."

Cooper aimed his sad basset eyes her way, and she shifted to scratch him with her toe, grateful she could bring her dog to work. "You're the best dog in the world, Cooper. Are you ready to move into Clay's place? You'll go nuts with all those smells from the diner below."

Cooper sighed a loud doggy noise, and Tandy reached to scratch his leg joints, knowing that was one of his favorite places to get lovings.

"Your old joints doing okay, boy? Did the glucosamine help? I don't think that lady at the shelter knew it would come on this fast."

Cooper rolled his head toward her, and she scratched his ears. "Poor little guy. Bet your basset ancestors dealt with the same problem."

She finished scratching and sat back up. "Let's get back to it, puppy dog. These details aren't going to take care of themselves!" Humming a Martina McBride tune, Tandy flipped back through the magazine. "I wonder where Clay's taking me on our honeymoon, Coop? You think he'll remember to make arrangements for you?" A quick glance down revealed Coop's shuttered eyes. He was solidly back in dreamworld.

Might as well make sure.

She dialed the diner and waited for Clay to pick up.

"Clay's Diner."

"Hey, sweetie, it's me."

"Hey, you! What's shaking?"

"Not too much. Just going through wedding magazines, and I realized I hadn't reminded you that we'll need to check Cooper in at the doggy spa for our honeymoon."

"Already taken care of."

"How did you already take care of it when we just settled the date this morning?"

"As soon as we had a date, I called them. Thought I'd remove any excuse you may come up with to change the date on me."

"Now why would I change the date?"

"Because you're female and that's what females do?"

"I'm hanging up now," she growled.

"Wait, before you go, are we going to Heartland tomorrow night?"

"Sure. Kendra and Darin are coming and, besides, I need a reminder of why I'm enduring these wedding-planning headaches."

"It's because you love me."

Tandy sighed melodramatically. "I suppose I do. It's my lot in life."

"Poor soul. Pick you up at seven?"

"See ya then."

Here came that silly grin again. The man's ability to make her giddy bordered on ridiculous. But in just two short months she'd be standing by his side, swearing to love him until death parted them. This time last year, nobody — including her, in all honesty — would have ever guessed that the next August would find her living in Stars Hill, running a business, and planning a wedding.

"Hey, sis!"

Tandy turned to see Meg coming in the back door. "Hey! What are you doing here in the middle of the day? Where are the kiddos?"

"At home with a sitter. I needed some adult time." Meg plopped down in Kendra's chair and propped her sandal-clad feet on the desk.

Tandy wrinkled her nose and pointed. "I can tell. What happened to your hair?"

Meg reached up and patted the oddly placed tiny ponytails that sprouted all over the front half of her head. "Oh! Savannah wanted to play beauty salon and needed a live model." She began taking out the small hair bands.

"And let me guess. You forgot they were even there when you left home."

"It's hard enough to get out of the house without them all knowing I'm leaving and pitching a fit to come with me. What my hair looked like was the least of my concerns."

"Ah, I see. Is this the fun married life I have to look forward to?"

Meg removed the last of the bands and stuffed them in the pocket of her khaki shorts. "Yep. Tempting, isn't it?"

Tandy knew she was joking but thought about it for a second. "You know, it really is."

Meg's eyes widened. "I think you've been looking at those magazines too long." She gestured to the piles of bridal magazines threatening to topple off Tandy's desk. "They make it seem like an effortless happily ever after, but you've got to know that it isn't that way in real life. It's like Martina sings, *'I beg your pardon, I never promised you a rose garden. Along with the sunshine —,'*"

Tandy joined in. *"There's gotta be a little rain sometime."* They laughed together, and Tandy closed the magazine in front of her, kicking her feet up on the desk as well. "Yeah, I know it's not all sunshine and roses, but I'd rather be with Clay during the storms than live back in Orlando with sunshine all the time. Aren't you that way with Jamison?"

"Most of the time, yes."

"Most of the time?"

"Well, yeah. There are some days I'd like nothing better than to lock the man in the basement and have the whole house to myself for a few hours."

"I think they already did that on *Desperate Housewives.*"

"That wasn't her husband; it was her son. And I wouldn't keep him there for days, just long enough so I could take a long bath and a nap." Meg wiggled her eyebrows, making Tandy laugh.

"If you're so tired, how could you summon the energy to wrestle him to the basement?"

"Ah, the logical lawyer still lurks, eh? I

guess you're right. I don't have the energy to do my own hair, much less manhandle my husband into the basement."

"Are you still tired all the time?"

Meg sighed and leaned back in the red leather chair. "Yeah. I try hard to get eight hours of sleep like all the magazines tell us to, but that's almost impossible with three kids, one of whom still doesn't sleep through the night. And even when Hannah does make it through the night, I still feel exhausted the next morning." She shrugged. "I guess my body isn't getting into deep sleep because my subconscious is waiting on a kiddo to wake up and need me."

"But Hannah's almost a year old now!"

"Yep, a year at the end of this month, actually."

"And she still doesn't sleep through the night?"

"It comes and goes. We'll go a couple of weeks with no nighttime waking; and then, *bam,* she's back to getting up at three in the morning."

"Wow, that sounds tough."

"It can be, but I wouldn't trade a thing in the world for them."

"You're a better woman than I am."

"Nope, I'm just a mom. You wait. You'll get there, too, and then you'll be the one all bleary-eyed with ponytails sticking up all over." Meg rolled her eyes.

"No, I think I'll just shave my head when I have kids. Much easier that way."

"I tried. Joy refused," Meg deadpanned.

Tandy's eyes widened before she realized Meg's joke. "Oh, that's rich!"

Meg waved the idea away. "Yeah, yeah, it's just as well. Jamison loves long hair and would have totally freaked if I'd done it. Anyway, I didn't come over here to gripe about my home life. Savannah's birthday is at the end of this month, and I'm planning her party. Can you be there on the 30th?"

"Sure! What do I need to bring?"

"Nothing but your smiling self and the new VeggieTales video."

"Oh! *The Pirates Who Don't Do Anything*?"

"Yep!"

"No worries, I've got it covered. We're having this at your house, right?"

"Right again." Meg stood up and brushed the wrinkles out of her shorts. "I'm off to rent a jump-a-tron now for it." She turned to go.

"Hey, Meg?"

Meg turned back. "Yeah?"

"Did you buy Kendra's story?"

"About not having a pattern, or not being involved with that man that Joy saw?"

115

"Both."

"No."

Tandy dropped her feet to the floor and pulled herself back up to the desk. "Me neither."

Kendra stood in the shower, all vestige of sadness gone for now, replaced by the anticipation of seeing Darin in just a little while and the sound of John Legend telling her "Don't You Worry 'Bout a Thing" on the stereo. Much better than Al Green. She made a mental note to stay away from Al for a while. Her heart felt bruised and battered from yesterday's avalanche of emotion.

Dancing with Darin at Heartland would be a blast because he made things so *easy.* Of course, tonight might not be as easy as usual since he wanted to have "the talk." Kendra squeezed her body wash bottle and lathered up the poof. She simply wouldn't think about that right now. Right now, she'd focus on the fact that a gorgeous man with a heart of gold was set to pick her up soon. Right now, she'd remember that tonight this gorgeous man wanted to dance with *her.* And right now, she'd think about making herself pretty for him.

Singing along with the music, she made

quick work of the shower, allowing herself only a few minutes to stand in the massaging spray while the deep conditioner did its work beneath the plastic baggie on her head. No time for too much luxury right now. Tonight felt like an impending battle, and she had war paint to apply.

She wiped the steam from the mirror and took stock. Despite passing thirty, there were very few lines in her face. *Unlike Sylvia.*

No. No thoughts about her birth mother.

Another voice filled her mind: *"You haven't been acting like the confident, sassy woman I met four months ago."* There was a sting of rightness in Darin's words, and that demanded a change. She had been letting childhood wreak havoc with her present again. Time for that to stop.

She picked up a jar of moisturizer and applied it over her face and neck. The light scent of wisteria reminded her of Daddy and Momma's house. That was more like it. Childhood with Marian and Jack Sinclair had been light-years better than her days with Sylvia.

Stop thinking of her, Kendra. Focus on the here and now. She stole a quick glance at the small clock that rested on a ledge beneath the mirror. Darin would be here in twenty minutes — barely enough time to get her makeup on and her hair set. Thank goodness she'd picked an outfit before jumping into the shower.

Swiping eye shadow across her lids, Kendra mentally threw off the chains of her past. Again.

She finished both eyes, then picked up the mascara wand and enhanced her already thick lashes. No need for falsies tonight. No time even if she did want them. Blinking rapidly to dry the mascara, she made her way into the bedroom and eyed the ensemble lying on the bed. The pale yellow dress would accentuate her caramel-colored skin and dark hair. Its short skirt was long enough not to embarrass her if Daddy and Zelda were there yet short enough to show off her legs when Darin twirled her around the dance floor.

Perfect.

She pulled the dress over her head and turned to the full-length mirror in the corner of the room.

"Not bad. Not bad at all." She turned this way and that to ensure the dress looked good from all angles. If she was going to have a conversation she'd rather avoid, then at least she could look good doing it.

Sitting down on the bed, she pulled brown

boots on her feet. Dancing at Heartland demanded nothing less than broken-in boots with heels good for stomping. A few of her signature bangle bracelets and a pair of white hoop earrings completed her look.

Ready for battle or anything else the night chose to dump on her, Kendra left the bedroom. Miss Kitty looked up from her spot on the back of the sofa as Kendra sailed into the living room.

"Okay, Miss Kitty," Kendra twirled around, feeling the dress swirl around her legs, "what do you think of your momma?"

Miss Kitty opened one eye in her best imitation of the Cheshire Cat, then began licking her paws.

"Oh, sure, sit there with your high-and-mighty self. That's all right. That's okay. I don't need your affirmation."

Miss Kitty looked at her again, then began cleaning the other paw.

Kendra put her hands on her hips, "Hey, Miss Thang. A little attention to the one who buys that high-priced food you love and cleans your litter box."

Miss Kitty stopped licking, looked at Kendra, then hopped down off the couch. She pranced across the living room and twirled herself in between Kendra's ankles, purring all the while.

Kendra relented and picked her up. "There we go. That's what I thought." She rubbed the soft furry head. "Sitting over there like you're the queen of this castle. You keep in mind, I'm the queen." She nuzzled close to the cat's ear. "You're the princess."

A knock at the door stopped the lovefest, and Kendra set Miss Kitty back on the couch. "Now you keep an eye on the place tonight and don't let any of those street cats in the door, missy, you hear?" She opened the front door. "Hi."

Darin's purple button-up set off his dark eyes, which were sparkling at her. "Wow, hey. You look beautiful."

"Thanks." Her pulse kicked up. "Come on in. I just need to grab my purse."

Darin stepped inside, his brown cowboy boots sounding on the hardwood entryway. "Sure, take your time. I'm a little early."

Kendra went to the kitchen and snatched her purse up off the table. "Ready!" she called, coming back through the doorway. But Darin wasn't standing by the door anymore. He sat on the couch with Miss Kitty in his lap purring louder than an outboard.

Kendra stopped. Stared. What on earth . . . ? "You realize she hates men, right?"

"Yeah, I can see that." Darin tipped the cat back onto the couch and came over to her, palms in the air in innocence. "She came over to say hello, I promise. I was only returning the favor."

"Hmm, I guess she's gotten used to seeing you."

"Good." He reached around her and opened the door. "At least one of you has. Ready to hit the dance floor?"

Should she let that comment go? Maybe go ahead and have the tough conversation now so they could either get it behind them and have a good night, or break up and move on?

Is it a breakup if you aren't already exclusively seeing each other?

"Kendra?"

She blinked. "Sorry. Yes, let's go." She walked ahead of him into the hallway and down the staircase to the front door, her boot heels clicking with his on the hardwood stairs.

Outside the August air enveloped them like a warm blanket. Kendra's bare arms took in the warmth as they walked across the grass to his Barracuda. Should she say something when he got in the car? Wouldn't it ruin the evening to have this thing hanging between them the whole night?

Darin opened her door and helped her into the car, facts she barely registered as she debated in her mind. Darin was an honest, up-front guy. He'd probably appreciate her tackling the subject head-on instead of waiting around with bated breath. Then again, if she told him she wanted to keep seeing other people, he'd ask if she *was* seeing anyone else. And no way would the words "Yeah, but he's married" come out of her mouth.

Darin cleared his throat, and she realized they were sitting in silence.

"Something on your mind?" he asked.

His teasing tone was an open invitation to share. But sharing was dangerous right now. Dangerous most of the time, really. "Yeah, thinking about that painting for Tandy."

If I have to lie, shouldn't I question the relationship?

Darin turned the key in the ignition and backed out of the drive. "Don't worry about it. You'll finish it with time to spare, and it will be the hit of the reception."

He maneuvered through the streets of Stars Hill, turning off Lindell onto University, then Broadway, before taking a quick right onto the one-way street where the bright lights of Heartland's parking lot shone. Kendra watched his hand on the

122

gearshift, turning the steering wheel, adjusting the rearview mirror . . .

It wasn't right to be seeing someone else while this lovely man showed an interest in her. Momma would have a conniption fit. Probably was, up in heaven. And Daddy — well, Daddy would hang his head and shake it back and forth, and shame would come over Kendra like the humidity of a Southern summer night.

Inescapable.

Overwhelming.

Suffocating.

Inevitable.

"You've gone quiet on me again, woman. And don't try the 'I'm thinking about the painting' line again. I let you get by with it once. Is something wrong?"

Kendra twisted the bracelets on her arm. "No."

Darin quirked an eyebrow and gave her a crooked grin. "Want to rethink that answer? You haven't said ten words since we left your place, and you're twisting those bracelets so hard I'd think you had Indian burn by now."

She glanced at her wrist. He was right. "There's a lot going on right now. The wedding, getting the business going —"

"Having a boyfriend who doesn't want to

see other people." He reached over and touched her arm, stilling the bracelets. "If it's something you're not ready for, Ken, no problem. Just don't pull away from me without at least having the discussion."

She sighed. "I don't mean to pull away."

"And you don't want us to be exclusive."

"I didn't say that."

"Not in words, no. Have I misread you?"

"I don't know. I'm confused."

He sat up and twisted in the seat to lean his back against the door. "Okay, confusion I can help with. What are you confused about?"

Kendra closed her eyes. If only life could be as simple as Darin sometimes made it. Just make a list of fuzzy points, clarify them, and move right on down the line. Life, for her anyway, wasn't that simple.

"I don't even know what I'm confused about." Well, she did, but telling him that a married man was muddling her brain wouldn't be the wisest course of action.

"Have you enjoyed the last four months?"

"Of course!" When his cocked head showed his doubt, she rushed to assure him. "I love spending time with you! You're a wonderful man. Any girl would be lucky to go out with you."

"Why?"

"Seriously? You want me to list why you're great? Having a low self-esteem night, are we?"

He settled further into his seat and crossed his arms — those arms! — over his chest. "Let's just say a man likes to be affirmed every now and then."

"You know you're a fabulous catch. I can't believe you want me to sit here and —"

"Name three things." He held up three fingers, then crossed his arms again. "Three little things you find attractive in me, or three little reasons you've enjoyed the past four months."

"That's easy." She wriggled down in her own seat and ticked off items on her fingers. "You're a great conversationalist, and I've had fun talking with you for hours on end." Maybe not the same intensely personal way as Harrison, but still. She rushed on. "You're a musician, and I like coming to hear you play. And you know how to dance, which is something I'm about to continue to enjoy if we can finish this conversation and get in there." She gestured toward Heartland.

"Not so fast, lady. Now name three things you like about yourself."

"What?"

"Come on, it shouldn't be hard. Three

things you like about yourself that you notice when you're around me."

"That's ridiculous." She turned to open the door.

"Kendra?"

His quiet voice made her stop and turn to look at him.

"Humor me. Three things. What do you like about yourself when you're around me?"

That'd be so much easier to answer if she liked herself right now. But here she sat, a cheating, conniving woman about to enjoy a wonderful date with a fabulous man who deserved a much better woman than she. Harrison's face flashed in her mind, and her shoulders slumped.

"Darin, I'm not going to sit here and list for you my finer points. If you can't see them for yourself, then maybe we *do* need to see other people."

He leaned forward and took her hand, drawing her eyes to his. Thick, dark lashes framed the concern in those chocolate depths. She looked away but had to turn back when he squeezed her hand. "I'm not asking for me, Ken. Come on, three things, and then we can drop this entire conversation, go in there," he nodded toward the dance hall, "and have a good time."

She took a deep breath. "Three things, huh?"

"That's it."

"Why does it matter?"

"Because a good relationship means that the other person is better for being with me, just as I'm better for being with her. Not better as in earn-your-merit-badge better but better as in more aware, more happy, more fulfilled — more *something* because I'm around. You hear what I'm saying?"

She grimaced, hearing the truth of his words. It was the reason he probably should be with someone else. How could he be better by spending time with her? How could anybody be better by spending time with a child whose own mother didn't want her or protect her from a host of vile boyfriends?

But what Darin asked for now wasn't a difficult thing to provide. Three ways she was better for having known him. She could name a million if he wanted. The whole world felt like a better place now that he lived in it.

"I see the dream possibilities of my life when I'm with you." Her voice came out whisper-soft, all she could force past the lump in her throat.

"I —"

A knock at her window caused them both

to jump. Tandy stood on the other side, smiling and waving.

Kendra cast a rueful glance at Darin, then turned back to Tandy, half grateful, half . . . what? Disappointed?

Sighing away her confusion, she opened the door and stepped a boot out onto the gravel.

"Hey, you! Ready to get your groove on?" Tandy held her arms in the air and shimmied a bit.

Kendra tilted her chin down, hands on hips. "I don't think Heartland would know what a groove was if we brought the dictionary and pointed it out."

Tandy dropped her arms. "You're probably right."

"Probably?"

"Okay, okay, forget the groove thing. Ready to boot scoot?"

Darin's car door closed, and Kendra turned to see him.

"I don't know, T." She smiled at Darin. "Are we ready to boot scoot?"

"Please, woman. I haven't boot scooted since the nineties."

Tandy linked her arm in Kendra's and tugged her toward the entrance. "Then what do we call it now?"

Darin drew alongside them. "Got me."

"Let's make something up. Come on, Ken, you're good with this stuff."

"Uh-uh. Don't go putting this on me."

They reached the door, and Kendra pulled it open. The twang of a steel guitar washed over them, the happy notes of a fiddle weaving in and out of the guitar's whine.

"Y'all figure it out while I go find some caffeine. I'm going to need it tonight, I think." Kendra took off for the refreshment stand.

"Get me some, too," Tandy called, and Kendra waved her hand over her head.

She glanced around the room on the way. Daddy and Zelda were indeed there and dancing. A circle had formed in the middle of the floor, and the participants were in the midst of a schottische dance. The multicolored lights played off Zelda's flaming red hair, creating a bizarre kaleidoscope of color, as she twirled beneath her partner's arm, then rock stepped and moved to the next person in the circle. The floor vibrated slightly from a hundred boots shuffling and rock stepping.

Kendra reached the refreshment booth and ordered a Coke, then turned and leaned on the counter to keep watching Zelda. From the corner of her eye, she saw Tandy, Clay, and Darin talking — their heads bent as if in deep discussion. She frowned. What was *that* about?

"I'm pretty sure she's seeing somebody." Darin looked up to ensure Kendra still waited over at the refreshment stand.

"Why are you so certain?" Tandy worried her bottom lip. Kendra had told the sisters she wasn't seeing anyone else. Had she lied?

"I told her I wanted to talk about it tonight, about seeing each other exclusively. When I picked her up, she was more scared than Bill Clinton on judgment day. Didn't say a word the whole way from her place to here. When I brought it up, you should have seen her face."

"Maybe she's just worried about something else. We *are* getting a new business off the ground, you know."

Clay rubbed Tandy's arm. "The business is four months old, sweetie, not counting how long those girls up in Nashville had it before they sold it to you. Is there anything happening with Sisters, Ink that would cause Kendra to act this out of character?"

"No, not really."

"But she told you girls she wasn't seeing anyone else?" Hope rose in Darin's eyes.

Tandy met his eyes. "She did. But, Darin, sometimes Kendra can twist things to make it *seem* like one thing when really it's another."

"You lost me."

"Well, I can't remember now if she actually said the words, 'I am not seeing another man.' I know we talked to her about the strange man that Joy saw, and she made it sound as if we were crazy for thinking she'd consider seeing anybody while she's with you."

"But you can't think of her actual words?"

Tandy tilted her head and stared at the ceiling, trying hard to think of Kendra's exact words during their scrapping time. She lowered her head in resignation. "I can't, Darin. I'm sorry. Why don't you ask her?"

Darin sighed. "You tell her, man." He pointed at Clay. "I'm gonna go see if Kendra needs help carrying the drinks."

Tandy watched Darin walk off, a definite slump to his broad shoulders.

"What should we do?"

"Go someplace we can hear each other without yelling." Clay took her hand and pulled her out the door. Outside moths fluttered in clouds around the parking lot lights. Clay kept walking until they were at the corner of the lot. He boosted himself onto the back of her Beamer — still the only

BMW in all of Stars Hill — and patted the space beside him.

She obliged and pushed up from the bumper to sit next to him. "Come on, Clay, how do we fix this?"

He leaned forward, elbows on knees, and clasped his hands together. "We don't, sweetie."

"What?"

"I don't think we need to fix this for Kendra."

"What are you saying?" She tugged on his arm, and he turned to look her in the eye.

"She's a grown woman, Taz. If she wants to make a stupid move, I think she's allowed at this point."

"When you love someone, you stop them *before* the train hits."

"How many trains are you going to deal with? She's done this kind of thing for years. Are you always going to fix it for her? Is Joy? Is Meg?"

Tandy leaned back on the rear windshield and watched the bats swooping through the darkness, no doubt snatching moths in midair. They were shadows of shadows, barely discernible from the darkness of night, visible only when they swooped into the light for the kill. And gone an instant later.

"Clay, we can't just sit by and watch a train wreck. How is that loving her?"

"I don't know. Maybe it's not. Maybe I'm completely off-base on this. But I've watched her do this over and over with you guys, and I can't see how anything you've done in the past is breaking the cycle."

"If we could figure out why she does it, we'd have a chance of ending the cycle."

"I think she doesn't feel worthy because of Sylvia."

"I think you're right."

"And there's nothing we can do about that." He pointed up to the moths still circling the light. "Any more than we can teach those moths to stay away from the light or they'll get eaten."

"Noticed that, too, did you?"

"It's hard to miss. Lots of bats out to-night."

"But isn't there a group of moths somewhere that change colors or something to make themselves harder to see?"

"Yeah, but nobody changes the color of those moths from the outside. It was God letting them adapt from the inside."

"So we've got to hope that God changes Ken?"

"No." He took her hand. "We've got to hope that Ken *lets* God change her."

Tandy held onto the hand of this wise man God had used to change her and watched the moths.

Kendra and Darin twirled past Daddy and Zelda, and Kendra laughed. Darin's arms around her made the world feel right again. For right now she could let go of that part of her that wanted to be with Harrison. That part of her that wanted to throw morality to the wind and just take the thing in front of her that made her feel good, even though the other part of her — that part that leaned into Darin now and nuzzled his ear as the music switched to a slow love song — knew that Harrison wouldn't feel good in a few years. If he left his wife — *stop it, that's not a good thing* — how could she do anything the rest of her life but wonder when he would leave her as well?

"Penny for your thoughts." Darin's breath slid over her ear as he whispered the words.

"Just enjoying the dance."

"Mmm, me too."

She swayed in his arms, wishing she could be worthy of this man.

Knowing she never would be.

But that's not stopping you, is it? From taking what you can get now and worrying about the rest later? No surprise there. Just goes to prove —

Kendra closed her eyes, trying to push the dark voice away, finally succeeding, but not before it gave her one last jab.

Like mother, like daughter.

NINE

"Thanks for another fabulous night."

Darin stood outside the door to Kendra's apartment. She looked so amazing — full of life, fresh. Energy lit her eyes, and if she asked, he knew he'd spend another hour dancing despite the fact that his feet were killing him and his back screamed for an Advil.

"You're welcome." She looked at the floor, and he grinned at the paradox of a suddenly shy Kendra.

"Well, I guess I should be heading on home." He touched her face, bringing her eyes to his. "I'll call you tomorrow."

Before she could think and that light could go out of her eyes, he closed the short distance between them and kissed her. She didn't resist, not even a hint, and he cupped her jawline in his hand. Could he be wrong about another man in her life? Would she give herself so fully to kissing him if someone else hovered in the wings? She'd been so hard to read all night, completely with him one moment and in another world the next.

He pulled away and looked into her mocha-colored eyes. "Kendra?"

"Mmm?"

Are you seeing someone else? He couldn't bring himself to say the words. It would kill their perfect evening; and, besides, what good would it to do have her admit it? There was still a chance she'd ended it. Or would be ending it. Or never had it to begin with, and he was suffering from a case of overactive imagination.

Along with all the sisters.

"What, Darin?" Her soft voice was a gift to his ears.

"Nothing. Never mind."

She let him get away with it. Because she needed to hide something? Because she feared his questions?

He stepped back, a little mind whacked from the unspoken words that floated around them.

"Thanks again. I'll talk to you later."

She smiled at him, touched his lips, and entered her apartment.

He stared at her door for a second. Would she talk to the other guy tonight? Or had she called it off by now? Or did she have a date planned with him for tomorrow?

Stupid! He should have asked her out for tomorrow.

He raised his hand to knock on the door but dropped it before he could make an idiot of himself. Turning on his heel, heart heavy with possibility and probability, he went to the grand staircase and descended.

Kendra sat down on her overstuffed white couch and pulled her feet under her. Miss Kitty came over and settled in the crook of her mistress's legs.

This roller coaster of a love life couldn't continue. It just couldn't. She glanced at the clock on the wall. Midnight. About the time Harrison's wife would be going to bed. Would he e-mail her before the night ended? Send a text her way? Dare to step outside in the driveway and call her?

Why did she care so much? Had those first few months with him removed all vestige of the morality Daddy and Momma had instilled in her for years? Hundreds — thousands — of Sunday school teachings and sermons delivered in Daddy's slow Southern drawl from the pulpit of Grace Christian pushed against the questions in Kendra's mind.

Tigers can't change their stripes.

Sylvia's words cut deep. Had Kendra spent a lifetime learning ways opposite those of her mother's only to find herself destined to follow in Sylvia's footsteps? Did daughters have a choice?

She glanced at the cordless phone on the table at her side. She could call Harrison's cell right now and leave a message that ended everything. That's what Darin deserved. Sweet, precious, loving Darin. His kiss lingered on her lips, and she reached to touch them, to feel that tingle of anticipation.

The phone rang and anticipation leaped to anxiety. No one would call her this late except Harrison. Unless a family member had an emergency.

Another ring, and Kendra picked up the phone to check Caller ID.

Harrison.

She must have gone to bed a few minutes early if he felt safe enough to call her already.

"Hello?"

"Hey, doll. How was your day?"

She snuggled into the couch and pushed Darin to the back of her mind, ignoring the twinge of guilt that caused the other Kendra answer. "It was okay. Yours?"

He sighed. "Long. Very, very long. But getting better by the second."

"Oh, I'll bet you use that line with all the girls."

"Yeah, the thousands I see every week."

The smile in his voice didn't completely stop her mental question. Was this the first time he'd looked at a woman other than his wife?

"I'm sure. And does it work with all of them?"

"Most." He laughed. "Tell me about your week."

"Not much to tell. I don't think you snuck out to your driveway to call and hear about my boring life."

"On the contrary. I'm in my car, and your life is anything but boring. I feel better after ten seconds talking to you than I have all week."

She tucked the compliment away to savor later. "You're in your car?"

"I am."

"At midnight? Why?"

"I gave a seminar this evening on better business principles. And, yes, it was as awful as the title."

"A seminar lasts until midnight?"

"No, a seminar lasts until nine. A man who's trying to ignore his compulsion to drive to a little town south of Nashville and talk to a woman who makes him feel so much better about life in general leaves that seminar and takes in a late movie in a desperate attempt to rid his mind of her memory."

"Ah, and did it work?"

"I don't think so, since I'm now two exits from your place."

She blinked. "What?"

"I'm about five minutes from your front door."

"What happened to meeting in public places?"

"Guess I should have called you from the movie."

"Yeah, that would have been smart." *Except I would have said no. Because I'm cutting things off with you. See, I have this man who is wonderful and doesn't deserve my cheating self.*

"Sorry. Do you want me to turn around?"

"Yes." *No.*

"Really?" A hint of confusion colored his tone.

"Yes. Go back one exit, and I'll meet you where we were before in about ten or fifteen minutes."

"Scared to have me in your apartment?"

"Too wise to have you in my apartment,

mister. Fifteen minutes." She disconnected and looked down at Miss Kitty. "Looks like I'm not in for the night after all."

Kendra checked her face in the living room mirror. Most of her makeup was gone now, sweated off on the floor of Heartland with Darin, who would be so hurt if he knew where she was headed right now.

But Harrison had driven an hour to see her. She couldn't just tell him to turn around. It would be rude. And friends didn't treat each other that way. Even if they were friends with an attraction, she and Harrison had chosen to keep things as friends. Only friendship was allowed.

Of course, they'd also *chosen* to restrict their meetings to public places, and here he came driving to Stars Hill in the middle of the night.

What had he told his wife? Was she lying in bed right now, wondering why her husband hadn't come home yet?

Kendra grabbed her keys from the table by the door and walked out. Descending the staircase, she tried hard to forget her steps on them not fifteen minutes ago. The man walking beside her then was honest, forthright, and undeserving of the kind of ugliness she walked in right now.

Maybe she should end things with Darin, not Harrison. If she truly cared for Darin, then the only caring thing would be to let him go so he could find a good woman.

A woman much better than she.

A woman who wouldn't dream of meeting a married man on an old country road in the dark of night.

Kendra crossed the yard and got into her little RAV4. Shards of pain cut deep into her heart. If the very thought of leaving Darin hurt this much, how would she survive the act of it?

Her cell rang from its place in the cup holder as she backed out of the driveway. Who was calling her at midnight?

"Hello?"

"Hey, Ken, it's me."

"Tandy? What's wrong? Is someone hurt?"

"No, no. I'm working on the wedding. What do you think of white lilies?"

"I think they're great if you're going to a funeral or playing the White Queen in Narnia."

"So that'd be a no?"

"Um, yeah. Why are you up at midnight working on this wedding?"

"Because it's when I have some time with Clay. I'm over at his place. We just got back from Heartland."

143

"Ooh, don't tell Daddy you were in Clay's apartment, just the two of you, late into the night."

"Oh, stop. Darin's here, too. We're fine."

"Darin's there?"

"Yep. Hey, you should come over here and help us plan!"

"Look at the clock, sis. It's after midnight. My going-out shoes are in bed for the night."

"But you're not at home."

"What do you mean?"

"I tried your house. You didn't answer. You're not home, are you?"

"Well . . . no." Kendra scrambled around for an excuse. "I needed to think, so I'm out driving around."

"That's perfect. Drive on over here."

"Not exactly conducive to thinking, you know?"

"Come on. I could really use a female perspective here. Clay and Darin have rolled their eyes at me at least fifty times since we sat down. And they're making fun of all the bride models in the catalogs. You could save your sister from a night of wedding-prep torture."

Kendra stopped the vehicle at the red light on Lindell. If she turned right, Harrison was less than ten minutes away. If she went straight, Darin sat one block ahead and on the left.

She groaned, too tired to face this decision right now.

"Ken? You okay?"

Oh, shoot. "Yeah, yeah, I'm fine. Tired and confused. But fine."

"What are you confused about? Come over here, and we can kick these guys to the curb and talk about it."

Protests from Darin and Clay sounded through the phone. Darin didn't deserve what she intended to do.

"Okay, I'll be there in a few." She tried to focus on the part of her that had wanted someone to stop this meeting with Harrison in the dead of night on a dark country road.

"Yay! I'll get the caffeine going."

Kendra hit the End button and dialed Harrison's cell the long way. If she ever lost her cell, there was no trace of Harrison on it in her speed dial numbers or phone book. Unless they checked the "numbers dialed" screen, her secret was safe.

"Hey, doll. You close yet?"

Kendra sighed. "Something's come up. Tandy needs help with wedding planning, so I'm headed over there."

"Wedding planning at midnight? Are you avoiding me?"

"I think I'd come up with a better story, don't you? Seriously, she called me as I was leaving. I couldn't very well tell her I had just left my house to come meet you, could I?"

"Why not? Tell her you have a friend in need and you can't leave him in the lurch."

"At which point she'll ask which of my friends, and I won't have an answer."

"You know, sometimes these sisters of yours can get in the way."

"Hey, watch it, mister." She was only half playing, grateful that he had made a wrong move. Then she wished he hadn't and would keep being perfect. Perfection made it easier to excuse the relationship. Because what woman rejected perfection?

"Kidding! I was kidding. How long do you think this wedding planning will take?"

"Why? Are you going to wait for me?"

"Perhaps."

He'd *wait* for her?

"Wait, how can you do that? I get that you can tell her you were in a seminar until late, then went to a movie, but your time frame won't work out."

"Relax. She's at her mother's. Won't be home until tomorrow night at the latest."

"Oh."

He could wait for her.

"Well, um, I'm not sure how long I'll be with Tandy. How about I call you when I leave there?"

"And try to get out soon?"

"And try to get out soon."

"Is there anywhere to get a bite around here?"

Kendra chuckled. "Sorry, we roll up the streets at nine. There's a twenty-four-hour truck stop one exit south of Stars Hill, though."

"Truck-stop food. Yummy."

"Oh! And there's a Wendy's. It's the weekend, so the drive-thru is open until two."

"Where's Wendy's?"

"Remember Lindell? Take it to University. Wendy's is about four blocks down on the left."

"Great. I'll go eat and be waiting on you at your place."

So much for public places. "Sure. See you soon."

She folded the phone closed again and dropped it into the cup holder. The red light before her had gone through its signal change about three times now. She eased through the intersection and drove down Lindell to College Street. Turning just before Clay's Diner, she rolled to a stop by the curb and looked at the windows in the upper level of the old building.

Light glowed through the glass and welcomed her. Up there were three people who cared more about her than Sylvia had ever thought about. Which left her wondering why she acted more and more like her birth mother these days. Had Sylvia cared for the men in her life? Had she shared with them the stimulating conversation that Kendra shared with Harrison? In a perverse way, Kendra almost hoped she had. Because that, at least, would give some logic to the situation.

Opening the door, she stepped out of the RAV4 and looked up and down the street. No cars marred the picture-perfect evening. Pretty much everyone in Stars Hill was asleep by now.

The stairs creaked as she made her way up to Clay's door. It opened before she'd climbed the last step.

"Hey, Ken!" Tandy stood in the doorway, golden light pouring from behind her to pool on the landing. The edges of her red hair glowed copper. "Come tell these guys that serving cheese puffs at a wedding reception isn't going to happen."

Kendra beamed and the bands around her chest loosened a bit. "Cheese puffs? Let me guess. Darin's idea."

"I heard that, woman!"

Kendra came into the apartment and noted the bridal magazines scattered around the living room. Darin sat in the corner of the couch, an open copy of *Bridal Magazine* on his knees. Clay nestled in his recliner, thumbing through *Travel+Leisure,* no doubt planning a honeymoon. Norah Jones's smooth voice came from the speakers.

Tandy tugged Kendra into the mess. "Tell him, Ken. Save me from the testosterone craziness."

"Cheese puffs?" She looked at Darin. "You've got to be kidding."

He smiled at her, and his eyes told her he was thinking of their kiss just a few minutes ago. "I was, actually. But Bridezilla here takes everything so literally these days."

"Hey, I am *not* Bridezilla! Why does everybody keep calling me that? Just because I don't want cheese puffs at my wedding reception? Crab puffs, sure. Cheese puffs? No." Tandy sat down and snatched a copy of *Modern Bride* from the floor.

Darin laid his arm across the back of the couch and tilted his head to Kendra. "Come here and tell this woman to lighten up."

Kendra stepped over the magazines and settled beside him. The warmth of his arm just above her shoulders set her tingling again and put the other Kendra to rest.

This was good.

This was smart.

This was nothing like Sylvia.

Sylvia would be out there in the dark somewhere with Harrison, ignoring the repercussions of her actions, throwing caution to the wind, and reaping the results in the morning.

"Sorry, no can do. It's her wedding day, and if she's smart, it'll be the only one she ever has. Better get it right the first time."

Darin winced, and, too late, she remembered his first wife. "Oh, sorry."

His smile didn't quite reach his eyes. "No problem. Can't stop a woman from leaving if she's dead set on it, right?"

How could she be so insensitive? If he found out about Harrison, he'd relive the ending of his first marriage all over again. The irony of the moment settled on Kendra's shoulders like a fine rain.

Darin gave her an odd look, and she wiped the emotion from her face.

"I'm about ready for some sugar and caffeine." He stood up from the couch and walked toward the kitchen. "Anybody else?"

Clay folded a corner of a page down in

his magazine and said, "Yeah, bring me a Coke."

"Sure thing. Tandy?"

Tandy waved him off, circling pictures like mad in the magazine before her.

"Ken?"

"I'll come help." Kendra unfolded herself from the couch and followed him into the kitchen.

"Hey, I'm really sorry about that. I just — it's just — you don't mention your ex all that often, and I forget you were even married before."

Darin glanced at her, then opened the fridge door. "I'm okay." He pulled out a two-liter bottle of Coke and shut the door. "It's been long enough that I know she's not coming back. And with the assistance of one very fine woman," he wiggled his eyebrows at her, "I've found my way back to the land of the living."

She crossed the kitchen and took glasses down from the cupboard. Being at Clay's house was as familiar as being at her own; they all spent so much time here these days. "Good. Happy to help."

They fixed the drinks and were taking them back into the living room when Darin's "Hey, Kendra?" stopped her.

"Yeah?"

His eyes had lost their normal joking sparkle. "No matter what happens with us, thanks for . . . well . . . for this."

He knew. He had to know. The weight settled back on her chest. "What do you mean what happens with us? You going somewhere?" Her attempt at being flippant fell just short of success.

"Me? No."

She turned back to the doorway. "Good."

She had to end things with Harrison. Darin had lived through one cheating woman, and she'd not be the next to hurt him that way.

TEN

Saturday morning cartoons blared throughout the house as Meg wiped down the kitchen table. White cords snaked their way up her blouse and into the buds in her ears. Smart moms knew how to combat the sounds of VeggieTales. A woman can only take so many singing cucumbers before she resorts to her iPod.

She hit the Play button, and the opening guitar notes of "Footloose" filled her head. *There we go.* She danced to the rhythm, dropping dirty breakfast dishes into a suds-filled sink and twirling. She and Jamison danced to this song at their high school prom. Meg closed her eyes for a second, reveling in the beat, remembering the feel of Jamison's hesitant hands on her shoulders as they danced together. On the football field, he'd been the most confident thing on the planet. But with her, he'd never seemed certain of his next word or act. She found it charming then and only more so as she grew to know him.

Jamison's face held a lot more wrinkles now, almost twenty years later, but his dedication to her had never wavered. He was more certain of them as a couple, maybe even took her for granted some days. No, that wasn't right. It was their life that they *both* took for granted at times.

Meg plunged her hands into the hot soapy water and fished around for the dish rag. Others didn't have it nearly as good as she did, and she'd do well to remember that. Take Kendra, for instance. Here she was, probably running off after another man while she had a perfectly fine man right there interested in her. Meg shook her head. Sometimes her sisters drove her crazy.

At least Tandy had finally seen reason. Meg would have bet Hannah's diaper money that when Tandy headed south for her home in Orlando four months ago they wouldn't be seeing her for another three years. But Clay's love had proven too irresistible for Tandy, and here she was, a diamond on her finger and a wedding planner filling up more each day.

Meg bobbed her head in time to the new song playing in her ears. "Danger Zone." Mmm, *Top Gun* with Tom Cruise. Now *that* was a movie. They didn't make them like that anymore. Military men rocketing through the air in fighter jets, then opening themselves up to the vulnerability of love once they hit the ground.

"Danger Zone" . . . that could be Kendra's theme song these days. Why couldn't the sisters see the wisdom in music? These artists sang about *life.* She sniffed. Oh, well. Let them try to figure out life without the wisdom of musicians and singers.

The shrill ring of their home phone sounded over Kenny Loggins's voice, and Meg popped out an ear bud to answer it.

"Fawcett residence."

"Hi, Meg. It's Joanie Hopkins over at Dr. Brown's office."

"Oh, hi, Joanie. How's your momma?"

Joanie's loud sigh came through the phone line "She's having a good day today, thanks for asking. Knew who I was when I went to see her before work."

"Good, that's good. You hang onto the good memories, now. No matter how much her memories fade, you can hang onto them for the both of you. And remember, we're praying for you."

Joanie sniffed. "Thanks, Meg. Alzheimer's is no walk in the park." A beat of silence passed as Meg fumbled with the iPod to pause it and Joanie got control of her emotions. "Anyway, I'm calling to remind you of your appointment on Monday at nine for your regular physical."

Meg looked on the family calendar hanging from the refrigerator and saw the notation in red. "I've got it down, Joanie. I'll be there at nine with bells on."

"All right. See you then."

"Bye."

Meg hung up the phone and went back to the dirty dishes. See, right there was another example of the preciousness of life: Joanie's momma had taught hundreds of kids at Stars Hill Elementary, and now she could barely remember her ABCs.

Meg wiped her hands on a dish towel and retraced her steps to the phone. Picking up the receiver, she dialed Jamison's cell.

"Jamison Fawcett."

"Hi, honey."

"Hey, you. What's up?"

"Nothing much. I was just cleaning up here and thought I hadn't said I love you lately, so I decided to call."

"Well, I'll take that kind of call any day. You okay?"

"Yeah, just worried about Kendra. You know how she can get." Tootsie came trotting into the room and stopped by Meg's foot. She obliged with a quick toe rub.

"I do, and I also know how much you let her stupid choices get to you. You've got to let her grow up, Meg. All you sisters do."

"I know, I know. She's not my child. But I'm almost sure she's seeing that man Joy spotted the other day."

"You asked her; she said no. What else can you do? Let it go for now."

Meg stopped rubbing the terrier, and Tootsie walked away in search of more love. "I know you're right. It's so hard, though, to let her do this."

"Yeah, but you're going to have to. Listen, I hate to do this, but I've got a client coming here in about five minutes."

"Never mind, we'll talk about it later. I just called to say I love you."

"Ah, Stevie Wonder. A legend."

"You said it. Bye, hon."

"Bye."

Meg hung up the phone and leaned against the wall. *Let it go, he says. Huh. Can't think of one good song that tells me to let my baby sister run headlong into a burning building.*

Kendra cracked one eye open and looked at the clock. Ugh. Nine in the morning? How did that get here so fast?

She tossed the covers back and slid out of bed. Her feet sank into the carpet as she stumbled to the bathroom. She was standing in front of the mirror, checking out her sorry excuse for a reflection, when she realized how nine had come so quickly. It tended to do that when you didn't get in bed until 3:00 a.m.

Images of Darin's laughing face collided with those of Harrison's sparkling eyes, and Kendra groaned. Reaching over, she pulled back the shower curtain and turned the faucet handle. Maybe a long, hot shower would clear her mind.

Fifteen minutes later her brain had regrouped the images into their respective folders in her brain, but the heart seemed to be having difficulties. Kendra stepped out of the shower, inhaling the cloud of steam that billowed around her. Wrapping a thick, white towel around her frame, she glared into the mirror and dared it to give her back the previous image.

The mirror obliged with a cleaner, shinier version of a woman who still didn't have her act together. Kendra grinned at herself, pulling the plastic cap from her head. "Woman, you are a mess."

She reached for the toothbrush as Miss Kitty came strutting into the bathroom.

"Morning, Miss Thang. How are you this fine day?"

The fluffy white cat meowed its breakfast appeal, then sauntered back out of the bathroom.

"Huh. I'll get to you in a second," Kendra turned back to the mirror, "just as soon as I get my face put on. I'd hate for somebody to see this mug without some cosmetic assistance."

As she worked, turning this way and that to ensure the makeup had gone on smoothly, she forced thoughts of Harrison away. Darin didn't deserve a conniving woman. And if that meant she wouldn't talk to Harrison anymore, then fine. Darin really cared about her. Really, really cared about her. He listened when she told stupid stories from childhood, and he didn't care about Sylvia, whatever he knew of her. Clay had probably told him whatever Tandy told him. That meant Darin knew enough of her childhood to know it was bad.

And yet he still called. He still picked her up and took her dancing so that all of Stars Hill could see. He treated her like a real person with feelings and dreams, and he didn't make fun of either whenever she dared to share them.

And things were over with Harrison. He

159

hadn't been amused that, after two hours of waiting for her last night, she showed up only to tell him they had to end things. This time for good.

She put the finishing touches on her makeup and sailed out of the bathroom. A quick perusal of her closet reminded her it was time to do laundry. Oh, well. There were no plans to leave home today anyway. Just a lazy Saturday at home, working on Tandy's painting and finishing up some articles whose deadlines were looming.

No Darin.

No Harrison.

Just her and Miss Kitty.

Sounded boring.

Boring but safe.

And a waste of the very expensive makeup she'd just applied.

She pulled on paint-stained shorts and a T-shirt and headed down the hall to the kitchen. Passing the second bedroom that served as a study, she decided to stop in and check her e-mail.

She waited through the start-up routine, then clicked on the Outlook icon. E-mails poured into her in-box, most of them the usual offers for Viagra and money from Nigeria. She deleted them even as more poured in, trying to keep up with the onslaught of spam. She almost missed Harrison's name and deleted the e-mail. That might not have been a bad thing.

"About last night" the subject line read. Kendra looked at it for a second, grateful she had turned off the function that let her see the content of e-mails without double-clicking on them. She should delete this e-mail before reading it. No good purpose would be served if she did anything but.

Her treacherous hands, formed in Sylvia's womb, double-clicked the mouse.

```
    Hi, doll. I'm writing this
in the hope that you won't
delete it before you even read
it. I don't know what happened
last night, but my hope is
that you feel differently in
the light of day and won't end
things with us. I know it's a
hard situation, and I'm not
saying I have any answers. I
only know that the future of
my days seems unbearably dark
without the hope of seeing you
again. I'm a horrible man for
even typing that, but it's the
truth. Take some time if you
need it, but call me when you
```

want, and I'll be here.

Miss Kitty came to the study door and gave a plaintive meow. Kendra blinked and stood up, deleting the e-mail before she could read it again.

"Poor baby," Kendra cooed. "Is your momma starving you this morning?" She followed the cat to the kitchen and retrieved a can of cat food. "We should call somebody about that. The ASPCA would swoop in here in an instant and rescue you, I'm sure."

Kendra scooped cat food into a bowl ringed with small white paw prints.

Now for her own breakfast. There was nothing convenient in the fridge.

A trip to the grocery store wouldn't take long. She'd have plenty of time to work on the painting and write her article even with a little trip to E. W. James.

Thinking like that is why you don't have a good start on that painting yet.

She rummaged around in the refrigerator, pushing aside old Chinese takeout cartons and Ziploc bags with chemistry experiments growing inside. Ah! There in the back sat breakfast. Kendra retrieved the small carton of half a dozen eggs.

Miss Kitty purred her approval of the morning meal as Kendra poured olive oil into a skillet, then turned the burner on. Blue gas flames transferred their heat to the cooking pan as Kendra cracked eggs into a bowl.

Grabbing a mini whisk, she whipped the eggs into a froth.

"Hmm, we need something green, Miss Kitty." Something green with every meal. The mantra had kept Kendra consistently healthy over the years, despite the occasional attack by a Krispy Kreme or Joy's cooking. Spying a green pepper in the crisper drawer, she pulled it out and chopped it into pieces.

The bit she dropped into the skillet sizzled, and Kendra — satisfied that the oil was hot enough — picked up the bowl of mixed eggs and poured it in.

She hummed a tune from Heartland as she stirred the eggs, oil, and pepper with a wooden spoon. She left it cooking and snagged a couple pieces of bread from the bag on the counter, then dropped them into the toaster.

Stirring the eggs some more, she continued to hum her tune.

Miss Kitty sat up, licked her lips, and went to twine her gratitude about her owner's legs.

At precisely the moment Kendra turned

to grab the butter.

This sent Kendra crashing to the kitchen floor, eggs and green pepper raining down like brimstone.

It took a second to register the searing heat on her thigh. She looked down, almost in a daze, and noted the egg burning her skin, the edge of a hot skillet resting on her leg, searing olive oil coating her flesh.

The moment her mind accepted the reality of the moment, she jerked away.

Screamed in pain.

Swiped at the oil and tried to stand up.

Her brain was too consumed by the torture of heat to make the injured leg work. She crumpled back to the floor. She shook her head. Miss Kitty crouched on top of the table, her cry loud. The cordless phone! Beside the cat.

Kendra lunged for it.

It clattered to the floor, and Kendra fought to ignore the agony engulfing her thigh. The oil slid to the back of her leg as she scooted, pushing the hot oil into her pores. *Oh, God, help.* A foot closer to the phone, she grabbed for it.

Her hand closed around the instrument. She got 911 dialed — *please, God, let me have hit the right buttons* — and again tried to stand. She was going to make it this time.

Her muscles were working.

But a few degrees from vertical, Kendra's foot slipped on the grease and she went down again, her head hitting the corner of the table . . .

And the world went to black.

Meg put away the last dish and turned to survey her now spotless kitchen. She had just decided the bathrooms would be next when the phone rang.

"Fawcett residence."

"Meg, it's Tandy. Is Jamison working today?"

"Yeah, he's behind. Can you believe that? Tax season is almost a year away, and the man's already behind again. It's just us chickens around here. Why? What's up?"

"So you're home alone?"

"The kids are here. What's going on? You sound funny." A frisson of alarm rang through her.

"I need you to be calm, okay? No one is dead, and she'll recover from this."

Meg's morning waffles settled into her stomach like lead. "*Who* will recover?"

"Ken had an accident. She was making eggs and she tripped. The pan fell on her, and she's burned. We're on our way to Vanderbilt."

The waffles reversed course and tried to fight their way back up and out her throat. She swallowed hard. "What? Eggs?"

"I can't get into details while going a hundred miles an hour down the highway. She's going to be fine. They're taking her to Vanderbilt."

"Does Joy know?"

"No, and neither does Daddy. I need you to call them and get up here."

Meg snapped into mom mode. Her mind cleared and began making a list of what to accomplish. "Okay, I'll take care of it. We'll be there. Call me as soon as you get stopped."

"Will do."

Meg heard the click and reset her phone. As she punched the buttons to reach Joy, she couldn't help thinking, *Wasn't she just saying that life was precious?*

ELEVEN

Tandy flew into the emergency room parking lot of Vanderbilt Medical Center in Nashville. Her seat belt was off before the car settled into park. Two steps away from the car, she remembered her wallet and turned back for it. They would need an ID to get into Kendra's room.

She raced across the parking lot, the hot sunshine mocking her with its bright intensity. People didn't end up in the ER on a beautiful day like today. It never happened this way in books and movies.

Great, I'm getting hysterical. I'm expecting the weather to tell me when life's about to take a turn for the worse. She burst through the sliding double doors and stopped long enough to spot the nurse's station. *Slow day in the ER.* Five people sat in waiting chairs. None of them looked emergent to her.

"Hi, I'm Tandy Sinclair. My sister was just

flown here from Stars Hill. Kendra Sinclair?"

"One moment, please." The nurse moved like molasses in January. What was her problem? She tapped computer keys and acted like this was just another task to be completed and not like Tandy's world had just spun off its axis. Tandy considered strangling her, but she didn't know the hospital's computer system, and there was no one else behind the desk to find her sister if she rendered this woman unconscious.

"Could you hurry, please? I'm sure she's scared and —"

"One *moment,* please."

Tandy stared in shock. Strangulation was fast becoming a distinct possibility. She tapped the desk and bit the inside of her jaw. The bitter taste of blood touched her tongue.

"She's in ICU. In the burn unit." The nurse's monotone gave no hint if that was good or bad. She looked over black-rimmed bifocals. "Are you a family member?"

"Oh, yes," Tandy fumbled with her wallet. "I'm her sister." Hadn't she said that already? Her driver's license stuck behind its plastic backing. "Here." Tandy threw the wallet down on the desk. "There's my license."

The nurse picked up the wallet, eyed the license, then kept Tandy waiting for another eternity.

"Hmm." She placed the wallet on the raised counter in front of Tandy. "Eleventh floor south. Follow the hallway until you see a bank of elevators on your right, then go to the eleventh floor, and turn right. Nurses' station is right there."

"Thank you!"

Tandy raced down the hallway. No use trying to get further information from Nurse No-Help. She prayed the ICU nurses would be better.

Her cell rang as she waited for the elevator.

"Tandy Sinclair."

"Tandy?" Daddy's voice almost broke the thin veneer of control she had on her emotions. "Anything new on our girl?"

"I just got here, Daddy. I'm on my way to find her now. She's in ICU. The burn unit."

"Well, that might be a good thing. Good care in that ICU."

Tandy pushed away memories of Momma lying in a bed in this very hospital, fighting with everything she had to beat a cancer that had spread like kudzu in the Southern rain.

Focus on Kendra. Focus. Focus. Focus.

"I know, Daddy. I'll call you soon as I get up there."

"Okay. We're twenty minutes out."

"The elevator's here. I'll probably lose you."

"See you soon."

"Bye, Daddy."

Tandy slipped her phone back in her pocket and jabbed the eleven on the elevator panel. Whose idea was it to put the slowest elevators in the universe in a hospital? How could this be happening? They were together just a few hours ago, planning her wedding and joking with each other about fuchsia bridesmaid dresses.

Antiseptic air wafted into the elevator as the door swished open. Tandy pushed away the memories of death that the smell conjured up and hurried to the nurses' station. *Not everyone who enters a hospital dies.*

A youngish nurse with jet-black hair pulled back into a bun sat at the desk. The name tag on her carnation-pink top read "Naomi."

"I'm Tandy Sinclair. I believe you have my sister Kendra here." The calm voice shocked her. Had that been hers? She looked over her shoulder. Yep, hers.

"Yes, Miss Sinclair. She's in room 1108."

Wow. Naomi hadn't even checked the computer before knowing the room number. Because Kendra's case merited special attention? Was it that bad? "Can I ask, why is she in ICU?"

"Most burn victims end up in ICU. Kendra's here specifically because she had an allergic reaction to the morphine they gave her in the ER. She'll recover completely, but she's up here at least until they remove her tube and can determine surgical course of action for the burns."

"Surgery? She needs surgery?"

Naomi stood and came around the desk. Placing one arm behind Tandy, she put small hands on either of Tandy's elbows and steered her gently down the hallway. "I'll get Dr. Phillips to come explain things for you. Right now, know that your sister is hurt, but she will make a full recovery with time."

They paused outside a door, and Tandy saw 1108 on the panel to its right.

Naomi continued. "The allergic reaction necessitated that we put a breathing tube in the patient's throat. Do not be alarmed. She can breathe on her own; the tube is just helping her until the swelling in her throat

171

from the allergic reaction subsides."

Tandy scrambled for composure. Her stoicism slipped like bald tires on black ice. Kendra with a tube down her throat? It couldn't be possible. How could she boss people around and tell everyone her opinions with a tube down her throat?

Naomi gave a small smile and pushed open the door to Kendra's room.

Tandy tiptoed in, trying not to recall the dark days of Momma's stay in this place, of walking with catlike stealth so as not to wake her. The chemotherapy had made Momma feel like a thousand needles pricked her skin, and any noise could sound to her like an avalanche, squeaky tennis shoes like a million crying birds.

The short entry wasn't lit. Shadows played along the walls. She could see Kendra's feet beneath a sheet. Tandy would have sworn the shadows were whispering. Suddenly consumed with a need to protect her sister from whatever they planned, she rushed forward.

And stopped short.

Kendra's dark spiral curls lay against a stark white pillow. Her face, always animated with light and laughter, fell slack. A large round tube came from her mouth, secured to her face with tape that pulled at the skin.

She's gonna be mad about that when she wakes up. Bet it will hurt to pull off.

The light blanket on top of Kendra rose and fell, reassuring Tandy with its rhythm. Naomi had said Kendra could breathe on her own, right? Why then the tube? Tandy wrinkled her forehead and tapped her temple, struggling to remember the few words the nurse had shared.

But the sight of her loud, boisterous, mile-a-minute sister lying in a hospital bed shut down the logical portion of Tandy's brain. If there existed something in the world that could render Kendra this silent, this *small,* then the world wasn't what Tandy had always believed. It was a much more cruel place. A place full of hidden danger.

She walked around to the foot of the bed and rested her hands on its edge, not daring to touch, better to let her sleep and heal.

Minutes ticked by. Tandy registered the low-pitched whine of a clock on the wall behind her as its second hand swept end-lessly around the face. A patient moaned down the hallway. Tandy thanked God that Kendra wasn't awake to feel the pain.

Actually, except for the tube in her throat and the lack of light in her eyes, Kendra looked normal. Tandy peered at Kendra's legs, noting that one thigh was larger than the other. They must have wrapped the burn. She prayed it wasn't too bad.

The door opened, allowing in a cool draft of air that swirled around her ankles. Tandy looked up. A short man entered the room, his white coat embroidered with "Dr. Phillips" in black thread. He adjusted his glasses and reached out a hand to her. A clipboard was wedged beneath his other arm.

"Hi, I'm Dr. Phillips. I'm treating your sister."

Tandy's hand automatically went to his, shook it, then released. How odd to be engaging in the formalities of society while her sister lay in a hospital bed. More for her brain to fumble over.

"Hi. Yes. I'm Tandy Sinclair. Can you tell me . . . ? Is she . . . um . . . , I'm not quite sure what to ask."

Dr. Phillips smiled at her and tilted his head. "That's perfectly understandable. How about I tell you what we're doing to take care of her, and you let me know if you have any questions, all right?"

Tandy nodded.

"Miss Sinclair came in —"

"Kendra." Tandy's voice was soft, but the doctor stopped speaking anyway. "Her name is Kendra."

Dr. Phillips cleared his throat. "All right. Kendra came to the ER via helicopter. She dialed 911 after falling in her kitchen. She appeared to have been cooking at the time of her fall and the skillet and contents fell on her thigh, burning the skin. The emergency personnel found her unconscious, presumably from a blow to the head when she fell. She awoke during her air transport to the hospital and was in quite a bit of pain. Morphine was administered, and an allergic reaction resulting in anaphylactic shock immediately followed."

Tandy's throat seized at that. Shock?

The doctor must have noticed her fear. "It sounds worse than it is. Miss — Kendra — is allergic to morphine. When it's administered, the tissues in her throat and face swell. Her airway is constricted, and she struggles to breathe. The good news with anaphylactic shock is that it is immediately diagnosed and treated. She was intubated — that's the tube in her throat — and has had access to oxygen ever since. The tube will be removed in a day or two, depending on how long it takes her body to let go of the swelling."

A lump lodged in Tandy's throat, and she fought to breathe normally. Kendra was right here. Lying in front of her. She was fine. Or she would be fine. The nurse had said so.

Dr. Phillips continued. "Her burns are severe but treatable. At this time we don't think that the burn has gone through to the bones, which will make her recovery infinitely easier."

"People can burn clear through to their bones?"

"Oh, yes. It's quite common in the case of grease fires because grease doesn't roll off the skin; it spreads. Your sister is very fortunate. She was cooking with olive oil, not lard or butter. Olive oil is thinner and dissipates more quickly."

"She's a health nut," Tandy murmured.

"That will work in her favor as well. Kendra is a healthy woman. Her vital signs are terrific, and we expect her to make a full recovery."

"How long will she be in the hospital?"

"That's a little hard to say. Somewhere in the vicinity of three to five days. Then, of course, she'll need to return for skin-graft surgery and physical therapy."

"Surgery? I thought the nurse said she already had surgery." Or was it that she *needed* surgery? Tandy rubbed her forehead, feeling the beginnings of a headache.

"She's had emergency surgery, but burns

require time to heal. The initial surgery removed the dead tissue. We'd like to wait until her airway is healed before we perform further surgery to replace that dead skin with grafts."

Tandy struggled to understand all he was saying.

"What's the physical therapy for?"

"Her burn went into the bend of her knee. When burned skin heals, it loses elasticity. We'll need to work with Kendra to ensure that her skin heals in a way that gives her knee full mobility. She'll wear pressure garments for a few weeks to help keep the skin from scarring."

"Pressure garments?"

"Think of them like a big ace bandage."

Tandy looked back at Kendra. Why had God let this happen? Because she was seeing that strange man? Did God act like that? Throw down punishment like lightning bolts from heaven if you stepped outside His will?

Tandy shook her head. No, the God of love she knew wouldn't do that.

Would He?

Did people get hurt because they did things they knew God didn't allow?

It made sense. People who tried drugs got addicted and either had a downward spiral to death or a lifetime of addiction recovery. People who slept around contracted STDs or unplanned pregnancies. But did people who lie pay a price? People who stole?

Better to ask Daddy when he got here.

Tandy looked up to find Dr. Phillips's eyes on her.

"I'm sorry. It's just a lot to take in."

"You're doing fine." The doctor's voice was kind. "I'm going to check on some other patients, and I'll be back in to answer your questions in a few hours. Do you have more family coming?"

"My dad and sisters."

"Good. Write down any questions that come up. I'll answer them when I come back."

He tucked the clipboard back beneath his arm, and Tandy realized he hadn't consulted it once during their entire conversation. Did the man memorize the details of all his patients? Naomi had done the same thing though.

They must really know their stuff. She tucked a curl behind her ear that had fallen loose from her haphazard ponytail. *Thank heaven.*

Dr. Phillips left the room, and the cool air again swirled like tendrils around her ankles. It reminded Tandy of the sculpture Kendra created for the Iris Festival Art Contest this year. The first-place trophy now rested inside a glass-enclosed cabinet at Kendra's apartment, keeping company with other prizes she had been awarded for her art.

The sculpture of a woman running with all her might, even while fighting vines that were hopelessly tangled around her legs, had been a visual embodiment of Tandy's life just six months ago. Now Tandy couldn't help but wonder, had Kendra become the runner?

A light knock at the door drew her attention. Daddy, Meg, and Joy tumbled through. Daddy's overalls were covered in dust, no doubt pulled from the tractor by a call to his cell.

"How's our girl?" He came around to the bed and touched Kendra's forehead.

"Dr. Phillips says she'll make a full recovery." Tandy's voice trembled a bit, the rush of adrenaline leaving her bloodstream and taking with it her staunch bravado.

"That's great!" Joy said. "You've met the doctor then?"

Tandy nodded. "He was just here. You missed him by about two minutes. He's coming back, though, in case we have questions or something."

"Well, give us the rundown. What happened?" Meg settled in on the vinyl-covered couch.

Couch *can be a relative term, right? Because* couch *may be giving that thing too much credit.*

Tandy related everything the doctor had said. As much of it as she could remember, anyway.

"She hit her head?" Meg dug around in her purse. "Does she have a concussion? James had a concussion last year when he fell in the gym. Remember that, Joy?" She pulled a piece of gum from her purse and unwrapped it.

"The doctor didn't say anything about a concussion, but we can ask him about it when he gets here."

"Wait, we should make a list of what we want to ask him, or we'll forget." Joy opened her planner and slipped the pen out of its holder.

Tandy sent up a prayer of thanks for sisters who were neurotic list makers. And who were more accustomed to dealing with emergencies, obviously, than she.

"So, first question: Does she have a concussion?" Joy wrote, then looked up. "What else?"

"How long will she be in the hospital?" Daddy's giant hand rested on Kendra's head, his thumb smoothing her forehead.

"That one I know. Three to five days. Depends on how fast she heals and some other stuff I can't remember."

"What determines when she goes home?" Joy mumbled, writing.

Tandy pulled a chair up by the bed and sat down. "Hey, has anyone called Darin?"

"Clay did," Daddy said, not taking his eyes off Kendra. "He called me and said they'd be here shortly after us."

Tandy took Kendra's limp hand in hers. "Good. I think she'd want him here."

"I don't know," Meg said. "What about the other man? Has she told Darin about him?"

"Not as of last night." Tandy looked at Kendra's face. Satisfied her sister lay sleeping and oblivious to the conversation, she continued. "She came over to Clay's, and we all stayed up too late going through wedding magazines and stuff. Darin told Clay she hadn't said a peep to him about another guy being in the picture."

Joy sighed. "Perhaps I misjudged the scenario."

"It doesn't matter either way," Tandy said. "Darin cares a lot for her, and she cares for him. I watched them together last night. I don't know if something else is going on

181

outside of that, but I do know she's into Darin as much as he's into her. And that means he should be here."

"I agree." Meg pulled out her cell phone and stood up. "I'm going to call Jamison with the update. I'll be just down the hall, so get me if the doctor comes back or she wakes up, okay?"

"Okay."

Meg left, and Joy put the cap back on her pen and sat back on the couch. "This definitely isn't the day I intended to have when I got up this morning."

"Tell me about it." Tandy kissed the back of Kendra's hand. "I can hardly believe it. We were sitting on Clay's floor just a few hours ago, laughing at the hideous colors some women force their friends to wear at weddings."

"I thought we were wearing pale gold?"

"I'm not sure yet. After seeing fuchsia and teal taffeta, though, I'm leaning more toward pale gold."

"Ugh! They still make dresses in taffeta?"

"From the pictures in the magazines, yeah."

Joy shook her head. "I have never understood what poor fashion sense has to do with weddings. It's a day to be beautiful, breathtaking, and glamorous. How does that

182

necessitate bows on our backsides and fat rolls in satin?"

Tandy laughed, relieved that she still could. "Oh, Joy, stop."

"I will not stop." Joy raised her hand, mock indignation growing. "Not until someone tells these dress manufacturers that they are responsible for thousands of hideous wedding pictures through the years. And not until something is done to stop such atrocities from being perpetrated on bridesmaids around the world."

"Wow, passionate, are we?"

"Perhaps a tad bit."

"Well, no need to worry about atrocities at this wedding." Tandy looked at Kendra, lying so still on the bed. Would she be able to walk down the aisle? Dr. Phillips had said physical therapy would stretch the skin. But if Kendra's skin didn't stretch, would she limp? Kendra would hate that. She hated showing any sign of weakness. "Hey, add a question to the list, Joy. Will Kendra walk with a limp after this?"

"I thought you said she'd have physical therapy."

"She will, but I don't know if she'll limp anyway."

"Okay." Joy made a note on her paper. "Got it. Any others?"

"Yeah, when's she going to wake up?" Daddy's voice was deep and strained. He hadn't moved from Kendra's side since he entered the room.

"Daddy? You okay?"

Daddy face looked etched in stone as his unwavering gaze stayed on Kendra. "Soon as our girl wakes up and tells me she's sick of lying in the bed, starts pitching a fit about hospital food, and demands to go home, I'll be fine. Till then, I think I'll stay right here and pray."

Was this a good time to ask about a vengeful God? Kendra's eyes were still closed, so she couldn't hear the answer anyway.

"Daddy? Do you think God did this because, you know, Kendra's seeing that other man?"

"No, baby girl. I do not."

Tandy couldn't let it go. "Why not? I thought you always said that part of loving a child is punishing them when they do wrong. Couldn't this be punishment?"

"Tandy, human parents punish their children when they do wrong. Yes, that's a way to show love because you love them enough to teach them right from wrong. But God is so much more gracious and merciful than to sit up in heaven with a mighty stick and whack us on the heads every time we get

184

out of line."

Daddy paused, and Tandy waited while the breathing machine continued its hiss. "It's hard to understand because we can't wrap our minds around just how loving God is. But know this: God knew Kendra before He even made her. He knew every choice she'd make, every action she'd take. And when Kendra chose to believe in Him, to accept that Jesus is God's Son and that He died for her sins, then she was made blameless in God's eyes. There's no reason to punish Kendra because she — and you and Joy and everyone else who believes in Him — is blameless in God's eyes. Is He using this for His will? Yes. God uses even the bad stuff to bring about good works. But did He reach down from heaven and turn that skillet over on her this morning? No, I don't think He did. He loves her too much."

Tandy wrestled with Daddy's words, not entirely sure she believed them. If God didn't do this, then how did it happen? Wasn't God in charge of everything? Didn't the Bible say *nothing* happened to God's children without it first being filtered through His hands?

She bit her lip, looking down at the beautiful caramel skin of her sister's hand. Time enough later to figure it out.

■ ■ ■ ■

"Man, this can't be happening." Darin eyed parking spaces as Clay drove up and down looking for an empty one. "Did they tell you anything else?"

"I've told you all I know. She's burned. She's in the hospital. That's it."

"You'd think they would have called us with an update by now." Darin ran his hand down his face and sighed. "There! Right up there." He pointed to an empty space, and Clay whipped the Mustang into it. Darin went to unbuckle his seat belt, but Clay stopped him.

"You sure you want to see her? We don't know who else is up there or what kind of shape she's in."

"Doesn't matter." Darin shook his arm free and released the safety belt. "If there's another guy, then I'll deal with it and be grateful she's got so many folks pulling for her. And I don't care what shape she's in so long as she's alive."

Darin scrambled out of the car, sparing a quick glance over his shoulder to ensure Clay was right behind him. For all his bravado, he didn't know for sure if he could handle what lay just ahead. If another guy stood there by Kendra's bed, holding her hand, whispering comforting words . . .

"Watch out!"

Darin stumbled backward as Clay's hand jerked his arm. He caught a glimpse of a motorcycle as it rounded the curve.

"Didn't you see him coming?"

Darin shook his head and resumed his driving pace to the emergency room door. "Nope."

They walked in tandem to the nurses' station, received the same information Tandy had a half hour earlier, and went to find the elevators. They stepped inside, and Clay pushed the button as the elevator doors slid shut. Darin tapped his fingers on the metal handrail that wrapped itself around the walls of the car. How long did it take to go up eleven floors? He probably could have run it faster than this ancient contraption got them there.

Finally a ding sounded and the doors whooshed open. Darin's heart was about to leap out of his body. Somewhere on this floor Kendra was lying. In pain. *Please God.*

He struggled to form a better prayer.

Just . . . please, God.

Clay got Kendra's room number from a nurse behind a circular desk. Darin followed him, no longer propelling them forward but

187

following along in his friend's wake. His friend who had a right to be here. No doubt Tandy sat beside Kendra, and that gave Clay entry into the room. But would Kendra even want Darin there?

Of course she would. She wanted you there last night, didn't she?

He realized they'd come to a stop in front of a door. Clay looked at him with a mixture of apprehension and sympathy.

"You sure?"

Darin drew a deep breath, steeling his heart as best he could for whatever his eyes would take in on the other side of that door. "Yep."

Clay pushed on the silver handle, and Darin caught sight of the sisters. Meg and Joy sat on an ugly plastic couch on the far wall. Tandy sat by Kendra's side, holding her hand. Mr. Sinclair was at Kendra's head, murmuring to her.

Thank you, God. It's her daddy.

Then he saw the giant tube coming from Kendra's mouth and gasped. A breathing tube? She needed help breathing? Exactly what had she burned? What happened?

"Hey, Darin." Meg got up and walked over to him. She pulled him to Kendra's bedside. "Don't worry. It looks worse than it is. She had an allergic reaction to the morphine, and her throat swelled up. They'll pull that tube out in a couple of days, and we'll have our bossy Kendra back."

Darin swallowed hard. A couple of days? "What happened?"

Tandy, now nestled in the crook of Clay's arm, told him everything she knew.

He swallowed again. "Is she going to wake up soon?"

"We're not sure." Meg patted his arm. "I'm betting they keep her sedated while the tube is in, but that's just a guess from seeing too many episodes of *House* and *ER.*"

He stared at Kendra, not quite able to believe the vivacious, sexy woman he met a few months ago was this person lying so still on the bed. He wanted to see her eyes, to assure himself that the sparkle was still there and that she was still as alive as she'd been last night.

Just last night? How did the whole universe change in less than a day? They'd been laughing a few hours ago. Well, laughing on the outside, anyway, while he tried not to ask her why she kept checking her watch.

He sucked in a breath. Had the other man been with her when this happened?

"Are you sure she was alone when it happened?"

The question was out before he had sense

enough to keep it in. Heavy silence filled the room, and Darin's eyes opened wide. He looked to Mr. Sinclair, but Kendra's daddy wasn't looking anywhere other than his daughter's face.

The silence lengthened, and Darin mentally slapped himself. Who walked into a hospital room and accused the patient? It felt like everyone in the room held their breath, waiting for somebody to make a move.

"That's a good question." Tandy's subdued voice released the tension, and Darin breathed again. "I hope she was alone."

"Me, too." Joy crossed her arms over her chest and tapped her ballet-slippered foot on the floor. "Because if that Tommy-Bahama-wearing jerk let her get hurt and then left her there, I'm going to find him and kill him myself."

"Joy!" Meg's voice held shock. "You are not going to kill anyone."

"Look at her, Meg. Look at our sister lying there in that bed with a tube in her throat, and Lord only knows what wrong with her leg," Joy's perfectly modulated voice slipped a bit, "and tell me you won't strap that man to a chair and let him see the business end of a stick if he left her alone."

The hiss of the breathing machine filled the room. Darin looked at his lovely Kendra, so still. So serene. So un-Kendra.

He cleared his throat. "I'll help you tie him down."

The response was swift. "Then you can stay."

TWELVE

Kendra's throat hurt. Water. She needed a tall, cold glass of water. That would stop the burning in her throat. The feel of desert sand being stuffed down her.

She coughed.

Don't do that again. Just stirs up the sand.

She swallowed.

Or that.

"Kendra?" Tandy's voice filled Kendra's mind. Tandy was in the desert with her? Why were they in a desert so close to Tandy's wedding day? Tandy probably wanted a tan so she'd look good in her wedding dress.

Kendra heard a moan, realized it was her own, and moaned again.

"Kendra, honey, wake up."

Another moan. Who would want to wake up in all this heat?

Except that there was no heat. The air felt cold. Only her throat burned. And her leg.

Her leg felt like someone was holding hot matches to —

Oh, no.

Kendra's eyes opened wide, the memory of what happened in her kitchen flooding back. Her moan became a groan, and she struggled to sit up. Her leg! Get the oil off her leg!

"Hang on. Wait, sis, wait. I'll get the nurse."

Nurse? There's a nurse in my kitchen?

An annoying ding sounded.

"Can I help you?"

It sounded like they were in a drive-thru. Kendra closed her eyes. Nothing made sense.

"My sister is awake, and I think she's in pain. Could you send someone, please?"

Awake? Or course she was awake! Wait . . . *nurse?*

Kendra opened her eyes again. "Tandy?" Her voice sounded like a frog after an all-night binge.

"Shh. Hang in there. The nurse is going to come, and we'll make you feel better."

"Where? What?" She tried to get whole sentences out, but somebody had relocated the Sahara to her throat, and only a couple of words escaped.

"Just be still. Do you remember anything

193

that happened?"

Kendra thought back to the kitchen. The oil. The eggs. She'd been making breakfast. Miss Kitty wanted some love, and Kendra had turned . . . and then felt like she was sitting in hell.

She groaned again.

"The pan fell on your leg. You were burned, but you're going to be okay, Kendra. I promise. You're going to be okay."

Kendra locked eyes with Tandy. Saw the truth there. She *was* going to be okay. Tandy's eyes said so, and Tandy couldn't lie to save her own life.

Kendra breathed and tried again to remember. Eggs falling. Slipping on the floor. Dialing 911. Falling.

"Well, look who decided to wake up!" An impossibly chipper woman bustled into the room, chubby fingers waving in the air as if to scatter the demons of sickness. Her face looked like that old cartoon dog, the basset hound with the jowls. "Dr. Phillips will be pleased you've rejoined the land of the living."

Kendra tried to be happy that she'd pleased Dr. Phillips, whoever he was.

"Are you in pain?" Small brown eyes peered at her from beneath a pile of dark brown hair shot through with wiry gray corkscrews. Bobby pins were jammed in all over the woman's head, and Kendra wondered how long it took to get all the pins out at night. Might be worth it for the three inches it added to this woman's frame.

"If you can smile, then your pain isn't a ten. On a scale of one to ten, with one being no pain and ten being the worst, where would you rate it?" The nurse took Kendra's wrist and pressed her fingers down on the pulse while keeping an eye on her watch.

Kendra reached down to her leg — bandages. A fire simmered underneath the gauze, but Kendra could feel where the fire ended and started. She looked back to the nurse — Judith, according to her name tag — and croaked a response. "Eight."

"Hmm, let's see if we can get that closer to a five. I'll be right back with some happy juice." The short woman rushed out of the room as fast as she'd come in.

"Nobody is that happy without pharmaceutical help," Tandy deadpanned, and Kendra laughed. Or tried to laugh. It quickly evolved into a hacking cough.

"Now, now. None of that." Nurse Judith scurried back into the room, a syringe in one gloved hand. She laid the needle on Kendra's bedside table and poured water from a pitcher. Holding a bendable straw to

Kendra's lips, she instructed sternly, "Drink."

Kendra dared not disobey. No telling what tricks Judith had up her sleeve to enforce her commands.

The cold liquid felt like heaven running down her throat. Before she knew it, she was sucking air.

"Good, good. Let's start slow now." Nurse Judith picked the syringe back up, and Kendra had a momentary bout of panic — needles! — before seeing that the needle was inserted into her IV instead. "This will take the edge off the pain but keep you awake for a little while. Tomorrow you'll see Dr. Phillips and get started on PT."

The efficient woman dropped the used needle in a red carton hanging on the wall and exited the room.

Tandy looked at Kendra and smiled. "I think you're in, um, capable hands."

Kendra grinned and chose to ignore the fire in her leg and focus on something she could control. "Where's Daddy? The sisters? How long have I been here? What time is it? Shoot, what *day* is it?" She gave in to another coughing fit, and Tandy poured more water.

"Drink. And stop talking so much. I get that it's hard for you, but try."

She would stick out her tongue, but she couldn't summon the energy.

"It's Monday night. We're at Vanderbilt Hospital, where you were airlifted after you dialed 911 from your apartment." Tandy told her the whole story, all the parts she knew of it, including Dr. Phillips's fabulous prognosis.

"So you'll be good as new in a few weeks, provided you listen to the doctors and do what they say."

"Hmm, we'll just see about that." Relaxation flowed into her limbs, and Kendra thanked God for good drugs. "Wow, that stuff she gave me really *works.*"

"Good! Feel better?"

Kendra nodded, and Tandy continued. "Daddy just ran down to the cafeteria to get some coffee. He's been here every second, and it took me hours to talk him into leaving your room. So if you could pretend to wake up again when he gets here, that'd be great."

"He hasn't left my room?"

"Nope." Tandy shook her head. "Nor, for that matter, have I. Which explains the state of my hair." She tucked more stray curls behind her ears. "Darin's been here every day but didn't want to take off work until you woke up. He said we could do the silent watch; he'd be by your side when he could hear your voice."

"Awww."

"Yeah, we thought it was pretty sweet, too. Joy, by the way, has decided he's a keeper, so I hope you were planning on having him around awhile."

"Why is Joy so approving of him?"

"I don't know." Tandy shifted in her chair and looked away. "You'll have to ask her."

That wasn't the whole truth, but Kendra felt too tired to go into it. "Okay. Has somebody been to take care of Miss Kitty?"

"Yep. Meg took her home and is keeping her locked in the laundry room so the kids don't inflict permanent harm."

"Poor Miss Kitty."

"That's what I said."

Kendra's eyelids were heavy. Must be the drugs. She closed her eyes.

Tandy watched as Kendra went back to sleep, then slumped back in her seat, feeling infinitely better now that they'd talked. No mention of a man being at her apartment when this happened. No request to call and let someone know what had happened. The only male-related conversation had been about Darin.

They'd misjudged. Whomever Kendra had

been seeing on the side apparently now fell into the realm of history. Tandy breathed a little easier and pulled her cell phone from her pocket. Checking to ensure Kendra walked in the land of dreams, she moved a few steps away from the bed and dialed Clay's number.

"Hey, how's Kendra?" The clattering of dishes made it hard to hear him, and Tandy realized she had called during the dinner rush.

"She woke up, talked for a couple of minutes, and is back asleep."

"Thank God."

"You said it."

"Did she tell you what happened?"

"I told her what happened. She doesn't remember a lot, I don't think. But get this: She didn't mention another man at all."

"Really?"

"Nope. Didn't ask if someone had been to see her other than Daddy and the sisters. I told her Darin had been here every day, too."

"He's going to be so relieved to hear she's awake."

"Yeah, I'll call him now. Just wanted you to know I think we misjudged the strange man situation. If she *was* seeing someone, it must be in the past now."

"Then I'll thank God again."

"Amen, sweetie. Got to run. I need to give Darin the good news."

"Okay, I'll drive up with him as soon as the rush dies down."

"Sounds good. Be careful."

"Will do. Love you."

"Love you."

She then dialed Darin and gave him the latest.

"Is she still awake? Can I talk to her?" Darin sounded like a kid on Christmas morning staring at a new bike.

"She's asleep again. They gave her pain meds."

"I'll be up in an hour."

"Whoa, there, Casanova. Clay wants to drive up with you, but he's dealing with the dinner rush right now."

"Oh. Um, okay. I'll call him and work out the details. Never mind. I'll just drive over to the diner and pick him up. We'll be up there soon."

Tandy hid her amused laughter behind a cough. "Okay. See you in a bit."

She flipped the phone closed and turned to look at her sleeping sister.

"Excuse me?"

Tandy turned at the male voice.

"Yes?"

"Is this Kendra Sinclair's room?" He walked in, and Tandy drew in her breath at the sight of a Tommy Bahama shirt.

"Yes, it is. And you are?"

"Harrison." He held out his hand, and Tandy shook it. "I'm a friend of Kendra's."

"That's odd." Tandy took her hand back, resisting the urge to wipe it off. "I know just about all of Kendra's friends, but I don't think we've met."

The man quirked a smile at her. Tandy could see how he'd charmed Kendra. That smile was good.

"She's told me a lot about you. About all her sisters, actually." He walked into the room, right on up to Kendra's bedside. Tandy's lips compressed. Should she throw him out? Or let Daddy deal with him? She suppressed a smile at that.

"Is that right? I'm sorry to say, then, that she hasn't said a word about you."

He angled to focus on her, and Tandy could see the sadness in the downward turn of his eyes, the slight slump to his shoulders.

"No, she wouldn't have."

He turned back to Kendra, and Tandy tried not to feel like an ogre for having hurt the man's feelings.

"I'm sure she will when she wakes up, though." *Because I'm going to grill her until she does.* "Anything specific I should mention?"

He was silent for a moment, and again Tandy regretted having spoken. Who *was* this guy? This Harrison who walked over to her sister's bedside as if he had every right in the world to be here? She saw his hand come up to Kendra's face, caress it, and pause on her chin. There was emotion in that touch. Raw emotion.

Tandy held her breath, scared of what she'd stumbled on. Her gaze flitted around the room, seeking an escape from the display, and landed on a simple band around the man's left hand.

Her breath escaped in a rush, and her mouth opened before she could tell it otherwise. "You're *married?*" No wonder Kendra kept this man a secret.

He turned, and the heartbreak in his eyes was so real, so plain, that Tandy knew. She knew this wasn't another of Kendra's flings with a man unworthy of her. It wasn't some cheap, fake romance Kendra entered into in a sad display of her birth mother's pattern.

It wasn't what Tandy had thought at all.

This man loved her sister. He had no right to, and Lord knew Kendra had no right to love him, but Tandy was suddenly as sure of that as she was that Kendra would be healing from this accident.

Oh, Kendra. The impossibility of the situation struck Tandy, and her heart ached for everything her sister lived with. No support from the girls. No understanding conversation around the scrapping table. Just raw emotion invading her life with no way to accept its presence and hang on to the person she'd been raised to be. The person she'd agreed to be the day she gave her heart to Jesus.

The hopelessness of the situation forced soft words from her. "Oh, no."

The man's smile looked like it better belonged on a hundred-year-old man. "Don't tell her I was here."

Tandy understood. He was saying goodbye. She bowed her head, unable to conspire with him, yet knowing the wisdom of his action.

"Your sister —"

She looked up again and saw Harrison glance back once at the bed, then meet Tandy's eyes.

"She's the most amazing woman I've ever met." He touched Kendra's cheek and then stepped back. "Too amazing for this."

With that he walked out of the room.

Tandy stood very still, watching the door to see if he would return. Seconds ticked by. The clock on the wall hummed. And after a little while, Tandy began to wonder if she'd made the entire thing up.

She walked back over to her plastic chair by Kendra's bedside and sank down into it. Taking her sister's hand, she held it, looked again at the door, then at her sister's face.

The lone tear trickling down that beautiful, caramel-colored cheek told her.

It was real.

THIRTEEN

Kendra's feet sank into thick, white, familiar carpet, and she breathed a sigh of gratitude. So much better than cold hospital tile. Her muscles flexed as she rose from bed, and she grimaced at the pain still present in her left thigh.

An entire week home and not one word from him. Not one. Despite three e-mails and two voice mails.

Snatching her silk robe from the corner of the bed, Kendra jerked the sash into a knot and strode into the bathroom. She came to a stop before that reflective honest pane and stared herself in the eye. "Kendra Sinclair, you've gotta let it go." Her lips were set in a firm line, and she noted with approval their resemblance to Momma on days when a sister got caught in a lie. "Let it go."

Seven days. Long enough to stop waking up with the thought of why he hadn't called. Or e-mailed. Or, shoot, dropped by. Not like he didn't know where she lived now.

Squeezing toothpaste onto the toothbrush, she savagely brushed until her gums cried for relief. Great, more pain. She rinsed, closing her eyes against the pain and relief of icy water against freshly bruised gums and cold-sensitive teeth. A conniving, cheating man doesn't deserve this much mental energy.

The phone rang, and Kendra wiped her mouth. That'd be Darin. The man who *did* call or come by every day, sometimes multiple times, to ensure she had everything close at hand. To tell her scars didn't matter. To say how sorry he was this had happened. To help her with bandages. Or just to listen.

She padded through the carpet and snatched up the phone on its third ring.

"Hello?"

"Good morning, beautiful. Did I wake you?" Darin's voice smoothed her ruffled feathers and sent shivers down her back.

"Ten minutes earlier and you might have."

"Then I'll have to thank *The Today Show* for a particularly good interview this morning. It's the only thing that saved me."

"Give Ann Curry my love."

"She is particularly fabulous, isn't she?"

"Watch it, mister."

"Not nearly in the same ballpark as a certain artist I know."

"Now we're talking." She sank back into bed, pulling the thick down comforter up to her shoulders and snuggling in among the pillows. Darin didn't deserve a scarred woman, both outside and in, but for now she'd enjoy his attention until he came to the realization. The thought left her cold and she pulled the covers tighter to her chest.

"Got big plans for the day?"

"I think if I don't spend some time at the office, Tandy might come push me out of this bed herself."

"Ah, no rest for the weary."

"You know, I've never understood that saying. No rest for the weary? What does that mean?"

"It means those who do the work rarely rest because there's always more work to do."

"Those who do the work are dummies then."

His chuckle rumbled low and deep. "Perhaps so."

"So what do you have on tap for the day?"

"Got to run up to Leiper's Fork. We're looking at a site up there, and I've got to meet with the owner, get the details."

"Oh, Leiper's Fork is gorgeous! Wave to any celebrities you see." She pictured the rolling hillside of the famed small town that so many country music stars called home.

"Well, I was kind of hoping a certain beautiful sculptress could join me for the drive."

"Oh! I'd love to!" Miss Kitty jumped up onto the bed. She pawed at the comforter, circled around a couple of times, and settled in directly on top of Kendra, who chuckled and scratched the fluffy cat's ears. Miss Kitty would never suffer for lack of attention.

"I thought you needed to go get some work done at Sisters, Ink."

"That can wait." Tandy wouldn't like it. She'd get over it, though. Just like she somehow had gotten over the idea Kendra was seeing someone else. Hmm, come to think of it, Tandy hadn't mentioned that subject since Kendra got home from the hospital. Odd. Kendra shoved the thought to the back of her mind.

"You sure?"

"Sure I'm sure. I do need to get some work done on Tandy's painting, though." That'd be the perfect excuse if Tandy asked why she hadn't come into the office today.

Couldn't get mad if the wedding was the reason.

"Okay, how about I pick you up in an hour or so?"

"That'll work." She shoved Miss Kitty off the bed and stood by the bedside table. "In which case I need to get off this phone and get cracking."

"Paint, woman, paint. See you in an hour."

"See ya." Kendra placed the phone in its cradle and twirled in a circle, ignoring the painful twinges in her leg, grateful for the change to today's plans. The sun shone in her bedroom window, and Kendra didn't fight the bubble of laughter working its way up her throat. Why worry about a man who didn't call, who didn't have the right to call in the first place? Who wore a gold band around his finger but didn't let that band keep his heart in check?

Much better to spend the morning with Darin. Sweet, honest, kind Darin with the gorgeous hands and tantalizing voice. And free heart.

She walked down the hallway to the studio and went inside, squaring her shoulders to face the blank canvas whose stare had been eyeing her for weeks now. Picking up a paintbrush, she held it parallel to her eyes.

"You and me, kid. We're going to get some

work done in the next half hour, and I don't want to hear a thing out of you but art. You got that?"

Yep, she'd lost her mind, She was talking to a paintbrush. But it was about time she took charge of *something* instead of letting men call all the shots.

Letting Harrison call all the shots.

Who did he think he was, making her wait around for a phone call whenever he could get free of his wife and other obligations? Who was she to let a man turn her into that? When exactly had she gotten to the point where that sounded all right? That wasn't her. Hadn't been for a long time.

Squeezing red paint into her paint wheel, she dipped the paintbrush in and applied it to the canvas. Red. The color of passion. Intensity. Emotion.

Feeling her heart at last open onto the canvas, Kendra painted with a frenzy, determined to capture this feeling and transfer it to the work before it disappeared again. The confusion, hesitation, second-guessing left her, and for these moments in time she felt blissfully free of life's entanglements.

Her brushes took on a life of their own, interchanging in her hands — she always painted with both — and transforming the whiteness into a scene of utter escape and safety. Minutes flew by and still she painted. Hours with Darin flitted into her mind.

Darin looking at her and laughing.

Darin opening the door for her.

Darin dancing with her at Heartland.

Darin playing the bass.

Darin twirling a straw at Clay's Diner.

Darin laughing at bridesmaid dresses.

Darin wrapping her leg.

Darin helping her walk.

Darin.

Just Darin.

The paintbrush stilled in midair, and she took in the work before her. It was other-worldly and amazing, and she couldn't believe she'd painted it. Couldn't believe all the pandemonium inside her became *this* whenever she just closed her eyes and thought of Darin.

What would happen if she did this when Harrison filled her mind?

She paused. The confidence blossoming in her demanded nothing short of daring, of seeing what would happen.

She turned to another blank canvas on an easel in the corner. Might as well find out. Let the canvas tell her what her mind hadn't been able to work out for these long months.

Staring at the canvas, Kendra tried to

focus on Harrison's face. It remained frustratingly blurry, having dimmed in its vividness over these long days of silence. He hadn't visited her in the hospital, despite her voice mails on his cell. He hadn't left a message to find out how she was doing with rehab, if she was adjusting, if she needed anything.

She tried to push away the anger and self-doubt, tried to remember the intimate conversations in his car, sitting on a hilltop overlooking the beauty of a crop ready to harvest.

Her paintbrush began to move, and Kendra gave her hand the power to translate her thoughts.

Shades of gray and lavender quickly filled the canvas, the strokes hesitant at first but growing with intensity the more she gave them control. Is this the color she saw as Harrison? This pale, wishy-washy, undefined color?

Don't analyze. Just paint.

More minutes ticked by, and she was vaguely aware of needing to stop. Needing to take a shower, put her face on, prepare for Darin.

Don't think of Darin. Think of Harrison. And paint.

Before her eyes a tranquil lake emerged.

Far off, in a distance so great she could barely make it out, floated a small boat. Not a sailboat, that would be too dreamy, too romantic for these feelings. A dinghy. A washed out, gray dinghy that wouldn't withstand many waves, if any. A woman, tiny as an ant, sat at one end. Her back was turned, but her shoulders gave away the lost feeling. A great depth of water, full of grays and lifeless blues, separated the woman from a shore not even within viewing.

Kendra took in the scene and felt tears trickle down her cheeks. For all their intelligence, for all their witty banter, she had to admit no future could exist with Harrison. Nothing could come except this, a great expanse of nothingness with no safe shore in sight.

She laid the paintbrush down, her arms exhausted and splattered in paint. Gingerly, she pulled this easel next to the first and glanced back and forth between the paintings.

A knock at the door cleared the artistic cobwebs from her brain, and she threw a look at the clock on the back wall.

How had an entire hour passed?

"Coming!" She cast about for somewhere to put the Harrison painting. Darin was perceptive. He'd know something was up when he saw that. *Anybody* would know. But the paint glistened with too much moisture to shove into the closet.

Nothing to do about it now. Stupid to have let herself paint it in the first place.

She tossed the paintbrush among a scattered grouping of others, wiped her hands on a stained cloth, and left the room, shutting the door with resolution.

The knock came again.

"I'm coming! Just a second!" Walking down the hallway, trying not to limp, but very aware now of the past hour she'd spent standing, Kendra reached the door and gave a grateful sigh as she opened it.

"Hey."

Darin gave a low whistle. "Well, this is a good look for you."

Kendra glanced down, belatedly realizing she still wore her robe and her hair must be as wild as Phyllis Diller's.

"Oh, shoot. I was painting, lost track of time. Come in, come in." She stepped back and let him enter the apartment.

"Must have been a good session. Can I see the results?"

"It's, um, not quite finished. Maybe in a day or two." *When I can hide the other one.*

"Come on, I promise not to judge."

"Nope, not happening."

"Chicken."

"Just call me Tyson-certified. Have a seat. I'll be right back."

She left him in the living room and went for the bathroom as fast as her hobbled leg could move.

No time for a shower. She reached for a hair wrap and tried to push her dry spirals beneath the fabric, but it was a no-go. Her hair, always with a life of its own, was having none of this hiding idea as dry as it was these days.

She threw the hair wrap on the counter, huffed her disapproval, and reached for the extra virgin olive oil. She coated the ends of her curls and pulled it all back in a low ponytail, then tied a colorful scarf over the whole thing. Not great, but good enough for now.

"Okay, I'm ready," she said as she entered the living room.

"I take back everything I ever said about high-maintenance women who take forever in the bathroom." Darin got up from the couch, pushing Miss Kitty off his lap.

"Hey, I wasn't in there longer than ten minutes."

"I know, and you look like one of those women who spends hours getting ready."

"Is that a compliment?"

He came to her and touched her face, the look in his eyes so tender and playful that she held her breath just to take it in more fully. "Definitely."

She struggled to remember what they were talking about. Oh, her looks. "Good. Ready to go?"

"I was born ready."

They left the apartment and descended the stairs. As always, Darin opened the front door and she walked ahead of him to the 'Cuda.

"So where in Leiper's Fork are we going?"

"I thought we'd run by the property I'm considering, then grab lunch at Puckett's Grocery."

"Oh, I love that place. It's like going to Mayberry."

"Yeah. Then if you don't have anything to get to this afternoon, we could hit the art gallery and see if Uncle Lester's doing a jig today."

"Is he still clogging at the drop of a hat?"

"He's what makes Leiper's Fork so great."

"Him and all the rest of those people who take care of each other like we do in Stars Hill."

"Yeah, minus the celebrities."

"Hey, we may not have celebrities in Stars Hill, but we take care of our own."

"Says the woman who cringes every time she hears anybody in town talking about her."

"I don't like to be discussed."

"And yet you value the fact that you live in a town where everybody is always talking about everybody else."

"There's a difference in relaying information and events and judging everybody for how they acted at those events."

"Sounds like you've been dissected a time or two."

"I've had my share of being raked over the coals, yes. All the sisters have. Guess we had it coming."

Darin shot a look at her, then focused on the on-ramp to the highway. "Why would you have it coming?"

Kendra's laugh sounded more like a groan. "Ask anybody who's lived in Stars Hill longer than two days."

"I could do that." Darin nodded. "Or I could just go to the source, which I'm trying to do here. Tell me about your childhood, Kendra."

She bit her lip, earlier feelings of happiness at spending the day with him flying out the window. "Why focus on such a depressing topic?"

"Because it's not depressing; it helped

make you who you are." He reached across the console and took her hand. "A very strong woman with an amazing artistic eye. Come on, I want to hear the real version, not the Stars Hill one."

Kendra settled into her seat, enjoying the feel of his thumb rubbing the back of her hand. "Okay, the long and short of it is that I had a mother who didn't want to be a mother but didn't know what to do when she got pregnant, so she had me and tried to raise me. Trouble was, that didn't fit in well with a revolving door of boyfriends who took one look at a scrawny, ugly kid in the corner and usually ran the other direction."

"I can't imagine you ever being ugly or scrawny."

"I'd show you pictures, but I don't have any. Trust me, this body is far removed from the one Jack and Marian Sinclair adopted."

"How long did you live with her?"

"Eight years. It wasn't all bad all the time, though. She had periods where it was just the two of us, and, for a couple of weeks, things would be good. Then she'd get a man, and things weren't good anymore."

His hand tightened on hers. "Not good how?"

"Different things. None worth mention-ing." She squirmed in her seat. If he knew all that had been done to her, he'd turn this car around and take her right back to her apartment. Because a man like Darin Spenser didn't have to put up with a past like she carried. He could have any of those shiny, sunny women who paraded in the aisles at Grace Christian every Sunday on the prowl for a good man like Darin, Bible and notebook clasped in their pale hands and a yearning for a family in their hearts.

"It's a long drive. We've got the time. Tell me."

Kendra looked out the window at the trees whizzing by. "Like I said, a kid was the last thing these guys wanted to be bothered with when they thought they were hooking up for the night."

"Did any of them hurt you?" His soft voice pierced more easily than any knife.

She let the question hang for a second, debating whether to share the truth. He deserved knowing what he was out with, she finally decided. No need in letting this go on further, hoping he wouldn't find out the details of her past. "Sometimes. Not always."

Darin's swift intake of breath drew her gaze to him. His jaw worked hard, and muscles stood out on his face. His thumb stayed gentle on her hand, though. What was he thinking?

"I'm sorry."

Her head jerked back, and she frowned. "For what?"

"That you were hurt."

"It wasn't you that did the hurting. You've got nothing to be sorry for."

"I'm still sorry you had to live through that. I won't ask you to share the details with me. But if you ever want to tell me, I'm here to listen."

Ever wanted to tell him? Shouldn't his next move be to run as fast and far in the other direction as possible? No man wanted damaged goods. And no man wanted to be needed when he could be worshipped and adored. Sylvia's lesson rang clear in her mind.

"I'll keep that in mind."

They drove in silence. Trees kept whizzing by, but Kendra wasn't focused on them. Instead, she waited for the inevitable words of separation to come from Darin's mouth. Were there any words that would undo the awful images that must be filling his head right now? Any possible way to undo the idiot thing she'd just done in sharing her childhood with him? She didn't harbor the delusion that Darin was a big enough man just to shrug off her childhood as if it hadn't happened. And there was no reason for him to settle for the likes of her.

Reality sucked.

Darin cleared his throat. "I'm sorry I put a damper on our day."

"I think that was me."

"Nope, I pushed you into sharing."

"I acquiesced."

"True. And I appreciate that. More than you can know."

"Why did you want to know?"

He glanced at her, then focused on the road. "Because I want to know everything there is to know about you, Kendra."

Kendra grimaced. "I'd advise against that."

"Why?"

Why, indeed. Why hide herself from him? "I'm not sure, really. I guess I'm just so used to not sharing that it's become a habit."

"One I intend to break, just so you know."

"Thanks for the warning."

"You're welcome. Kendra, have you been seeing someone else?"

The suddenness of the question caught her off-guard, and her answer came out before she had a chance to stuff it down. "Yes."

She watched his Adam's apple bob and hated herself for hurting him like this.

"I see."

"I'm so sorry, Darin. You deserve better."

He squeezed her hand. "I deserve a whole lot worse, Kendra."

Before Kendra could puzzle out his meaning, he continued. "Are you still seeing him?"

"No."

"How long has it been over?"

"Since before the accident. Since the night before the accident." Might as well get all the details out there while they were talking about it. No need to hedge around the truth now.

"You saw him that night? You were with me until two in the morning."

"He waited at my place until I came home."

"Oh."

Tires hummed on the pavement, and she waited, her heart in her throat.

"I told him that night that we couldn't keep seeing each other. That it wasn't right."

"How'd he take it?"

"Not well. He left mad."

"Does he know about the accident?"

"Yes. I called and left him a message. He hasn't called back."

"Do you wish he had?"

"I don't know."

Silence reigned again, and she took deep breaths, eyeing the off-ramp, waiting on him to slow down.

"Careful."

"What?"

"You need to slow down." She pointed to the off-ramp.

"Oh." He slowed the car in time to make the off-ramp, and her heart hit her toes. He really was turning around. A part of her had hoped — stupid, stupid girl — that he would want her anyway. Even after he found out she was no better than his ex-wife.

He pulled into a gas station parking lot and killed the engine.

"Go ahead, I'll wait here."

She looked at him, daring to meet his eyes, her forehead wrinkling. "What?"

"You need a bathroom?"

"No."

"Then why did you —"

"I thought you would want to turn around."

His brow creased. "Why would I do that?"

"So you could take me home?" The hopeful part of her sprang to life again.

"Kendra, I'm not taking you home." His eyes were those of an older man, and she wondered at the amount of pain he'd had to bear the past few years. Funny how she

223

hadn't thought of that since getting involved with Harrison again. "You thought I'd leave you when I found out?"

She bobbed her head, feeling like an idiot. A miserable idiot.

"I've known for a while."

"What?"

He shrugged, not meeting her eyes but not letting go of her hand either. "I knew something had changed with you, and I thought it was probably somebody else. I've been waiting for you to tell me and hoping you'd end things with him."

"You *knew?*" Why did she feel so betrayed by that? She had no right to feel anything other than remorse right now. Which didn't make the feeling go away but did stop her from speaking the angry words on her lips. Instead she just studied him. "Why didn't you say something?"

"I don't know. I guess I wasn't ready to deal with being cheated on again." Defeat filled his voice, and she reached out to him, desperate to stem the flow of hurt from his voice.

"I am so sorry, Darin. I didn't want to hurt you. I knew him before you, if that matters. Not that anything makes this right, but you need to know that I knew him before I met you."

"Were you seeing him when we met?"

She shook her head, needing him to understand. "No. We had ended things." Her mind skittered past why, unwilling to tell Darin the depth of her betrayal. "He called me up a couple of months after you and I started seeing each other. I wasn't sure if you were serious about me, and we hadn't said we were only seeing each other, so I agreed to see him again. I should have told you, but I couldn't figure out how."

She watched his bald head bob up and down and hoped he wouldn't ask more questions. Questions that would force her to reveal that she was no better than his first wife. No more deserving of his affections.

"I guess I can't much blame you," he finally said. "We never said we weren't going to see other people, and I know better than to make assumptions." He raised his head and pinched the bridge of his nose. "The way I see it, I know now, and you're not dating him anymore, and that's gonna have to be enough."

Not a complete acceptance, but not a rejection either.

"Okay." Her voice revealed the uncertainty that strangled her heart. She waited a few beats. Did he have more? The silence accused her, ridiculed her for Sylvia's past.

"Where do we go from here?" The hated question had to be asked.

His eyes, now red from the emotion of the moment, met hers. "Where do you want to go?"

"I think, given the situation, that's entirely your call."

"Let's pretend I don't have a say. What do you want, Kendra?"

To turn back the hands of time. To pretend I never met Harrison. To be born to a different woman, born into the loving home I eventually grew up in. To be a woman who feels entitled to a man like you.

"Oh, Darin. I want things I shouldn't."

The grin that stopped her heart on a routine basis began to spark. "Don't we all." He maneuvered the gearshift into reverse and backed them out of the gas station. "For now, though, this is what we've got." He jabbed the power button of the radio, and she let the easy jazz fill the silence. Sometimes music was just a better idea than words.

They drove the rest of the way to Leiper's Fork in silence, their heads moving in time with the beat, and Kendra wished they could ride like this forever, hand in hand. All too soon, Darin pulled off the highway again and drove down a two-lane country highway.

She stared out her window. Giant tobacco leaves waved in the breeze, their field broken up by tall stalks of corn with golden tassels on top. A blue sky hung like a canopy over it all, granting sunshine to the hungry crops. A smile crossed her face as she noted the line of blue on the horizon, saw the dark green bleed into it. That would be a beautiful line in a painting. Giant white wisps of clouds moved lazily, nowhere to rush, nowhere to be but here.

Her shoulders inched down, tension unwelcome in this tranquil place, and she noted from the corner of her eye that Darin was affected by the setting as well. His neck lost its stiffness. The lines around his mouth softened into a small smile.

He slowed the car to a crawl, and she rolled her window down just to feel the breeze against her skin, cooling the boil of residual shame, washing her clean, and lifting her hopes again for the day.

"Are we close to the site?"

Darin nodded. "It's about half a mile ahead. Close enough to the interstate for an easy commute, far enough away not to hear the highway traffic." He allowed the car to coast down the slight incline.

Morning sun dappled the leaves of a stand

of oak trees along the back of the property. It had to be at least a hundred acres, just lying there. No crops, just bright green grass blanketing the ground like a green wave.

"That's beautiful," she breathed.

"Mmm," Darin agreed. He pulled the car to a stop beside a slick white Lexus, and Kendra turned to see a short blonde sitting in the driver's seat, talking on her cell phone.

"Who's that?"

"That's Lorena." Darin opened his car door, and Kendra followed suit. "She's the realtor we're working with on this project."

Kendra assessed Lorena as the realtor held up one red-lacquered nail to signal she'd be with them in a minute. Pretty. Could stand to lose a few pounds. A ready smile, but sadness lurked beneath the surface.

Kendra trailed behind Darin as he stood on a rise looking over the property.

"Picture five to ten acre lots, two- and three-level brick homes, circular driveways, fountains, roundabouts. This will be *the* place to live if we do things right."

A part of Kendra wished the land could just stay the way it looked right now. But somebody was bound to come along and develop it. Might as well be Darin because he'd make sure those oak trees were still standing after the bulldozers left.

"Darin, hi." The blonde toddled toward them, hand outstretched. Aigner loafers bearing the signature brass *A* wrapped around tiny feet. Wide-leg ivory pants made the woman dumpier than she had to be. A matching jacket, cut right at the hip as if the designer *intended* to emphasize the woman's widest point, was buttoned snugly around her waist. Pearl studs completed the dowager image. How had this woman made it in the cutthroat world of south Nashville real estate?

"Hi, Lorena. This is my friend Kendra."

Kendra shook the woman's hand, noting the slight pudge of skin around her wedding ring. Ah, so she'd gained all that weight since the wedding.

Lorena flipped her hair — at least it was a natural blonde — and swept her hand across the view. "Breathtaking, isn't it?"

Darin's eyes were razor sharp as he looked at Lorena, and for the first time Kendra saw the business side of the man.

"It's a beauty." He slid one hand into a pocket and gestured up the road with the other hand. "Just like a lot of other tracts up and down this road."

"True, true. But the farther we get down

there, the longer your residents must drive to the interstate, right?" Lorena tucked a lock of hair behind her ear, and her hand trembled a bit. Was she nervous? New to the real estate game?

"Oh, I agree." Where had that come from? Kendra's eyes widened at the sound of her own voice. "This is the perfect distance from the highway." Lorena's hand stopped shaking, and Kendra felt better about opening her mouth.

Darin watched the two women, shared a look of understanding with Kendra, and held out his hand. "Thanks for meeting us out here, Lorena. I've got a couple of calls to make Monday." He shook the realtor's hand. "We'll be in touch."

He strode back toward the car, and Kendra quickly followed while Lorena scrambled to keep up.

"Um, do you have any questions?" The tremor in Lorena's voice made Kendra glance back. The woman looked panicked. "I've got plenty of information here on the property if you'd like to see it."

"Darin, we just got here." There she went again, butting in. Hadn't Darin just brought her along for the ride? It's not like the man's ability to pick properties wasn't proven. "Don't you want to walk the property? Get a feel for the place?"

Darin swung around to her, his easy smile in place. "I've been all over it and, thanks, Lorena, but I have the information you faxed to the office." He leaned toward the woman, who by now was all but shaking. Kendra's heart went out to her. She had to be new.

Extending his hand, he took Lorena's small one in his and bent lower to her level. "I wasn't kidding. I'll call you on Monday for details about the contract."

Kendra blinked. He was buying the property? That fast? Lorena recovered more quickly than Kendra. "Oh! Oh, that sounds fine. I'll wait for your call, then. You two have a lovely afternoon!" She wiggled her fingers in the air and plodded off to her car.

Kendra waited until they were ensconced in the relatively soundproof Barracuda before turning to Darin. "What was that?"

"That was me buying a new property." He started the car, his air of nonchalance at odds with what had just happened.

"You knew you were buying it before we got here."

"Yep."

"Then why make that poor woman schlep all the way out here?"

He maneuvered the car back onto the

231

road and waved good-bye to Lorena, who was now talking with great animation into her wireless ear piece. "I wanted to make sure the realtor had enough hunger to get the deal done fast. I've worked with a lot of them who act like they're doing me a favor by selling the property. I'd never met this woman, and I just made sure she wouldn't give me any grief in the process."

Kendra sat back in her seat, a fresh wave of appreciation going through her. "You're good at this."

Darin's eyes cut to her, then back to the road. "Thanks."

"You're welcome."

"So now that business is out of the way, how about lunch?"

"Good idea."

Ten minutes later they walked into Puckett's Grocery, and Kendra looked around, expecting to see Andy Griffith.

"Mr. Spenser?"

Kendra and Darin turned at the same time. "Why, you're going to think I'm stalking you or something!" Lorena adjusted her jacket and smoothed the front of her pants.

"Leiper's Fork is a small town." Darin winked. "Guess it was inevitable we'd run into you during the lunch hour."

"Well, don't let me interrupt your lunch."

"Oh, join us." What was it about this woman that made Kendra want to reach out and take care of her? She spotted Darin's confused look but didn't see a way out of the invitation now. "We'd love to hear more about the real estate up here."

Lorena smiled, and Kendra stared. That was a killer smile when the woman let it go. "Now *that* I can tell you a ton about. But are you sure you two want to spend your whole lunch listening to me prattle on?"

Kendra nodded, eager to give the woman confidence in what was so obviously a new career. "You bet. Come and tell me everything I've ever wanted to know about Leiper's Fork."

Forty-five minutes later Kendra pushed back from the table and groaned. "Ugh, Lorena, I'm holding you personally responsible for letting me eat all that food."

The realtor giggled — a sound like little bells chiming — and pointed across the table. "I can't take credit for that. You're the one that asked for the pie menu even after I warned you about the expanding dumplings."

Kendra moaned. "You weren't kidding. I'm going to have dumpling hangover tomorrow."

Darin chuckled and picked the check up from the corner of the table. "And you'll have nobody to blame but yourself."

The lunch had been better than Kendra would have guessed up front. Lorena was a delightful, if inexplicably sad, woman. Married for three years, she had yet to have any children and had decided to focus on a career in real estate until a baby came along. Darin would be her first major sale — major being something in seven figures, Darin had whispered when Lorena excused herself for the restroom.

"You're right, you're right." Kendra pulled herself upright. "I'll be good tomorrow."

Mischief crinkled Lorena's eyes. "You sound like me. Except that tomorrow comes, and somebody puts cookies or peanut brittle or pie in front of you, and you think, *I'll be good tomorrow.*" She patted her pants, visible now that she'd unbuttoned that tight jacket. "Pretty soon, you're wondering who shrunk your pants."

"You're a nut." Kendra laughed. "Honey, that's why God made kimonos."

Lorena scrunched up her nose. "Do you see me in a kimono? I don't think so."

The women joined in laughter while Darin pulled bills out of his wallet and laid the money under their check on the corner of the table. "Lorena, I'm glad we ran into you here. It's going to be a pleasure doing business with you."

"Oh, phooey on you, Mr. Businessman." Kendra shoved his shoulder. "Lorena, don't you let him get all stuffy on you. You let me know the next time you're near Stars Hill, and we'll go have some fun together. I know a certain diner whose burgers are to die for."

Lorena pointed a finger at Kendra. "You've got yourself a deal." She picked up her purse and stood up. "Well, I think I've taken enough of y'all's day, and I've got another appointment to get to. Thank you very much for lunch, Mr. Spenser."

"My pleasure. Anybody who keeps this lady smiling," he hugged Kendra to his side, "is always welcome at my table."

"Aww, you two are so sweet." Lorena's eyes turned down, and Kendra wondered again at the sadness that entered the lovely blonde's face every time talk of relationships arose. "Bye now."

As Lorena wandered off to her next meeting, Kendra turned to Darin. "Do you think she's in a bad relationship?"

Darin rose one eyebrow. "Who? Lorena?"

"No, dummy, the other blonde we just had lunch with. Of course Lorena!"

"How'd you pick that up? We talked about

real estate for forty-five minutes."

"Not the whole time. And besides, every time you smiled at me or said something nice about me, she got this sad look on her face. I think her marriage is on the rocks."

"Sure, Psychic Madame, you read her perfectly."

"Hey, don't make fun. I'm serious here."

Darin rolled his eyes and stood up. "Come on, woman. Let's get over to the art museum before you line up a marriage counselor for my realtor."

Kendra beamed and followed him out the door, happy to have made a new friend.

FOURTEEN

Joy slumped on the toilet seat, staring at another negative test as thunder rumbled outside. Did a quest exist that could be more degrading than trying to get pregnant? What other pursuits in life required the adventurous one to pee on a stick every month and watch the clock's slow second hand sweep, dread and hope building as one, until the answer became obvious?

She sighed, then straightened. Another month down the drain. After twelve months of the same answer, the time had come to try a different tack.

Throwing the offending test in the trash, she stomped out of the bathroom in search of her husband.

"Scott!" Her voice bounced off the marble floor of the foyer as she passed through on the way to the kitchen. Lightning slashed the dark sky outside, sending eerie blue light flashing through the front windows. The

237

gong of the grandfather clock started, reverberating off stone and making it hard to count out nine separate tones.

"Scott! Where are you?" She raised her voice above the clock's sound. When were they going to get that intercom fixed?

"In here, Princess."

Joy turned off into the library. Scott clung halfway up the bookcase ladder, about ten feet in the air. "What are you looking for?"

"I had a hankering to read some Roethke." He reached out from the ladder and plucked a leather-bound volume from the shelf, then gingerly made his way back down. Thunder rumbled outside.

"Roethke, hmm?" Joy hated to disappoint him when he was in such an amorous mood. Roethke was for newlyweds, lovers full of passion. Not couples trying to conceive a child only to confront failure every thirty-one days.

Scott reached the bottom step and sauntered toward her, a confident man unperturbed by the months of faulty tests. She ignored the spurt of anger at that.

"Yes. I watched you lying in bed this morning, and a Roethke line popped in my head. All day long I've been trying to remember the rest of the piece, but I finally gave up and came in here to find the book."

"What line?"

" 'Lovely in her bones.' You looked lovely this morning, Princess." He kissed her lightly, assured of her response before making the gesture.

"I took another test." *Dial down the harshness.*

"I take it we didn't get the answer for which we hoped?"

"Do you see me jumping up and down, bouncing around this room?"

"Joy . . ." His arm came around her waist, and she felt the corner of the book dig into her back. "It will happen when God wants it to happen." Rain pattered the windows.

"When is that, Scott?" Shoving against his chest, she parted them and moved to the other side of the room. "Next month? The month after that? When? Next year? Next decade? When is God going to hear my prayer? When is He going to deign to listen to me? When is He going to listen to *you?*"

"Now wait just a minute. God's not ignoring me."

Joy clenched her hands over her barren stomach. "No? It sure feels like it to me. I've got a serious lack of pink lines in my life, and I think that's because God's ignoring the both of us."

"Joy, He's not deaf. He's just not giving

239

you the answer you want." The lightning flashed on his face, and he looked like an emissary from God Himself.

"Is this the answer *you* want?" she goaded. "Are you fine with having no child, no son to carry on the Lasky name? Are you perfectly okay with the way your mother eyes me every time we go to their house for dinner? Or the way your dad reminds me of the five sons his perfect wife provided him? Exactly what are you all right with here?"

"I'm not all right with any of this, but I'm also not going to lose my faith over it."

"How about your temper? Could you lose that? Or do you not care enough to lose control over your precious universe?" The shrill in her voice frightened her into silence. They stood, sparring partners caught in a freak light show.

Scott blinked, then closed the distance between them in three easy strides. He stood before her, not touching. Breathing through flared nostrils. Good, he was at least upset enough to breathe heavily. "Joy, I hate everything about this. But I'm not going to start yelling at you. There's a solution here. There always is. We just have to keep trying."

"I'm sick of trying, Scott. I want to be *doing.*"

Scott tossed the book onto his massive cherry desk. "I know you do. But right now all we can do is try."

"No, right now we could be going to a fertility specialist and finding out what the heck is wrong with me. Or you. Or us."

Scott sucked his breath in through his teeth and stared stonily out the bay window. "Joy."

His voice held a warning. One she was sick to death of heeding. "Scott." Her tone matched his. Let him know how close he was to starting something he didn't want to finish.

"We've had this discussion."

"I'm not an idiot. I am persistent, though. And a year of trying is enough, Scott. It's enough."

"Some women take years to get pregnant."

"I'm not going to be one of them. I'm calling Dr. Goodman on Monday. I'll go alone if I have to, but I'm going."

"Don't do this, Joy."

"Do what? Find a way to give you a child? How does that make me a bad woman?"

"No, don't make this a fight between us. We won't survive it if you decide to play opposite me."

"I missed where this became a game." Her voice could have frozen the raindrops that cascaded down the window, but she didn't care. Enough was enough.

She left him standing in his study, lightning cracking the sky at his back.

FIFTEEN

"Sisters, Ink," Kendra propped her sandal-clad feet up on the desk and tucked her long skirt into her knees. There it couldn't get trapped in the wheels of her chair, and she could still conduct business in a comfortable position.

"Kendra Sinclair, please."

"This is Kendra."

"Oh, hi! It's Lorena. The realtor? From Monday?"

"Well, knock me over with a feather. How's your day, Lorena?"

"It's all right. Listen, I had to drive about a half hour south of Nashville to show a property this morning, and I think I might be close to Stars Hill. Didn't you say you were an hour from the city?"

"That's right."

"Would it be presumptuous of me to ask if you had lunch plans?"

"Not a bit! I'm at the office now, but I

can wrap things up by the time you get here."

"You sure I won't be interrupting your day?"

"Please, woman. I've got one sister in the throes of wedding bliss, another about to maim her husband if they don't get pregnant soon, and another — well, I don't think Meg's got too much going on these days, but I'm sure her house is chaos with three kids running around. You wouldn't be interrupting; you'd be saving me from work and family visits."

Lorena chuckled. "All right, then. How do I get to Stars Hill?"

Kendra gave her directions, agreeing to stay at the Sisters, Ink offices until Lorena showed up. She hung up the phone, then speed-dialed Darin on her cell.

"Darin Spenser."

"Hey, guess who's on her way to Stars Hill?"

"Britney Spears."

"You're so funny."

"Brooke Shields. She heard Britney was coming and wants to come help her jump-start her career again."

"You've been reading *People* magazine again, haven't you?"

"Tandy left one behind at the diner, and

Clay took too long to get my burger to me yesterday."

"Well, you struck out on both counts. Neither Britney nor Brooke is on the way to our humble little town."

"Those were my best guesses. I give. Who is coming to grace us with their presence?"

"Lorena."

"Who?"

"Lorena."

"Lorena my real estate agent? Why?"

"Because she was showing a property close to here and thought she'd come on down."

"Did she say there were problems with the Leiper's Fork property?"

"No. I didn't get the impression she was coming for business at all."

"Then what's she coming for?"

"My witty conversation?"

"Honey, realtors don't drive an hour from their office to make conversation. There's got to be an issue with the property."

"Then why didn't she call *you*, hot shot?"

"Because you two bonded over lunch? Because it'd be easier to work a woman than a man?"

"I'm hanging up now."

"Wait, that didn't come out like I meant it."

"So you didn't mean to sound like a chauvinist pig?"

"Right. Exactly. I meant to — shoot, I don't know what I meant. I just don't want there to be anything wrong with that property. I've already gotten bids on the development project. I'd hate to throw all that work away."

"Let's not borrow trouble. She'll be here in a few minutes. I'll call you if she's coming down for work."

"If she even hints about work."

"Got it."

"Okay, but I don't like this."

"You like me. That's enough."

"For now."

Kendra smiled as she shut the phone and went back to answering member e-mails. Sisters, Ink's membership was growing more and more each day. Scrapbookers loved being able to find like-minded individuals online who were just down the road or around the bend in real life. Kendra had to give it to her sister — Tandy's business idea was proving to be a winner.

Twenty minutes later the bell over the door sounded, and Lorena trundled into the room. Today's outfit fit her no better than Monday's. Maybe worse.

A navy pencil skirt cut her legs off at mid-calf, and Kendra thought again of the crazed designer bent on highlighting the widest parts of Lorena's body. Navy and ivory-colored stripes wound their way around her busty frame, the fabric held together by giant brass buttons with anchors embossed in the centers. *Yeah, let's put images of very heavy objects right over a woman's heaving bosom and thick waist.* A wide white headband held Lorena's full blonde locks back from her face, which shone red with exertion.

Kendra inwardly shook her head. Did the woman not own a full-length mirror?

Lorena scanned the office, her cornflower-blue eyes lighting up when she spotted Kendra. "Hi!" Lorena weaved through the store fixtures — they'd put them in yesterday, deciding to sell some product on the side — and came to a stop at Kendra's desk. "You were so right about this town! It's got the charm of Leiper's Fork."

"And about the same nightlife as Mayberry." Kendra came around the desk and rested her hip against its corner. "So welcome to our little town. Want me to show you around?"

"I'd love it. Do you know if there's a realtor in town?"

"That'd be my brother-in-law, Scott."

"Oh, whoops. Don't worry." Lorena made an *X* over her heart. "I promise not to be any competition at all to him. I just couldn't believe a town like you described at lunch that day actually existed this close to Nashville outside Leiper's Fork. But from what I saw on the drive in, I guess you're right."

"Yep, it's small, it's intimate, and it's home. At least until the yuppies find us."

"I can't believe they haven't yet."

Kendra walked Lorena toward the front door. "They're starting to. Scott's sold a few pieces to some young professionals working in Brentwood and Franklin."

"I'll bet the land prices here are a whole lot better than we can offer in the Fork."

"I don't know about that. Haven't sold any land here myself." They left the shop, and Kendra turned left toward College Street. "Have you had lunch yet?"

"I haven't. I was hoping you'd help me find that diner with the great burgers."

Kendra motioned in front of them. "It's right here. Clay's Diner. I have to confess, though, I'm a bit biased. The owner is about to become my brother-in-law."

"Is that so?" They crossed College and stopped in front of the door to Clay's. The wind kicked up, swinging the sign above their heads. "I'll keep that in mind when forming an opinion."

On entering the restaurant, Kendra tried to see the setting through fresh eyes, the way Lorena would be seeing it right now. Well-dressed women and less-dressed teens packed almost every table. The men sported overalls or plaid shirts, cups of coffee hooked securely on one finger. A congenial hum of chatter filled the room.

"What a charming place," Lorena said, and Kendra had to agree.

"Thanks."

"Don't mention it. You said the owner is about to be your brother-in-law?"

"Yep. He's marrying Tandy, my younger sister." As they plopped down in the only available booth, Kendra gave her the brief rundown of Tandy's legal career and subsequent return to Stars Hill after falling in love — again — with Clay Kelner that very spring.

Lorena's eyes were misty and her voice hoarse as she said, "What a wonderful love story." She gazed out across the patrons, shaking her head slightly.

Kendra considered pursuing the matter, decided it was none of her business, and let it drop. "So tell me how you met your hubby."

"What?" Lorena's gaze jerked back to

Kendra, then down to her wedding rings. "Oh. We met at a singles social at church. He was sitting in a corner, looking like a lost puppy, and I wanted nothing more than to get out of that meat market and never return, so I went over to talk to him."

"Instead of leaving?"

Lorena shrugged. "If I left, they'd just keep inviting me back, and I'd keep giving excuses about why I couldn't come. I figured if I stayed for one whole function I could tell them I didn't have a good time, and I'd never have to go to another one."

Kendra took a second look at the woman. "And you ended up meeting your husband instead."

Lorena's smile was slow and melancholy. "Yeah. I asked him if he came to these things often, and he looked at me like I'd just asked him to go to Mars. It took about three minutes for us to declare our mutual hatred of both the single life and the quest for the 'right' partner. Three hours later the event ended, and we were still sitting there, talking and talking. Three days later he proposed."

"Wow, that was quick." She caught Clay's eye and held up two fingers.

"It was, but we had a long engagement. It took a year for me to plan the wedding."

"And you never had doubts?"

Lorena shook her head, her blonde hair falling into her face, too heavy for the headband. "Never. That year only reinforced what I'd known in those first three minutes. He's the one for me. Forever."

"That's amazing."

"It is, isn't it? You search your whole life for that special one and then, *whammo*, when you least expect it, there he is, sitting in a corner."

"Remind me, how long have you been married?"

"Three years."

"Ah, the three again."

"Yeah, except I'm not sure the magic of three is helping us right now."

"Really?"

Lorena shook her head, and Clay appeared at their table, bubbling drinks in each hand.

"For my favorite soon-to-be sister-in-law." He set a drink down in front of Kendra. "And for . . . ?" He set the other drink before Lorena.

"Clay, this is my new friend, Lorena. Lorena, this is Clay."

"You're the Clay on the sign?"

"One and only." Clay wiped his hands on

his apron. "Anything else I can get you ladies?"

"This'll work for now. Thanks, Clay." Kendra waved him off and focused again on Lorena. "You were telling me the magic is losing its touch?"

"I was?" A flustered Lorena teased her straw. "Oh, never mind. I can't believe I brought this up."

"No, it's fine." Kendra reached out a hand and laid it on Lorena's arm. "Sometimes it's easier to talk to a stranger than to your closest friend."

Lorena's head dipped in embarrassment. "You're right, but unloading on the girl-friend of a client is pretty bad form."

Kendra took her hand back. "I don't know about that. Darin will be happy to know this isn't about a problem with the property."

Lorena's head snapped up. "What? No! There's no problem. None at all. Why would he think that?"

"Relax. He's just paranoid."

Lorena slumped into her seat. "Gosh, don't scare me like that. I need this sale to go through."

"So you'll know you're a good realtor?"

"So I'll have some money in case my husband leaves me."

Kendra stopped chewing. "Come again?"

"I think he might be planning to leave. There, I said it. No more denying."

"Why do you think he's leaving?"

"Lots of reasons." Lorena waved a pudgy hand in the air. "Out all hours of the night, late meetings, unexplained gas receipts, an emotional distance from me. They say a woman knows, and you know what? They're right. I know. I just don't want to know." She rolled her eyes. "Gosh, I sound like such an idiot."

"No, you sound confused, not dumb. I'm sure there are perfectly good explanations for all those things."

"Yeah, he's cheating."

"You don't know that. Have you asked him if he's cheating?"

"And give him a reason to go ahead and end our marriage? Are you nuts? No. I'm holding out hope that he finds a reason to leave her and stay married to me."

"You're just sitting around, hoping?" Kendra struggled to understand. "Lorena, I mean, I know this is really none of my business; and I have no idea what you must be going through. But I can't believe you're just lying beside him every night, wondering if he's left the side of another woman."

Lorena was a pretty woman. Blowsy and

overweight, yeah, but sweet and kind and cute. She certainly didn't deserve a cheating husband. Especially with the love story they shared so far.

Lorena shook her head. "I know you mean well, but you don't get it. As long as I play dumb, I've got a chance."

"But what if he *does* come back? Are you going to spend the rest of your life pretending you didn't notice everything you just told me?"

"Yes." Lorena took a sip of her drink.

"Seriously?"

"Yes."

Kendra sat back in the booth, not sure how they had gotten into such an intimate conversation to begin with but certain that she was the least qualified person in existence to offer marital advice. Though if she ever did get married and her husband cheated, not only would she confront him, she'd do it in the middle of Lindell Street for the whole town to see. And he'd rue the day he so much as looked at another woman, much less went for her.

Lorena tucked strands of hair back into her hair band. "I'm sorry, Kendra. Here it is, a beautiful day in an idyllic little town, and I go and ruin it all with talk of my philandering husband."

"Honey, you talk about him all you want. Just start talking *to* him, too." She couldn't help it. Giving advice came second nature.

"I'll think about that."

"And let me know if you need some backup to confront him. I've got some sisters who are more than qualified to assist in a confrontation."

Lorena grinned, and Kendra's heart lifted at the sight. "Thanks. It's good to know I've got some backup."

Kendra's cell phone rang, and she fiddled around in her giant purple bag to find it. "Where is that stupid thing? Hang on, hang on." Shoving aside mints and receipts, she saw a corner of shiny silver. "Aha! Kendra Sinclair." She held up a finger to Lorena and mouthed the word, "Sorry."

Lorena waved her off and pointed to the signs for the restrooms, then scooted out of the booth.

"Hey, girl, it's me."

"Hey, T, how goes the wedding planning?"

"Ugh, I'm weddinged out. I need a night of romance to remind me why I thought this was a good idea in the first place."

"I think you misdialed. Clay's number is —"

"Yeah, yeah, very funny. I'm serious. Remember when we kidnapped the guys a few months ago?"

"You planning a reenactment?"

"Something like that. I hear Joe's is open on Thursday nights now. Want to go hear some moody jazz?"

"Like you have to ask."

"I thought I'd at least pretend you had a life apart from me."

"You're a barrel of laughs today."

"I try."

"Seriously, I'm not sure I can dance very well yet. My leg still acts up if I stay on it too long."

"So sit and listen instead of dancing. Won't hurt my feelings a bit. Come on, Ken, I need to do something besides work and plan this wedding."

"You *did* do something. You were at Heartland just last Friday."

"Where I spent an hour sitting on the hood of my car talking to my fiancé about the wedding."

"Oh, wow, you do need a break."

"Thank you. So you'll get Darin on board?"

"I'll try. Call you back in a few."

"Great. Thanks, Ken."

"Yeah, yeah, I'm the best sister in the whole world."

"Keep that humility going."

"Wouldn't have it any other way." Kendra snapped her phone closed, then opened it again and dialed Darin, then grimaced when the call went to voice mail. She waited for the beep. "Hey, Darin, it's Kendra. Tandy's having a wedding cow and wants to go out tonight to Joe's. Call me if you can make it." She snapped the phone closed and rubbed her thumb across the back of it, thinking.

"He's got James Dean pictures in the bathroom!" Lorena sat down hard in her seat and scooted into the booth, everything on her jiggling a little in the process.

"Yeah, Clay's a bit of an old movie buff." Kendra tapped the phone on the table, knowing the idea she was about to voice could end in disaster. And knowing just as much that she'd do it anyway. What's life without some risk? "Listen, that was my sister on the phone. She wants to go to a little jazz place tonight."

"Oh, then I better be moseying along." Lorena began pushing her way back out of the booth.

"No, no, that's not what I meant." Kendra swallowed. "I wondered if maybe you'd like to join us. You . . . and your husband."

Lorena looked down. "Oh, I couldn't possibly. I'm sure he's working or already has

257

an appointment or something."

"Never hurts to ask, right?"

Lorena's blue eyes met Kendra's. "Yeah, sometimes it does."

Kendra held her gaze for a long moment. Her place should be supporting her new-found friend, but here she sat goading Lorena into a confrontation with her maybe-cheating husband. "Never mind. It was a suggestion. A dumb one at that."

Lorena whipped a cell phone out of her purse, pressed two buttons, and held it to her ear. "No, I think you're right. I don't have to ask him about the other woman. I can just remind him of the good times *we* have. Nothing wrong with that, is there?"

Kendra gave her the thumbs-up. "Not a thing."

Lorena held up a hand to stop Kendra as she spoke into the cell. "Honey? I've made us plans tonight."

"I'm somebody nobody loves," Cassandra crooned from the stage, as Joe tickled the ivories with skilled fingers and a small brass band kept time.

"I love this place." Kendra leaned against Darin as they walked into Joe's Jazz Place. Cassandra's voice filled the room with its smoky rasp, and the tension that had coiled so tightly in Kendra's belly as Lorena bemoaned her husband's infidelity began to loosen.

Darin patted her hand, which rested in the crook of his arm, and looked down at her. "Good." The tightness had left his voice as well, and Kendra relaxed further. Despite her admission of seeing someone else, it looked like Darin was ready to forgive and forget.

"Hey, you two." Clay's voice from behind caused Darin and Kendra to turn around.

"Look at you!" Kendra walked over to Tandy, who stood in the navy dress she'd worn the first time they'd come to Joe's together. "I swear, that dress was made for you."

Tandy executed a quick twirl. "I kind of like it."

"And she's not the only one." Clay's grin was only for Tandy.

"Hmm, looks like these two may want to be alone," Kendra warned Darin. "Maybe separate tables are in order?"

"Not on your life." Tandy tucked her hand through Clay's arms, mirroring her sister. "I want a night with my fiancé and my sister, and I'm getting it."

"I'll just trail along, if you don't mind." Darin's playful voice cut in.

"I don't mind at all," Tandy joked in return.

The band broke into "Taking a Chance on Love," and the foursome made their way into the crowded jazz hall.

Tandy leaned over to Kendra as they walked to "their" booth in the corner. "Did you say your friend Lorena was coming?"

Kendra nodded. "Yes. I called her on the way over. She had to drive back up to Franklin to change clothes and pick up her husband."

"Do you think he's cheating?"

"I don't know. I told you all she told me this afternoon." They reached the table and slid into the shadows made by low-hanging Tiffany-style lamps and black leather. "But I don't see me sitting at a table with a cheater all night long and not saying anything."

"Kendra, it's not your place to go butting into their marriage."

"Hey, I'm not the one who unloaded all my personal details to a virtual stranger over lunch. I think she *wants* someone else to confront him."

"I think you want her to want you to confront him."

"Well, I think I want you to want to talk to *us* for a little while." Clay's smile took

260

the bite out of his words. "Come on, Tandy, let's dance."

"I thought you'd never ask."

Kendra watched her sister, nearly glowing with love, hit the dance floor with Clay. They looked so happy together, joining hands and moving in time to the music. Clay's face radiated sheer pleasure just for being in Tandy's company. Kendra sighed.

"You all right?" Darin brushed her bare shoulder with his knuckles, and she tilted her head to see him better.

"Yeah, I think so. You?"

"Yeah." He dropped a light kiss where his knuckles had brushed. "Yeah."

She leaned her back into him, and they sat together, watching Tandy and Clay move across the dance floor as one. "They're perfect together," Kendra said.

"I think that's how it's supposed to be right before you get married."

"Mmm." Kendra watched them a moment more, then saw Lorena come in.

Alone.

"Oh, no. Look."

"What?" Darin moved his eyes from the dance floor and saw Lorena, looking like a chiffon banana in head-to-toe yellow, wobble over to them on chunky white heels. "Uh-oh. I don't see the mister."

"Tell me he didn't refuse her," Kendra murmured, then stood to greet Lorena.

"Hey, girl. Look at you!" She took Lorena's hands in hers and held her arms out. "All dolled up!"

Lorena's smile didn't quite reach her eyes. "Thanks, Kendra. I'm afraid it might be just me tonight."

"Your husband isn't coming?"

Lorena smoothed her hair back and adjusted her upswept do. "I'm not sure. He said he had a work thing tonight but that he'd try to make it."

"Well, let's just hope the man has a sensible bone somewhere in his body," Darin stood as well and reached a hand out to Lorena, "and sees fit to join his beautiful wife at a swanky jazz club." He kissed the top of Lorena's hand, and Kendra shot him a grateful look.

"Thanks, Darin. You're right. This place is divine." Lorena looked around and folded onto the seat — well, folded as well as her tight yellow dress would allow. "Has it been open long?"

Darin and Kendra resumed their seats, while Darin filled Lorena in on the history of Joe's. "That's about it," he finished.

"I had no idea you were so multitalented." Lorena smiled at him. "You develop property by day and play bass by night. A regular Renaissance man."

"Careful," Kendra patted Lorena's arm, "I've got to fit his ego back through that door at the end of the night."

They shared a laugh, and Kendra noticed Lorena check the door . . . again.

"I'm not the only one with hidden talents," Darin said. "Kendra here has a voice that'll make a man stop in his tracks."

Lorena turned to her. "Oh, really? Do you ever sing here?"

"I do occasionally. When I need somewhere easy to perform or when they're short a voice."

"Don't let her fool you." Darin clasped Kendra's hand in his own, and she basked in his look of approval. "They ask her to sing all the time; it's just that she's rarely available."

"Tom loves jazz," Lorena said, checking the door again, and Kendra noted that she'd let his name slip. "We went to all kinds of little hole-in-the-wall clubs during our dating years. We scoured *The Scene,* following new bands all over town, buying up indie CDs just to have something our neighbors didn't. Those were good times. I wonder whatever happened to those CDs?"

Kendra looked at Darin, but his eyes were

focused on Lorena's face. The pain on Darin's features stilled her. His sadness, when it broke the surface, consumed whatever other emotion might lie in the room. Clearly Darin's own failed marriage was rearing its head and lashing out. Kendra felt the blow as sharp as any hand on her face.

Inviting Lorena, while well-intentioned at the time, seemed wholly insensitive now. Why must Kendra continually remind Darin of his wife's betrayal?

She reached out, daring to cross the inches of chasm between them. "Darin?"

He jerked, looked at her. Blinked. Wiped his hand down a haggard face. "Yeah, sorry. Sorry."

Lorena's puzzled face registered on the periphery as Kendra touched Darin's mouth and whispered, "Me, too."

He could never know she'd spent time with a married man. If any doubt about that existed, the lost look on his face at this moment cleared it away. She would not, so long as it remained under her control, hurt him the way his first wife had.

He captured her hand in his, pressed his lips to it, then raised those chocolate eyes to hers. "Okay."

"Hi, Lorena. Good to see you again."

Clay's happy voice broke Kendra's gaze on Darin, and she looked up to see Lorena offering her hand.

Clay gestured to Tandy. "And this is my fiancée, Tandy. Kendra's sister."

Lorena shook Tandy's hand and looked from Tandy to Kendra and back again, clearly flustered. Kendra gave Tandy a look of confusion, then it dawned on her.

"My *adopted* sister, Lorena."

"Oh! Oh, my. Well, of course." Lorena took back her hand and patted the table. "I wouldn't have dreamed otherwise. Not that anything otherwise would be bad, I mean. I just wasn't certain how you two were, um, ah, well, sisters, being —"

"Different races?" Kendra saved her from a spiel she'd heard all her life. "Yeah, I tend to forget about it sometimes."

"Me, too," Tandy said. "So in case you ever meet our other sisters, be prepared to meet another white girl and a Chinese chick."

"Really? I'll bet you all look like the United Nations when you get together!" Lorena popped a hand over her mouth. "Oh my goodness. Was that insensitive?"

Tandy laughed. "Nothing we haven't heard before, let me tell you."

Lorena looked to Kendra, her eyes wide.

Kendra laid her hand on Lorena's and offered a smile. "Seriously, we're used to it."

"Oh, well, all right, then. I didn't mean to offend."

"Trust me. You couldn't."

Lorena gave her a grateful smile, then checked the door. "Hmm, it appears as though my husband might not be making it after all."

"No worries," Tandy said. "You can just hang out with us for a while."

"Oh, I'd hate to be a fifth wheel. You four look so cute together."

"Yeah, but we were missing a blonde. Now we've got all the colors covered," Kendra teased, and Lorena primped her hair.

"Oh, you."

"So, tell us all about you," Tandy said as Clay signaled for the waitress. "You're Darin's realtor?"

Lorena explained her connection to the Leiper's Fork property, which led to a discussion of the charm of the little town, which segued into stories of growing up in small Stars Hill, which gave Tandy the opportunity to tell a few stories on Kendra, which left them all shaking with laughter.

"Heavens to Betsy." At Lorena's laughing exclamation, Kendra realized the woman hadn't checked the door throughout the entirety of Tandy's story. "Kendra, I can't believe you jumped on the back of a pig."

"You'd be surprised what a girl will do to own her own horse."

"That sure was smart of your daddy, seeing if you could stay on a pig before letting you up on a horse."

"If you can keep a momma sow from knocking you off her back, you can stay on anything." Kendra drank her Diet Dr. Pepper and watched Tandy start her nightly fade into dreamland.

"Words to live by," Darin deadpanned.

Lorena checked her watch, and her eyes widened. "Oh my, it's after ten! I need to head on back. It's a long drive up to Franklin."

"You sure you should drive it tonight?" Kendra asked. "You can crash at my place."

"No, no, I wouldn't want to put you out."

"It's no bother, really. I'll worry less knowing you're not out there driving on a dark highway, as tired as you look."

"No, I'm fine." Lorena waved away her concern, but her eyes were about as heavy as Tandy's. "I'll put on NPR and be all caught up on world events by the time I pull into my driveway."

"Ugh, that would put anybody to sleep," Clay said, and Tandy smacked his arm halfheartedly.

"Hey, don't hate on NPR. I happen to be a fan of Morning Edition."

"Yeah, you tell him, T," Kendra said.

"Okay, okay." Clay put his arm around his sleepy fiancée. "NPR rocks. There, happy?"

Tandy melted into him with a sloppy grin and a yes, and Kendra realized her sister was getting loopy. Yep, ten o'clock had arrived. Tandy would never be a night owl.

"How about we all pack it in for the night?" she suggested. "I'm beat anyway, and Miss I-Fall-Asleep-at-Ten-on-the-Nose over there is going to conk out on us any minute."

"First NPR, now my sleeping habits. You people aren't very nice." Tandy laid her head on the table, her lids heavy. Clay patted her back.

"Mm-hmm. That's what I thought." Kendra chuckled. "Say good night, Gracie."

"Good night, Gracie," Tandy mumbled, her face pointed toward the table.

"Wow, she's really tired." Lorena stood and tugged her dress down.

"Yeah, she does that. She'll be up at five, though, more chipper than anybody has a right to be at that hour." Kendra got out of the booth, too, and the guys followed suit.

"You're kidding."

"I wish. She and Joy, one of our other sisters, used to come in my bedroom at five in the morning singing at the tops of their lungs to wake me up."

Lorena shook her head as they made their way to the door. "You're so lucky to have sisters."

"You tell her."

At Tandy's comment Kendra rolled her eyes. "Hush, Sleeping Beauty."

"Bye, Joe!" Darin called over his shoulder as they made their way to the door, and Joe lifted a hand from the piano to wave.

They spilled out onto the parking lot where Clay and Tandy split off to his car, Tandy's sleepy good-night drifting back to them.

Darin and Kendra turned to walk Lorena to her car.

"Thanks for coming all the way down here," Kendra said. "I know it's a long drive, but it was fun having you here."

"Didn't they tell you? Blondes have all the fun." Lorena patted her hair and opened the door of her white Lexus, which now sported a thin layer of highway grime.

"In that case you should come down more often."

"I just might do that." Lorena settled herself on her white leather seat and started the car. "Thanks for a good night."

"You're welcome." Kendra leaned down so that only Lorena could hear her. "And don't hesitate to call if you need backup."

Lorena winked, then put the car into gear.

Kendra felt tired to her bones. Her leg ached, and her heart hurt for Lorena, going home to a distant spouse, as Darin must have night after night toward the end of his marriage.

"Did you know your ex was cheating before she told you?"

Darin's steps slowed further, and he waited until they'd reached his car before he said yes.

"How did you know?"

"You just know, Kendra. When you're one with somebody, and they suddenly aren't sharing the details of their day or looking at you right, you know."

"Did you ask her about it?"

He opened her door and leaned on the window glass. "Not for a long time."

"Why? I don't get that. Lorena won't ask her husband, either. She just goes to bed with him, every single night, and lies there wondering if he's cheating on her."

"She's not wondering if he's cheating. She's wondering who she will be if he leaves her."

Kendra stopped. *Oh.*

"Anyway, I need to get you home and get home myself. I've got meetings in the morning."

Kendra let it go. No, Darin could never know all the details of Harrison. It was over anyway, so what would be accomplished by telling him?

Sixteen

Kendra pulled her RAV4 to a stop by the curb and peered out the windshield. Her hair would be a complete disaster by the time she dashed into Sarah's, but it couldn't be helped. Tandy was determined to get her bridesmaid dresses ordered *today* or die trying.

Kendra cracked open the door and popped an umbrella out. Pushing the button to expand its protective shield, she stepped out of the car and into the deluge. She hopped her way around the various puddles forming on the old pavement of College Street and scampered up to the sidewalk on Lindell. The hem of her long skirt was soaked by the time she escaped through the front door of Something by Sarah.

"Tandy!"

"Back here." Sarah Sykes's country tones carried from the fitting room area.

Kendra folded up her umbrella, left it sitting on the floor to dry, and hurried to the back. "I'm sorry I'm late. This rain isn't helping my day at all."

"Tell me about it," Sarah drawled, coming to the front of the room. "Your sister's in the big dressing room. I think she's on her third dress so far."

Kendra smiled wryly and walked toward the rear of the fitting area. "Tandy? What are you doing trying on dresses? I thought they were for us?"

Tandy opened the door and stepped out. "They are. But you were late and I didn't want to waste time, so I thought I'd start trying stuff on."

Kendra appraised the tangerine-colored silk number that hugged Tandy's curves and set her hair off. "Please tell me that one's not in the running."

Tandy looked down. "What's wrong with this?"

"Orange? You want a University of Tennessee wedding?"

"Hey, orange is the new red."

"Orange is the color of the seventies." Kendra pushed Tandy back into the dressing room. "That's a no. I'm here now. Get your clothes back on, and let's go look at dresses that are within the realm of possibil-

273

ity." She shut the door firmly and turned to see Sarah smiling. "What?"

"Nothing, nothing." Sarah began gathering up dresses that Kendra now noticed were scattered all over the fitting room. "Just thanking the good Lord you're here."

"Has she been awful?"

"Oh, I wouldn't say that. I think she's just stressed about the wedding. It happens with every bride."

"I can *hear* you!" Tandy's voice floated over the dressing room door.

Kendra scrunched her nose at Sarah. "Good. Then you'll know we love you enough to tell you when you're going off the deep end."

"I am *not* going off the deep end." Tandy came out, now in street clothes. "This is my *one wedding day,* and it will be *perfect,* and we will find the *perfect dress* today, and everything will be —"

"Perfect," Kendra finished for her. "Yeah, yeah, we get it. Go sit over there and prepare to judge." She grabbed up a handful of dresses and entered the room Tandy had just vacated. "Where are Meg and Joy anyway?"

"Meg's taking the kids over to Daddy's, and I have no idea where Joy is. Probably got hung up at the salon."

Kendra slid a soft-blue sheath dress over her head and struggled with the back zipper. A quick look in the mirror caused her to shudder. *Sheathing* and *dress* should not be used in the same sentence. She opened the door and stepped out. "Can we eliminate this one, please?"

"Why? The color is great on you."

"I look like a piece of dark meat encased in blue wrapping. Trust me, sweetie, you're not going to end up with scrap-worthy pictures if you wrap all your sisters in baby blue."

"You're right, you're right." Tandy shooed her back in the fitting room. "Joy suggested the color. I should have known it was more about a nursery."

"Speaking of which, don't you think it's a little odd that they've been trying for months and aren't pregnant?" Kendra pulled the dress off gratefully and put it back on the hanger. She unbuttoned a plum-colored number and put it on. "I mean, it's been, what, six months?"

"At least. They were talking about a baby last Christmas, if I remember right." Tandy nibbled her lip and motioned for Kendra to turn out. Kendra obliged.

"I like that one. What do you think?"

Kendra walked over to the three-way mirror and checked the dress out from all angles. Dusky purple silk hung softly across her backside, making her curves look feminine instead of fat. Small round buttons emphasized the arch in her back, at least as far as her shoulder blades. There the material ended. A fitted bodice gave her straight, smooth lines in the waist area, and the halter neckline brought the eye off her body and onto her face.

"Not bad." She spun, keeping her eyes on the mirror. "Not bad at all."

"That color works well on all of you."

"Ooh! That's pretty." Meg came into the room and dropped a large tote bag on the nearest chair, pulling a digital camera from its outside pocket. "Turn around, Kendra, let me see the front." She snapped a pic. "I've got the perfect paper to go with that dress."

"Get the kids dropped off?" Tandy asked from her chair in the corner.

"I did. Daddy's got them outside pulling weeds in the pumpkin patch." Meg turned to Tandy and clicked the camera's shutter once again.

"Ooh, they'll be nice and tired when you pick them up."

"That's my plan." Meg checked out her picture on the camera's built-in screen. "I really do like that dress, Ken."

"You'd love it if you had seen the one Tandy had on when I got here."

"Was it bad?"

"Picture a Tropicana carton."

"Tandy!" Meg stomped her foot. "You know I look hideous in orange."

"Yeah, yeah. We got rid of it, okay? Focus on the moment. You like the purple one?"

"I do. Except that neckline is going to make Joy look even shorter than she is."

"You think?"

"I do."

Kendra shrugged and went back to her dressing room. "It's not like we don't have a thousand more to try on." She tugged the dress over her head and set it to the side. Wedding or no, that dress was going home with her today.

"Hey, where's Joy?" Meg's voice came from the cubicle next door.

"We were just wondering that very thing," Kendra pushed her spiraled locks back into place. "Tandy, why don't you call her? It's not like her to be this late without calling us."

A few moments later Kendra and Meg stood before the three-way, each assessing their dresses. "Well, it could be worse."

Kendra pulled a face at Meg. "Yeah, we

could put a pile of fruit on your head and make you sing the Chiquita banana song."

Meg's willowy form was draped with pale yellow the same shade as her hair. Her light skin blended so well with the color that she looked like a yellow pole.

"Though I'll admit you look better than Lorena did last night. She dressed head-to-toe yellow, too."

"Who's Lorena?"

Kendra filled her in as Tandy wrapped her call to Joy.

"Joy's on her way. She had a color emergency to handle. Sort of like that dress. Gosh, that's . . . that's —"

"Not the dress you're forcing me to wear on your wedding day."

"Heavens, no. But —" Tandy held up a finger, then twirled and shot into Meg's dressing room. She reemerged brandishing Meg's camera. "It *is* the dress that's going to make a great OOPS layout!"

Tandy captured the moment before Meg could cover her face.

"Tandy Sinclair! You better delete that picture right now."

"Not on your life, sis. And you better not, either, or I'll tell James where you hide his candy."

Meg held up her hands while Kendra

278

laughed. "Okay! Okay! You can have your pic. Just give me the dignity of journaling my embarrassment on your layout, deal?"

"Deal." Tandy handed Meg the camera. "So did I hear you talking about Lorena?"

"Yeah," Kendra studied her mirror image.

Meg fussed with the flouncy bow at her hip. "And I'm trying to understand how a woman suspects her husband of infidelity and doesn't do a thing about it."

"*Thank* you!" Kendra slapped her black-silk-covered thigh. "I've been wondering that very thing. Seems crazy to me."

"Or like the world's worst case of denial," Tandy offered.

"But Darin said he did the same thing when he knew his ex was cheating. He knew but didn't say anything for a while."

"That's nuts. If I thought Jamison was out with another woman, much less sleeping with her, he had better look out."

"Shoot, Daddy would kill him before you had the chance."

Meg pointed at Tandy. "Exactly."

"I wonder if Lorena's parents know?"

Tandy looked at Kendra. "Are her parents alive?"

"I don't know. I'll have to ask her if I see her again."

"If?" Meg looked at her in surprise.

"You've got to stick by her side, Kendra. She can't go through this alone. Can you imagine knowing the love of your life was betraying you? That'd be so awful!"

Kendra squirmed. "I don't know, Meg. Maybe he's got a reason to cheat."

"Kendra Sinclair! What is *wrong* with you?" Tandy pushed herself up in her seat. "There's *never* a reason to cheat."

"Oh, Tandy. Sometimes life hands you events that force you to recognize the world has shades of gray."

"Gray or not, you don't step out on your spouse." The intensity in Meg's eyes bored into her. "You just don't, Kendra."

"Look, Darin told Clay you had been seeing another man, Kendra. But that's not the same as if you were married to Darin. Right, Meg?"

"Absolutely. You haven't pledged vows to each other, Kendra. Lorena and her husband are not in the same situation as you and Darin."

Kendra stared at them, amazed at how easily a situation could be misread. But also grateful for the out. "Yeah, I guess you're right."

Meg's eyes softened on her. "I know we are. Don't feel guilty about that, Ken. You're not seeing the other man anymore, right?"

Kendra nodded. At least that much was true.

"Then . . . *don't you worry 'bout a thing*," Meg sang.

"Oh, Meg, honey, you are no John Legend."

"Yeah, but the man sings truth. It's over, Ken. Let it go."

That was true, too. Things with Harrison had ended weeks ago, with not so much as a peep from him since the accident. Time to take Meg's advice and let it go. Granted, if Darin knew all the details, he might rethink his easy forgiveness, but she'd make sure he never knew that Harrison was married. Because no reason could present itself for bringing it up again. She'd said she dated someone. Darin hurt but forgave her, and they were back on track now.

Kendra shook her shoulders, leaving the shackles of her past behind her again. "You're right. You're totally right. Thanks, girls."

"We're always right, Ken." Tandy hugged Kendra, and Meg joined in. "Soon as you figure that out, life's going to get a whole lot easier."

They pulled apart. Meg beamed at her, and Kendra felt the vestiges of guilt wash away. *Let it go.*

"Looks like I'm missing a scrapping moment." Joy's lilting tones made them look up. "Can someone clue me in?"

"Nope, that's what you get for putting somebody's color emergency before your sister's wedding." Tandy sashayed back to her chair. "You get to stay in the dark."

"Hey, if you had seen the shade of green on that woman's head, you'd have begged me to keep her off the streets until I fixed it." Joy put little hands on petite hips, looking — in her black capris, fitted white top, kitten heels, and boxy purse dangling from one wrist — for all the world like a miniature, Oriental Martha Stewart.

"Green?" Meg gaped.

"Think Oscar the Grouch. When will people learn that sun-activated bronzer and lighteners do not work on all hair types? It took three different rinses to bring out a natural brown, and did she heap gratitude on me for my efforts? No. She complained that I had taken her right back where she started instead of leaving her with beautiful blonde tresses. Not that she had the coloring for blonde locks anyway, but what could I do?"

"Oh, my."

"Exactly. So I had to spend another thirty minutes giving her a color only Madonna would wear, and only in the eighties, but she left happy."

"Madonna or the customer?" Tandy smirked.

"Cute, sister."

"Sorry." Tandy held up her hands.

"She left happy, though, right?" Meg pulled Joy's gaze off Tandy's face.

"I said she did, didn't I? You think I would leave a customer anything but?"

"Never."

Joy looked at the three sisters, her eyes narrowing. "You all look as if you are about to explode. Go ahead. Enjoy a laugh at your sister's expense."

With that, the girls lost control and collapsed into giggles.

"What's so funny back here?" Sarah came back into the room. "I hate to miss a good time."

"Joy was just telling us about her day," Kendra explained. "You had to be here to get it."

"Oh." Sarah slumped a bit. "I hate that I missed it."

"Trust me, Sarah, you didn't miss a thing." Joy slid her purse off her wrist and deposited it by Meg's tote bag. "At any rate, none of this conversation is helping us to find the exquisite dresses Tandy shall have us wear in her wedding."

At that Tandy snapped back into bride mode. "Right. Back to your fitting rooms, girls. We're burning daylight here. Meg, give me back that camera. I feel a scrapping moment or two coming on."

Meg groaned but tossed Tandy the camera before heading back to her dressing room.

Two minutes later all three sisters opened their doors and looked to Tandy for a reaction.

Joy's small frame was swathed in brown linen.

"Eww, no." Tandy clicked the camera, and Joy closed her door.

Meg wore a strapless pink number on her body and a look of chagrin on her face.

"Ditto." Tandy clicked again.

Kendra's red taffeta might as well have been a red arrow pointing to every ounce of extra skin. Tandy barely had the words "I don't *think* so" out of her mouth before Kendra shut the door.

The sisters tried on dress after dress. From green cotton to white linen, peach silk to red satin, strapless to strappy, sequined to plain, they paraded before Tandy for what felt to Kendra like hours. Each time Tandy shook her head, snapped a picture, and pointed back to the dressing room with a grin.

Kendra thought briefly of strangling her sister but decided instead to put on the last dress in her fitting room. At least the end was in sight.

The pale gold number fit her body as well as the first plum one had. Heavy fabric fell across her hips in a wave rather than a tug. A surplice bodice added soft lines to her chest and showed off her neck while hiding her thick waist. Discreet darts removed any hint of pulling or straining on the fabric. Kendra tossed her hair back. It didn't look as good as the purple one — pale gold didn't fall in her color family — but the finished product soared high above anything else she'd had on in the past two hours.

She opened her door and saw that Meg and Joy were already in front of the mirror wearing the same dress. The color looked great on Meg, with her blonde hair and fair skin. She looked like a golden goddess.

Joy's black hair set off the shine in her dress, and her blue eyes deepened the gold color so that it appeared richer than the fabric against Kendra's skin. The surplice neckline acted as a frame for Joy's tiny face and all but worshipped Meg's neckline.

Kendra knew it didn't work as well on her, just as she knew the purple number wouldn't work for Meg or Joy the miracles it worked on Kendra's body.

She sighed, trudging over to the three-way mirror. "Tandy, either love this dress, or I'm instituting a naked theme for your wedding."

Tandy walked over from her chair. She bit her lip, turning her head this way and that.

Finally she raised the camera. "Ladies, I think we have ourselves a winner." The lens shutter's click brought sighs of relief from every sister. "And a bona fide scrapping moment. Sarah!"

Sarah came into the fitting room. "Would you look at that. You girls look lovely."

"Thanks. Just needed a confirmation." Tandy gestured with the camera. "Will you get over there with them? I need a picture of all of you for the pre-wedding scrapbook."

Sarah, as familiar with the Sinclair sisters' scrapping habit as anybody, obliged without question.

Tandy snapped off a few pictures. "There. I think somewhere in there I got a good one."

"Good." Kendra stepped down from the raised platform and went for the dressing room. "Now who's up for a veggie burger?"

"Make that something that used to be a cow, and I'm in!" Meg said.

"Me, too!" Joy returned.

"I'll call Clay." Tandy pulled out her cell phone to make sure they'd have a table when they got to the diner.

Kendra's cell phone rang, and she pulled it from her skirt pocket. "Kendra Sinclair."

"Is this the one, the only, the beautifully luscious Kendra Sinclair?"

Darin's teasing tone made her smile. "It is. And who may I ask is calling?"

"Somebody looking for a lunch date."

"Aren't you in luck then."

"Only if you're joining me somewhere. I've got a two-hour break before the next meeting."

"I'm at Sarah's shop where we just found," she raised her voice and tilted her chin toward the dressing room door, "THE PERFECT BRIDESMAID DRESSES." Kendra returned to her normal tone. "And now we're headed to Clay's for lunch. Want to meet me there?"

"More than anything else I can think of."

"See ya."

She snapped the phone closed and hustled into her skirt and top, coming out with the gold dress on a hanger.

Sarah took the dress from her, then from Meg and Joy as they exited their stalls.

"Anybody mind if Darin joins us for lunch?"

"Nope. Actually, Jamison was in the diner when I called, Meg," Tandy said. "He's waiting around for us, too."

"Well, goodness," Joy pulled out her cell phone, "let me call Scott and see if we can't make this a regular date."

"*You're* going to have a greasy burger?"

Joy turned her back to them and spoke into the phone. "Hi, honey, it's me. The girls and I are going to Clay's Diner for lunch, and I wondered if you could join us. Darin and Jamison are there as well." She waited a beat. "All right. I'll see you there."

"Joy, you have got to be the most proper person I know," Kendra said as they made their way to the front of the store.

Joy tossed her shining hair. "There is nothing wrong with good manners, Kendra."

"Oh, I agree." They pushed out the door of the shop into the rain. "But the day I say 'all right then' to Darin, somebody call me on it, okay?"

They walked to where the awning ended and looked out at a cascade of raindrops falling between their corner and the opposite one, where Clay's Diner was situated.

"We're going to get soaked."

"And I just left my umbrella back at Sarah's," Kendra whined.

"Why do people avoid the rain?"

At Meg's question, the sisters turned to look at her.

"Um, because they don't want to get wet?" Tandy's forehead creased. "What kind of question is that?"

"It's an honest one. Think about it. None of us has anywhere to go after this. We can walk right out there, get soaked to our bones, and it won't matter a hill of beans."

"Except we'd look like drowned rats." Joy was scandalized. "What are you thinking?"

"I'm thinking we don't spend enough time embracing life." With that, Meg stepped out into the rain. "Come on. Remember when we did this as little girls?" She held her hands out, palms up, catching rain drops as she twirled in a circle on the concrete. "Who needs sunshine when you've got rain?"

Kendra looked at Tandy and Joy, whose faces reflected her own incredulity at Meg's behavior.

"I'm siiiiingin' in the rain," Meg sang at the top of her voice. "Come on, girls! Let's be crazy again — just for a few minutes."

She *did* look like she was having fun. Kendra shared a look with Tandy and saw her sister had gone into consideration mode as well. Why not? How often did the opportunity to play in the rain with her sisters come up these days?

Kendra stepped a hesitant toe out into the deluge and felt a fat rain drop hit her toe. Cold. She stuck her hand out, watching the drops pummel her hand. They were big splatters, falling with a satisfying *plunk*. That'd feel good on her face. Before she knew it, Kendra had walked right out into the weather, tilted her face up, and stuck out her tongue.

"That's my girl!" Meg cheered. "Come on, y'all. You're missing all the fun!"

Tandy looked at Joy, shrugged her shoulders, and jumped into the nearest puddle.

Kendra laughed hard, loving the cleansing feel of rain on her face. Why didn't they do this all the time? "Come on, Joy! You can clean up afterwards!"

"You three are going to be struck by lightning any moment. Momma taught us enough sense to come in out of the rain."

"She also taught us to enjoy the time we're given on this earth," Kendra countered. "Come on!" She held out her hand, dripping with water, to Joy.

Joy stared at it, then started untucking her shirt. "I can't believe the things I allow you girls to talk me into. I'm wearing a white shirt, for goodness' sakes!"

"If I know you, though, you've got a camisole on underneath it and a bra underneath that. Nobody's gonna see anything they shouldn't."

Joy frowned at her, then stuffed her purse under her shirt. "All right, but I'm not ruining a perfectly good purse."

"Fair enough."

Kendra closed her hand around Joy's and pulled her into the rainfall.

Pretty soon all four sisters were twirling around, hopping in puddles, laughing themselves silly. Kendra took the sound of their laughter deep into her soul, tucking it away to remember later.

The cold, cold raindrops pounded her head and shoulders, and she laughed.

Car and truck horns honked at them, and she laughed.

Joy's purse fell out of her shirt into a puddle, and she laughed.

Clay came out the door of the diner and asked what in the world they were doing, and she laughed.

She laughed and laughed and remembered how good it felt.

Ten minutes later a shivering group of Sinclair sisters huddled with their men in the back booth at Clay's Diner. "What's the air-conditioning set on in this place?" Kendra hugged herself. "Arctic?"

"It feels colder than it is because you're wet." Darin's mock correction made her smile. "Which is another reason people do not play out in the rain."

"Oh, don't fuss." Meg eyed the menu. "We were having fun."

Kendra pressed her arm against Darin's, enjoying his warmth. "Yeah, but all good things must come to an end, right?"

Meg snapped the menu closed. "Only if you let them."

"What is it with you today?" Tandy sipped on the Diet Mountain Dew Clay had placed in front of her a minute ago, promising to return soon with burgers for all of them. "You're nuts but not usually *this* nuts."

Meg ducked her head and avoided their eyes. "Nothing is with me. I wanted to embrace the moment. Sue me."

Kendra shared a look with Tandy and Joy, silently agreeing to let it drop for now but committing to pick it up again later.

"You'll be happy to know," Jamison said, "I managed to get a picture of you guys acting like goofballs."

Meg's eyes snapped up. "You did? That's great!"

"I did. You left the film camera in the car, and when I saw you four out there, I thought two words."

"Blackmail photos," Scott said, and Jamison pointed a finger at him.

"Exactly. The next time the kids want to run out in the rain and play, guess who's going to let them?"

Meg slumped in her seat. "That'd be me."

Jamison grinned, eyes twinkling. "Yep."

Joy peered at Jamison. "You're not serious, are you? You aren't intending to allow your children to play in the rain amid lightning and thunder?"

"What lightning?" Jamison gestured out the window. "The only thing out there is a whole bunch of raindrops."

"So long as you're not putting my nieces and nephew in danger."

"Thank you, parent police," Meg said. "We'll try not to kill our kids so we can stay in your good graces."

"Fine."

Scott put his arm around Joy and squeezed. "Relax, hon. I'm certain Savannah, Hannah, and James will make it through childhood — rain dances and all."

Joy leaned into her husband. "I know. I'm sorry, Meg. I don't mean to judge you. It just feels like everybody but us has kids,

293

and half the people who have them either don't want them or don't appreciate them."

"Whoa, sister, I love my kids."

"I know you do." Joy met Meg's eyes. "I know. I'm just touchy, is all."

Kendra took a drink of her Diet Dr. Pepper. "Have you guys talked to a doctor? Found out what might be making this take so long?"

Joy shoved away from her husband. "No. Scott thinks we don't need a medical opinion."

Uh-oh. Stepped right into that one. Kendra smiled at Scott. "Never mind. Not my business."

Scott returned the smile, but Kendra noticed the sadness didn't leave his eyes. "Not a problem. We'll figure it out."

Joy crossed her arms over her chest and sat back. "Yeah, when I'm ninety years old and have no eggs left, Scott will figure out we're *not* going to get pregnant without a little help."

"So, how 'bout them Packers?" Overly bright tones filled Jamison's voice. "I hear they're going to have a pretty good year."

"You know, I heard that same thing." Darin leaned into the table. "Got a good defensive line this year."

The men entered into a detailed analysis

of the defensive players for the Green Bay Packers, and Kendra turned to Joy. "Don't worry, Joy. If we have to hog-tie him ourselves and drag him to the doctor's office, we'll help you get this done."

Meg and Tandy bobbed their heads.

"We're with you on this, sis," Tandy said.

And Kendra watched her mannerly sister sniff.

SEVENTEEN

Kendra paused on her walk from the car to the church door Sunday morning and took in the beautiful blue of a Southern autumn sky. No trace of Saturday's raindrops lingered, their cleansing purpose complete in the resplendent sky today.

Kendra resumed her steps, grateful for the flat shoes she'd chosen that morning to go with her multicolored caftan. Dreams of Joy running around her house yelling, "Where's my baby?" had kept her awake for too much of the night. Kendra frowned and made a mental note to ask Daddy to talk to Jamison about going to the doctor. If a physical problem prevented them from getting pregnant, Joy needed to know sooner rather than later.

She climbed the stairs to the old wooden front doors that looked the same today as they had the past twenty-some years. Walking into the foyer, Kendra breathed in the familiar scent of Murphy's Oil Soap and rosewater perfume. Comforted and welcomed, Kendra moseyed through the sanctuary to the Sunday school rooms at the back. She hadn't been to church early enough for Sunday school since the accident, but the last Joy dream had ended at about six, and there was no use going back to sleep.

She stopped outside the door to the Grace Seekers class and took a breath. *Let it go.*

Pushing open the door, ten faces turned her way and she smiled.

"Hi, Kendra." Jerry welcomed her from his place behind the lectern. "Good to see you."

Kendra hoped her smile wasn't as tight as it felt. She sat down in a folding chair by the door.

The class continued taking prayer requests. Kendra read through the list of praises and requests on the whiteboard at the front of the room. Looked like the Smithson's adoption of a Guatemalan boy was almost complete. Barbara and Stacey were celebrating their ten-year wedding anniversary. Misty had a trip planned to South Carolina that week and had asked for traveling mercies. The youth group would be conducting their kickoff event that week and were asking for prayer for a good turnout. Kendra was surprised when she saw her own name at the bottom of the "healing" list.

"Anyone else have something to add?" Jerry's glance swept the room. "Anyone feel led to pray on behalf of the class?"

"I will," Stacey said and, everyone bowed their heads to pray.

Kendra bowed her head as well, realizing she hadn't done that a lot in recent months. Hard to talk to a God whose commandments you were openly breaking.

"Amen." Stacey finished the prayer, and Kendra raised her face.

"Today we're going to talk about consistency. Being the same person at work and home that we are on Sunday morning."

Kendra tuned out to open her Bible and read the Scripture focus of the day. She was the same messed-up woman regardless of the day of the week. And if anybody were to take a close look at her life, they'd know the truth of that thought.

She read Scripture as Jerry taught about the value of living a life that glorified Christ regardless of the circumstances we face. Kendra agreed with that. She could be at her apartment painting or sculpting instead of sitting here, being told things she already knew.

"I see a lot of you nodding, and I'm wondering, if all of us Christians agree that we should walk what we talk, why do we have so many godly folks doing the most ungodly things?"

Kendra's head snapped up.

"Hypocrisy's always been a problem in the church," Cam said.

"That's true." Jerry came out from behind the lectern. "But why? Is it just 'cause people don't really believe, that they weren't saved in the first place?" He looked around the room, but no one ventured a guess.

Jerry continued. "I don't think that's it. I look at people like Jimmy Swaggart and Sandi Patty and Michael English, and I see people who had great ministries for Christ. I don't think they were preaching something they didn't believe. I think they got caught in a web of sin."

"But that makes it sound like they didn't have a choice." Brent was frowning. "We have a choice whether or not to do wrong."

"That's right," Jerry said. "We always have free will, and we can walk away from temptation. But sometimes we don't have our guard up, and we get blindsided. Still our fault for not seeing it coming, but it changes the picture a bit, doesn't it?"

Kendra lost her place in her reading and looked up. "What do you mean, blind-sided?"

"I mean the Bible says that the devil plots against us. Think about it. He hates that we love and accept Jesus, and he wants nothing more than to see us fall, to see our witness for Christ ruined. So he plots. He starts with little white lies in your life. They seem harmless enough, right? Then maybe he brings a friend to you. A friend of the opposite sex, and that seems harmless, too. After all, friendship is good, right?

"And then you start talking about things with this friend that he really should be talking about with his wife or that she should be talking about with her husband. But by that point you're friends, and you don't want not to be a friend anymore, so you have the conversations. And pretty soon you find yourself smack in the middle of an affair, looking around, wondering how in the world you got to this big sin when all you did was tell a little white lie about a year ago."

Kendra went cold. Jerry always had a knack for teaching on topics that touched her life. It happened a lot. So she wasn't worried that he or anybody else in this room was accusing her personally. But Kendra couldn't deny the truth of his words. Now that she thought about it, it fit her relationship with Harrison well. Too well. She'd been singing, and there he sat. They'd talked about nothing that first night — the weather, their love of music, harmless things. But within a few weeks they were talking about more intimate topics, topics he should only discuss with his wife.

Even worse, just like Jerry had said, she excused it because Harrison was a friend by that point. She'd dismissed the tiny voice inside that warned her off. She told herself she was being a prude and a bad friend if she didn't help Harrison through this tough time in his marriage. She'd even let herself think that God brought Harrison into her life so that he would have someone to talk to about his bad marriage.

Kendra sat back in her chair, Jerry's voice fading into the background as her mind whirled. If all that was from the devil, not God . . .

Had she been deceived so completely?

The class stood for the closing prayer, and Kendra followed suit, in a daze. After the amen Kendra walked out the door behind Barbara and Stacey. She retraced her earlier steps, ending up in the sanctuary.

"Earth to Kendra." Tandy snapped her fingers and Kendra blinked.

"Sorry." She sat down in their pew.

"You look like somebody just decked you with a two-by-four. What's up?"

Kendra turned to her sister. "Have you ever wondered why Christians still commit the big sins?"

"There are no big sins, Kendra. You know that. All sin is equal."

Kendra shook her head. "That's not what I mean. I'm talking about when Christians in the public eye are caught in an affair or drugs or something. You ever wonder how they got to that point?"

Tandy squinted her eyes. "Can't say as I have. Why? You know of somebody doing something?"

Kendra turned and watched her daddy walk to the pulpit. "No, of course not. Jerry brought it up in Sunday school, and it got me to thinking, is all."

"You were here for Sunday school?"

"Yes, Tandy. I'm not a complete hellion."

"Excuse *me*." Tandy pretended offense.

Kendra relented. "I was up anyway, thought I might as well get a shower and come early."

"You were up?"

"I had dreams all night about Joy wandering around moaning, 'Where's my baby?' I spent half the night trying to help her find her child." Tandy chuckled, and Kendra glared at her. "Hey, don't laugh. She can't get pregnant. That's nothing to laugh about."

Tandy's humor faded. "I'm not laughing about that. Good grief, Kendra, of course I'm not laughing about that. I was just picturing you running all over a hospital, jerking open doors and interrogating people about the whereabouts of a nonexistent child."

Kendra smiled. "I was pretty good, actually."

Tandy pressed her lips together as the organ sounded. "I'm sure you were."

"You're still laughing."

"Only on the inside."

Kendra pulled a hymnal from the rack in front of her and turned to the first song of the worship service. "You are an evil, evil woman."

"Yeah, I should be shot."

The sisters grinned while they sang "When the Roll Is Called Up Yonder," and Daddy looked on, no doubt wondering what shenanigans his girls were up to now.

Kendra elbowed Tandy. "Look at Daddy. We better straighten up, or he's going to separate us."

That sent Tandy into another fit of giggles, which was fortunately covered up by the congregation's enthusiastic singing.

"Hey, where are Meg and Joy?"

"Meg's home with a sick Savannah. I have no idea where Joy and Scott are."

"Savannah's sick? Nothing bad, I hope. Isn't her birthday party next weekend?"

"Yes. Meg said it's just a cold, but she didn't want to give it to the rest of the kids in the nursery, so she kept them all home."

"Mighty nice of her."

"Think about it. If all the kids are sick, they can't come to Savannah's party."

"Ah, light shines in the darkness."

"Just call me incandescent."

They giggled again, and Daddy's look changed from mild disapproval to stern glaring.

"Uh-oh. Better chill." Kendra held her hymnal up high to hide her face from Daddy.

They went through several verses of "I'll Fly Away" and "Sweet, Sweet Spirit" before taking their seats.

Kendra opened her Bible and turned to the Scripture reference printed on her church bulletin. It looked like Daddy had picked loyalty as the preaching topic for this morning. Good. Kendra was loyal to a fault. Shouldn't be any more whammos like Sunday school.

"Have you ever had a friend betray you?" Daddy asked the congregation, leaning over the pulpit and studying the faces of his audience. "Ever been so close to somebody — thought you knew 'em like the back of your hand — and then find out they weren't what you thought?"

Several heads nodded.

"Ever turned to a friend in time of need, so sure he'd help you out, and been told no?"

More heads nodded.

"Ever been the one doing the telling?"

The heads stopped.

"It's easy to remember when we've been slighted or hurt. It's harder to remember and admit when we're the ones doing the slighting. But we've got to admit it, my friends. Got to go to our brothers and sisters who bear battle scars from wounds we inflicted and say we're sorry. We've got to get real with ourselves and admit when we hurt each other."

Should I call Harrison's wife?

The thought slammed into Kendra's brain like a freight train flying off its tracks. Where did that come from?

305

"You know when you're doing something hurtful, don't you?"

Kendra looked to make sure Daddy wasn't asking her directly. No. His eyes were on the Segers in the row behind her.

"You know when you've picked that perfect word to put somebody in their place or you said something about somebody in town, only not to their face. We've all done it, on one level or another. Don't go thinking you're better or worse than any of the rest of us sitting in this room.

"But when we wrong somebody, we have a responsibility as representatives of Christ's love to go and say we're sorry. Not for our own sake, but for the sake of the person you've wronged. You've got to let them know you value them, you were wrong, and you know it. You've got to humble yourself and ask forgiveness."

Kendra pictured going to Harrison's house and knocking on the door. She had no idea what his house or his wife looked like, but she pictured a pseudo-Southern McMansion and a heavy oak door. The woman answering it would be haggard, mousy brown hair hanging in dry clumps, angry eyes staring out from a gaunt face. What would that woman say if Kendra appeared out of nowhere? What would Kendra say?

What *could* she say? It wasn't as if she and Harrison had an affair. They shared one kiss months ago.

But it was more than that.

So much more. Harrison's words of praise rose up in her mind, and her responses, telling him what a good man he was — how smart, how professional, how undeserving of an uninvolved woman. Their relationship had become something it shouldn't, but that was as far as her definition could reach.

So really, what could she say to his wife? *Your husband has been talking to me.* Um, no.

Kendra tuned Daddy out, certain he wasn't preaching about a topic as convoluted as hers.

Eighteen

Kendra spent the week at the Sisters, Ink offices during the day and sharing phone conversations with Darin at night. He was hip-deep in development plans for the Leiper's Fork property and getting miffed that the paperwork wasn't complete on the sale of the land. Kendra listened to his struggles, loving that he shared this side of his life with her. She painted after their conversations.

She was amassing quite a collection of small, happy paintings.

Her lips lifted as she adjusted the green and yellow ribbon on Savannah's birthday present Saturday morning. Spending her nights on the phone with Darin had done wonders for her troubled sleeping habits, and she loved how the whites of her eyes held no more red from lack of sleep.

Darin. A truly great guy. His first wife had to be an idiot for cheating on him. Kendra hoped she never met the woman. Then again, it'd be good to know what that much stupidity looked like when packaged in human form.

The blade of the scissors curled the ribbons. Savannah would have a ball with the ribbon.

Kendra considered inviting Darin to the party, but as close as they'd drawn over the past few weeks, she didn't want to pull him that far into the family just yet. It was nice, having something to herself for a little while, not because it had to be hidden but because she chose not to share it all the way.

She curled the last ribbon and put the scissors back in their drawer. Better get on the road, or she'd be late to the party.

Enormous puffy clouds studded the sky when Kendra drove down the road toward Meg's house. Meg's behavior was very odd lately, Kendra thought as she tooled down Lindell. At times distant, then childlike, it seemed like Meg couldn't quite decide if she wanted to revisit childhood or rush headlong into being an adult.

Kendra shook her head. Achieving full understanding of her sisters would happen about the same time Jesus came stepping down from one of those clouds.

Minutes later she pulled into Meg's driveway, noting the various vans parked along the street and steeling herself for an on-slaught of high-pitched kid laughter and yelling.

Joy, dressed in long white shorts, a cham-bray shirt, and light brown sandals, opened the door before Kendra got there. "You're here!"

"I am. How's the party?"

"Loud. Very, very loud. Are kids always this loud? Savannah and James aren't this loud when they're alone."

Kendra chuckled. "The volume of kids increases in direct proportion to the number of children in the room."

"You're wrong. This isn't a one-to-one ratio."

"No, it's ten to one. For every one kid you add, ratchet up the volume by ten deci-bels."

"Now you might be on to something."

Kendra followed Joy through to the kitchen where Tandy sat at the bar cutting slices from a roll of cookie dough. Bits of dough dotted her sleeveless sweater in haphazard fashion, and a smear of chocolate slashed down the side of her khaki shorts. Meg stood at the sink, her arms covered in bubbles from the elbow down. Dark wet spots dotted the front of her navy sleeveless shirt, and tiny fingerprints marked the edges of its long hemline.

"Can I help?" Kendra set down her present.

"Yes." Meg's frazzled voice sounded exhausted, but happy. Wisps of blonde hair, escaped from the makeshift ponytail at her nape, curled around her face. "Go check the den and make sure nobody's bleeding or dismembered."

"Got it. Be right back."

Kendra turned on her heel and headed for the den. Ten toddlers were lined up on the sofa, enraptured by a green ogre on the television screen. Two others sat on the floor in front of the couch, each with a hand on a giant doll in the shape of said ogre.

Silently, so as not to disrupt their attention on the television, Kendra turned and went back to the kitchen.

"Twelve kiddos, present and whole," she announced. "Next task?"

Meg looked up from the sink, blowing hair out her eyes. "Twelve?"

Kendra nodded. "Ten on the couch, two on the floor."

"There are supposed to be fourteen."

"Uh-oh." At the frantic look on Meg's face, Kendra went on. "Don't panic. Just wash the dishes. I'll go find the others." She

311

hurried back to the den. Ten kids still sat glued to the television. Two others on the floor. Kendra came into the room, and twelve little pairs of eyes turned to her. "Don't mind me. Just on a kid hunt." She walked around the couch and found two tow-headed little boys eating dirt from a potted fern.

"Guys, seriously, that's disgusting." They looked at her and giggled, revealing mud-spotted teeth. "Ugh. Gross." That evoked more giggles. "To the bathroom with both of you before I find my Dirt-Eating Boy Time-Out Chair."

That got them moving.

Five minutes and three dirty towels later, fourteen kids sat watching the movie, and Kendra returned in triumph to the kitchen. "Your fern's going to need a little replacement dirt, but all kids are present and accounted for."

"Thank you," Meg breathed, then collapsed onto a bar stool. "What was I thinking having fourteen three- and four-year-olds at my house at the same time?"

"That you love your daughter and wanted her to have a happy birthday?" Joy guessed.

"Yeah, that's it. Keep reminding me of that." Meg wiped her forehead.

"Where are their parents? Your front lawn

looks like a Dodge Caravan convention."

"They all piled into two vans and went bowling."

"How rude!" Joy's eyebrows formed an angry *V.*

"Not really. I told them to go, enjoy their Saturday kid-free."

Joy's face smoothed. "Oh, then I suppose we can't blame them."

"I suppose not."

Kendra took a second look at Meg, noticing how pale her skin was and the lines of exhaustion around her eyes. "You okay, sis?"

"Fine as frog hair split three ways. Why?"

"You look tired."

"There are fourteen toddlers in my living room. I think you should worry if I *didn't* look tired."

"This is more than tired. You look like a truck hit you. This morning. Twice."

"Wow, don't hold back on my account."

Tandy stood and took the tray of cookies to the oven. "She's right, Meg. You getting enough sleep?"

"Not really," Meg admitted. "But show me a parent of three pre-K children who *is* getting enough sleep, and I'll show you three neglected kids."

"How about I take them off your hands for a day?" Tandy offered.

"Careful what you offer. Trust me, you don't have time to watch three kids while planning a wedding."

"The wedding plans are done. Dresses ordered. Flowers chosen. Music recorded. Decorations on the way. How about I come get them for church in the morning, and you and Jamison take the day for yourselves? I'll bring 'em back Monday morning before I go to the SI office."

"You're serious."

"As a heart attack."

Meg looked at Tandy for a second. "All right, but you bring them home when you realize you've bitten off more than you can chew."

"Oh, we'll be fine."

"Thanks."

"No problem. What are sisters for if not to meddle in each other's lives and offer help when it's needed?"

"Amen to that," Joy said. "Speaking of meddling, Kendra, how are things with you and Darin?"

Kendra smiled. "They're great."

"Look at that smile!" Tandy shaded her eyes. "Looks like more than great to me."

"Okay, it's fabulous. Wonderful. We talk every night, and he tells me all about his day, and I tell him all about mine, and then we talk about things that matter, and he's so intelligent and wise and . . . wonderful."

"I think I'm getting a cavity," Joy complained. "That was too sweet."

"Hey, weren't you the one reminding me of what a great guy Darin is just a few weeks ago?"

"That's when I knew you were seeing someone else behind his back."

Kendra shifted on her stool. "Yeah, well, that's over and done with." *Because no way am I stirring up trouble by telling Harrison's wife or telling Darin that Harrison is married.*

"Good. I like Darin. And I like that smile he puts on your face."

The corners of her mouth lifted, and Kendra gave in. "Me, too."

"Who was the other guy?" Tandy cut more dough and arranged it onto another cookie tray.

"What?"

"You never told us. Was it the guy Joy saw outside the office?"

Kendra cast about. Would it matter if they knew? They'd never run into Harrison anyway. "Yes. He came down to Stars Hill to see me."

"I knew it! I knew it!" Joy said.

"Came 'down' here? Where's he from?" Tandy nudged a cookie to make room for another.

"Nashville." Time to get out of this conversation. "Listen, let's not talk about it. Like I said, it's over and done with. Joy, how's the baby-making coming?"

"Ugh," Joy groaned. "I think I'm even getting sick of the trying now."

Meg turned to her sister. "Joy!"

"Well, it's the truth. I look at Scott, and all I want to do is scream, 'We need to see a doctor!' Not rip my clothes off and try to make a baby."

"Please, I can't see you ripping your clothes off *ever,*" Tandy said, and they burst out laughing.

"Still, it's hard to want to do that when you're constantly considering what day of the month it is, what time of day, whether you're ovulating, whether this is the best position to cause fertilization."

Tandy wrinkled her nose. "Sounds very . . . clinical."

"It is."

"Why won't he see a doctor?" Kendra said.

"I can't figure it out. My best guess is that he's never come against a problem he couldn't reason out, and he's still trying to reason this one."

"But he's not a doctor," Kendra protested.

"That's what I keep saying. But you try telling a man who has always figured out his own problems that he needs to ask for help, and see how far you get."

"Why are relationships so hard?" Kendra asked.

Meg's reply came instantly. "Because they involve people."

"Amen, sister," Joy said.

"And people," Meg stood up and went to the oven, where she pulled out the finished tray of cookies and set it on a hot pad, "are uncontrollable forces that react in ways we can't predict. So we're left reacting all the time and trying to figure each other out."

"Hmm." Kendra leaned her elbows on the counter. "If it's so hard, then why try at all?"

"That's easy." Tandy carried the other tray of dough to the oven and slid it in. "Because you love the person. You don't walk away from what you love. You keep trying until the easy times come again."

Kendra considered that. Already she and Darin had been through a hard time and were back on the easy side of things. They'd weathered a small storm and come out the other side intact. That felt good, knowing they could stick through the tough stuff.

Would he stick, though, if he knew she didn't just date another man but another *married* man?

Good thing he didn't ever have to know.

NINETEEN

A bell rang in Kendra's head, and she ran down the hall to find it. Joy came out of a room, yelling, "Where's my baby?" and Kendra vaguely knew she was stuck in a dream.

She struggled to consciousness.

And heard the phone ring again.

"Hello?"

"Kendra? Did I wake you?" Darin's deep voice brought her fully awake.

"Yeah. What time is it?"

"A little after nine."

Kendra pushed herself into a sitting position, knocking Miss Kitty from her sleeping position. "Seriously?"

"Look at the clock."

"I can't believe I slept this late."

"And here I hoped you'd be up and ready for the day so you could join me on my drive to Leiper's Fork."

"You're going up to Leiper's Fork?"

"Mm-hmm. Lorena has the final paper-work ready, and I'm going up there to sign it. Since you two hit it off so well, I thought you might want to come along."

"I can be ready in twenty minutes."

"See you in nineteen."

She scrambled out of bed. Dashing to the bathroom, she sent a hopeful glance to the mirror. Reality dashed any hope of a quick makeup session. "Ugh. Girl, you've got to get some cover-up on this mug."

Securing her shower cap, she turned the knob to get a warm water spray and stepped into the shower. Thank goodness she'd deep-conditioned her hair last night. Her spirals were under control. All she needed to do was fluff them up a little, dab some concealer under her eyes, and swipe on some mascara.

Shoot, the laundry hadn't been done. Anything decent and clean to wear? She turned off the water and quickly toweled off on the way to the closet.

"Please, please be clean . . ." She searched among the hangers for her long turquoise skirt. Her eye landed on the bright fabric. "Yes!" And she pulled the skirt and a pale yellow top with turquoise beads sewn around the collar from the closet.

"Perfect. Now where are my sandals that

go with this?"

Her eyes scanned the floor as she knocked over piles of dirty clothes and pushed aside books and handbags. *I've got to find time to clean this place up.*

"Aha!" The tip of a pale yellow strap stitched in the same turquoise as her skirt peeked out from beneath her Bible. Yep, she'd worn these shoes to church last Sunday and then dumped them, and her Bible, here afterwards.

Pulling off her shower cap, she hurried back to the bathroom and applied her makeup faster than a Mario Andretti qualifying run.

"There." She took a final appraisal in the mirror. "Good as it's getting for now."

She scurried back to the bedroom, threw on the skirt and shirt, and was buckling the final sandal on when Darin's knock sounded at her door.

"Coming!"

She hopped down the hallway, buckling as she went and thanking heavens that her leg was almost completely healed now.

"Hi!" she said as she pulled open the door.

"Okay, that's impressive." Darin's eye raked her up and down. "You were in bed," he held his watch up, "seventeen minutes ago."

"Call me Wonder Woman."

"You are Wonder Woman. Ready to go?"

"I need to put some food out for Miss Kitty."

Darin followed her into the kitchen and watched as she poured food and water into the cat's dishes. "I don't think I've ever seen you this domestic."

"Enjoy it." Kendra straightened. "This is about as domestic as I get." The bag of organic cat food crinkled as she rolled its top up. "Now I'm ready."

"Let's hit it."

"Bye, Kitty!" Kendra called as they left the apartment.

"How long have you had that cat?"

"Since the summer Momma died. Daddy got her for me so I'd have something to hold onto, something to love."

"Which makes her, what, about ten years old?"

"Almost eleven, yeah."

"How long do cats live?"

"They can stick around for almost twenty years. Why?"

"Just wondering."

They walked out into the morning sunshine, and Kendra caught the sound of birds singing while she walked to the car. A good day lay before her — a long drive with

Darin, catch-up conversation with Lorena, and a long drive back with Darin.

"What are you grinning about?" Darin asked.

"Oh, nothing. Looking forward to the day."

The lines at Darin's eyes deepened as he smiled back. "Me, too."

He started the car and backed out of the driveway. "Let's see, we haven't talked in, what, ten hours? Tell me everything I've missed."

"Well, I went to bed. Had more dreams of Joy searching for a baby, then you woke me up. Your turn."

"Checked e-mail. Went to bed. Woke up. Fixed eggs. Called you. Day got better."

"Gosh, we're boring people."

"Only when you take us in ten-hour chunks. Talk to us every three days, and we have great stories to share."

"I'll bet you have stories from way back that you haven't shared yet. Tell me a story. Tell me how you met Clay."

"It was a dark and stormy night . . ."

Kendra cuffed his arm. "Seriously. How did you two meet? You act like you've known each other forever, but you didn't go to high school with us, so I know that's not it."

"Nope. I met him two years ago when the band was looking for a new lead man. He auditioned, he had the skills, so we voted him in. The rest is history."

"Guys are so bad at sharing."

"Hey, I'm trying here."

"I know, but you left out the details! What did he play? Was there anybody else that you almost took instead? How did he go from bandmate to friend?"

"Oh, you want the Lifetime movie version."

"Yes, please." Kendra crossed her hands in her lap.

Darin shrugged. "Don't really have a whole lot of drama for you. My marriage fell apart a couple of months after Clay started playing with us, and I was working on some songs to get the emotion of the moment onto paper. I needed a bass line, called him up, he came and hung out one night." He shrugged again. "We clicked. He knew what it was like to get rejected, and we wrote some great stuff."

"Who was he rejected by?"

"Uh, your *sister?*"

"You mean right after high school? She didn't reject him. He rejected *her.*"

"Whatever. He saw it different, and it doesn't matter now because they're getting married."

"But —"

"No buts. We are so *not* arguing about who left whom in that relationship."

"Of course not, because we both know he left her."

"Whatever."

"So why haven't I heard this great stuff you two wrote?"

"We haven't ever played it in public."

"Why?"

"Haven't really had the right gig for it. It's some dark stuff, not good material for a community bandstand type thing."

Kendra waited until the silence brought Darin's eyes to hers. "I'd like to hear it sometime."

His reply was swift. "I'll play it for you when we get home."

She loved the sound of that. *When we get home.* Like they belonged in the same place at the end of the day. What would that be like? Going home to Darin after a long day. Talking about life, about what happened while they were apart. Making healthy meals together, her painting after dinner and him working on his music.

She could see it all, laid out there for her, and it looked mighty inviting.

Reaching across the console, she took his

hand. He looked over at her, a question in his eyes.

"What? I have to have a reason to hold my man's hand? We hold hands all the time."

"Yeah, but I've always been the one taking your hand." He raised their joined hands to his lips and planted a soft kiss on hers.

"Really?" She thought about it and realized he was right. Every time they'd held hands, he had been the one to take hers first.

She squeezed his. "Sorry."

"Don't be. I love that you reached for me now."

Settling into her seat, Kendra reflected on her dating history. The sisters had accused her of having a pattern, and while she doubted it was the one they'd accused her of, she had to admit she had a routine down.

Meet guy. Wait for guy to make move. Decide guy isn't right. Act out until guy gets the hint and leaves.

My word. I've been doing that for over a decade. I need a new plan. She shook her head slightly. *No, planning is what Tandy does. I need a new act.*

The vision of her and Darin in his kitchen came to her again. That scene would be easy to play. She'd love every second of it for as long as he'd let her play the role. Because it wouldn't really be a role. That could be her life. Her everyday, go-to-bed-with-it, get-up-with-it-in-the-morning, do-it-all-day life role.

He'd forgiven her for Harrison. He'd been there throughout the accident and her recovery. He listened to her stories, was patient with her tantrums. And he fit in with her family, at least the part of it she'd let him know so far.

Shoot, even Miss Kitty likes him.

It took five months, but for the first time Kendra looked at Darin and saw the complete picture that Joy, Meg, and Tandy saw. No wonder they were all over her to do this right.

Darin Spenser.

Kendra Spenser.

Oh my gosh, I can't believe I just thought that. What am I, sixteen?

No, not a teenager. But definitely in love.

"You got quiet on me." Darin glanced at her. "And when you get quiet, I worry."

"Now why is that?"

"Because you're not a person who thinks things through."

"Ouch."

"I didn't mean it in a bad way. I mean, you're a spontaneous, live-in-the-moment kind of woman. It's one of the things I like about you."

"Really? It doesn't bother you that I'm flighty?"

"You're not flighty. Who said you were flighty?"

"About four dozen people along the way."

"Four dozen people are dummies, then. You're not flighty. You're artistic."

"I'm goofy."

"Quirky."

"Undependable."

"Spur of the moment, and I'm not going to keep feeding your ego. You're a fabulous woman, and you know it."

Kendra grinned and pushed her hair behind her ears. "Yeah, but it's nice to hear every now and then."

"I'll say it every day if you want."

"That works with my schedule."

"You know, some people would think only an insecure woman would need so much reassuring."

"They'd think that?"

"They might."

Kendra took a deep breath. "They might be right."

Darin shook his head. "Kendra, I meant what I said. You're a fabulous woman, and I'm honored that you're spending time with me."

"The feeling's mutual."

"I'm a fabulous woman?" Clay mocked, and she silently thanked him for lightening the moment with humor.

"The best."

"Dang straight." He pulled off the interstate, and Kendra looked out the window as they drove once more past the luscious green countryside. Dilapidated barns stood sentinel behind rambling farmhouses with odd additions on the sides and tops. Families probably did exactly what Momma and Daddy had done — just build onto the house wherever and whenever you can as the family expands.

In no time they pulled into a blacktop parking lot in front of a white-brick building that squatted low to the ground. Its black shutters and shingles gave the impression it wanted to be colonial but couldn't quite shake off function for form.

Deep yellow and orange marigolds dotted the flower beds lining the sidewalk, their round color looking like miniature spots of sunshine. Behind them, mounds of white vinca piled up before giving way to rounded evergreen bushes.

"*This* is Lorena's office?" All that order didn't jive with Lorena's tottering, bumbling personality.

"I know. Weird, isn't it?"

Darin led them to a shiny black door complete with brass knocker and "212" etched on it. Ignoring the knocker, he twisted the knob and went in.

Kendra found herself in a lobby area that was as orderly as the flowers outside. Bold black and gold stripes lined the walls, broken by oil paintings that Kendra recognized as works by Campanile.

"Oh my word, Darin. Those are Campaniles."

Darin spared the paintings a look as he moved down the hallway. "I take it that's a good thing."

"What she dropped on one of those paintings would exceed my car payments and rent. For a year."

Darin stopped and stared at one of the paintings. A bowl of fruit and a piece of cheese, with a small bit missing, were captured in paint. It took him a second, but Kendra caught the moment he saw the mouse standing behind the bowl of fruit. "I can't believe I never noticed that. I like this!"

"For a measly six figures, it can be yours."

He looked at her, at the painting, then resumed the trek down the hallway. "I don't like it that much."

At the end of the corridor, he turned right, and Kendra walked into a miniature of the grand lobby in front. The same bold wallpaper lined these walls, and antique white furniture had been arranged into an intimate seating area. A young guy sat stiffly behind his mahogany desk, pencil in one hand and sudoku book lying in front. At the sight of visitors, he stuffed the sudoku in the top drawer and stood up.

"Hello. You must be Mr. Spenser. Lorena is expecting you. Come on back." He led them down a short hallway and, with a light knock, opened a door.

Lorena stood from behind a larger version of the kid's desk. "Darin, good to see you. And Kendra! I'm so glad you could come."

Kendra crossed pale blue carpet — her feet sank at least two inches into the pile — to meet Lorena at the corner of her desk for a hug. "Hey, girl. How are you?"

"Oh, better than some, worse than others. Have a seat. Do either of you need anything to drink?"

"No, I'm fine." Kendra took one of the two chairs upholstered in stripes of blue and gold. Small throw pillows with horses embroidered in the center and matching blue fringe around the edge sat in each chair as well.

"I'm all right, thanks." Darin sat in the chair beside Kendra, and Lorena resumed her place behind the desk.

"Well, tell me how you two have been. Kendra, it's been too long since we talked. How's your sister?"

"She's good."

"Wedding plans coming along?"

"She tells us it's done, but we'll see how many things she changes between now and the wedding."

"It's coming up soon, isn't it?"

"A little over three weeks, yes."

"How exciting!" Lorena clapped her doughy hands together. "I just love weddings."

"Me, too." *Wait, what?* She saw Darin's look of surprise. "I mean, I love that Tandy's having a wedding. It's great that she's marrying Clay, the man she loves, you know." She stumbled to a halt. *Good grief, get hold of your tongue, Kendra.*

Lorena watched them both for a second, her eyes sparkling. "Yes, I know precisely what you mean. Well, then, I guess we should get to this paperwork so that the two of you can enjoy the rest of the day up here in our beautiful part of the world, hmm?"

She swiveled around and reached for a manila envelope lying on the credenza

332

behind her, and that's when Kendra's world came crashing down on her shoulders.

No, it couldn't be.

Even *her* luck wasn't this bad.

But there, in a bright red frame on the second tier of the shelf behind the credenza, smiling at her like the whole universe kept right on humming, was Harrison Hawkings.

TWENTY

"Kendra, are you all right?" Worry creased Darin's forehead.

"Um, I'm fine," she lied.

"I don't think so. You look like you've seen a ghost." Darin eyes followed her stare to the picture on Lorena's shelf. "What's wrong?"

Lorena looked to the shelf and back to Kendra. "Kendra? What is it?"

She blinked, but the image of Harrison still smiled at her, oblivious. Made sense. Harrison and oblivious went together like winter and ice.

She would make sense of this later. For now she turned to Darin, smiling a false but reassuring smile. "I'm fine, really. Just remembered something I needed to do later."

"Lorena, could you give us a minute?"

"Certainly." Lorena bustled out of the room, shutting the door behind her.

Darin leaned in to Kendra. "Okay, spill it. What's going on?"

Uh-uh. No way in the world would she tell him she'd spent time with a married man. Kissed a married man.

Even Sylvia's daughter shouldn't inflict that much emotional damage in one sitting.

"Kendra." He read her like a book, voice full of empathy. "Whatever it is, you can tell me."

She shook her head. "Not this."

"Yes, this. Anything."

Tears pricked her eyelids. So close. She'd come so close to having her act together. Sisters, Ink was humming along; Tandy's painting stood in near completion in the studio; her leg rarely even twinged these days.

And now, with one picture, she stood to lose the biggest part of what made her happy. What she had just been dreaming about having for the rest of her days.

"Seriously, Darin. Let it go."

"I won't. You're in pain. It's written all over your face. Tell me."

He wouldn't stop. She knew that, sure as she knew he'd walk out of her life the second she told him the breadth of her betrayal.

And he'd be right to leave.

Right — but oh, so wrong.

Her chest hurt, constricted with the reality of her own behavior. Of the consequences she now knew she couldn't escape. How had she rationalized this just a few weeks ago? Sitting with a married man in a dark car, opening her heart and letting him open his. How had that been okay? Acceptable? Desired, even?

"The Bible says that satan plots against us."

Jerry's words echoed through her mind. Plotting. It had started with an innocent performance of a song.

But she'd let herself fall. A little bit more every day. She could see that now. Could see how, step-by-step, her worldview had shifted from a believer appalled at the lack of commitment in American marriages to contributor of a marriage's demise.

What a cruel joke. She balled her fists, felt her fingernails digging into the flesh there. Of all the men in all the world, Harrison Hawkings was Lorena's husband.

Sweet, bumbling, naïve Lorena who went to bed every night wondering if her husband was caught in an affair.

Kendra had the answer.

And she'd never wished more in her life for blissful ignorance.

"Kendra, you've got to tell me. I can help.

Whatever it is, we'll get through it." Darin reached out and touched her knee, and the kindness in that simple gesture crumbled her remaining composure.

Tears poured down her cheeks. She blinked, tried to brush them away, but they came faster than she could brush them off.

"Oh, honey." Darin came out of his chair, knelt before her, took her hands — cold, so cold — and warmed them with his own. "Talk to me."

Her head hung, and she shook it. There would be, could be, no talking of this. Even for her, a child of an immoral woman who had been so desperate for love she'd allowed a parade of men through her own home, her own child's bedroom — even for that child this sank too low. Kendra gasped, sobs wracking her body now as she pictured Daddy's face when he found out.

Because somehow he'd find out. Everybody would. The whole town would talk about it. Daddy, Tandy, Meg, Joy, Jamison, Scott, her nieces and nephews — they'd all be shamed. Not for anything they'd done but solely because of their association with her.

And Darin. Sweet, Darin.

Oh, Darin.

She heard his murmurings now, let the

sound penetrate through the haze of disappointed incredulity that twisted itself around her like coils of barbed wire.

"Jesus, I don't know what's happening, but I know Kendra's hurting."

He was *praying* for her.

Oh, God! Her soul cried out, having no words, no hope other than to cry what it knew. What every soul ever created knew to cry when nothing else could be done.

"Comfort her, God. Sustain her. Let her know Your love."

God's love? That couldn't happen, not for girls like her.

For betrayers.

For liars.

For adulterers. Might as well admit it. Doesn't the Bible say it's as sinful to think it as to commit it? And you thought it. You know you did. So did he. He told you he did. And you did nothing to discourage him. You ate it up. Loved every second of his adoration. Didn't care about his wife sitting at home. Didn't care, really, about him. Because, if you'd cared, you would have sent him home. You would have done what was good for him. Not for you.

Selfishness battled with acceptance. What her mind rejected, her soul embraced.

Being with Harrison — talking, sharing,

338

laughing, caring, investing, being — had always been more about her than him. About feeling smart. Chosen. Enjoyed.

All the things Sylvia never made her feel.

Was she that dumb? To have spent her entire adult life choosing men based on who could give her what Sylvia had not?

"Show her truth, God. Love her." Darin's intercession on her behalf continued.

Oh, Momma. Daddy and Momma, with their unconditional love. They'd tried to fill the hole carved by eight years of loneliness. But human beings can't heal other human beings. They can only introduce each other to the Healer.

Truth lay in that thought. Enough truth to pull her mind from the ghetto of self-hatred.

God. Truth lay there.

True love lay there. Not some hyped-up conversation with pseudo-sharing. But intimacy. Knowing and being known. That truth rang in her soul. To the depth of her marrow, her being recognized the rightness of the thought.

And in that thought lay freedom.

Could it be so simple? Could she know and not try?

"Darin?" Her voice, so small, trembling, stopped his prayers. She met his eyes, looked into their depths, and stepped to the edge of a very high cliff. "I need to tell you something. And I wish," she sniffed, "I didn't. I wish we could walk out of here and pretend we never came in."

He rubbed her hands, face open to whatever message she would share.

"Over there," she tilted her head to the damning picture, "is a picture of Lorena and her husband."

Darin waited, not taking his eyes from hers.

"I know that because I know her husband."

Darin's hands stopped moving.

"His name is Harrison Hawkings."

Darin straightened, his body going rigid. Face hardening into lines that aged him by decades.

But when you step up to a cliff, it's not so you can back down. There's only one reason to hang your toes over the ledge.

"I know this because he's the man I was seeing."

And with that her freefall began.

TWENTY-ONE

Kendra stood in her studio, shorts and T-shirt spattered with paint, getting her breath. The phone rang. Again.

She checked the caller ID. Ignored it.

Again.

As she would keep doing until the little screen reflected back to her the only number she cared to see. Desperately cared to see.

Darin. His eyes, full of a pain she'd inflicted with her actions and admission, were burned into her memory. He hadn't spoken the entire way back to Stars Hill yesterday. No amount of pleading, of explaining, of begging, had broken his silence. He'd offered only two words: "All right."

That's all he'd said in Lorena's office. Oh, he'd made excuses to Lorena about needing to leave, an urgent matter to attend to. And Lorena had let it go, albeit with a dozen quizzical looks cast in Kendra's direction.

But he hadn't spoken to Kendra past those two words. "All right."

The canvas before her vibrated with the intensity of color it held. This safe place for emotions that scared her with their depth served as therapist.

Obviously Darin had told Clay. Who must have told Tandy. Who would have told the sisters. Which explained the relentless ringing of the telephone.

She removed the canvas and picked up another. They were all probably talking about her right now, this very second. Shaking their heads in disappointment, pooling their thoughts to determine a course of action. Taking turns dialing her number.

Pretty soon she fully expected a knock at her door. Which also would go unanswered unless it was the knock of the only person with whom she wanted to speak.

Dipping her paintbrush into a violet circle, she closed her eyes and let the frustration pour out through the art.

Freedom through confession. Was it Tolstoy who lamented his inability to put principles into practice? Right now she could show him the safety of keeping principles ensconced in ink on a page. In practice the principle of confession only wreaked havoc with daily life. And not just hers. She

lay the violet brush down and picked up a
thicker one. Dipped it in crimson.

No doubt the sisters' lives were in turmoil
as well. She'd lied, and now they knew it.
Nothing to do but admit that as well.

Liar.

Adulterer.

The accusations came fast and strong,
tormenting with their accuracy. Yet not finding a home in the depth of her being. Their
vile purpose lay eradicated by the cleansing,
protective shield of forgiveness.

Confession wreaked havoc, yes, but it also
brought a balm of peace and healing. At
least a certain kind of peace. Not one that
would allow her to ignore the agony of
Darin's face or give up the pursuit of his
forgiveness.

She picked up the phone and hit redial.

*"You've reached the voicemail of Darin
Spenser . . ."*

Kendra dabbed color onto the canvas,
running out of steam with each successive
canvas. When Darin's greeting ended, she
said, "Hi, Darin. It's Kendra again. I know
I have no right to . . . well . . . to anything,
but please call me."

She disconnected the call and considered
the painting before her. This wasn't getting
her anywhere. Just another headache.

Calling Darin didn't get her what she wanted either.

Go over there? Did she have the courage for that? What if he slammed the door in her face? He'd be right to, but she couldn't see kind, sweet Darin slamming a door in anybody's face.

Okay, maybe that of his ex-wife.

Whom Kendra no doubt reminded him of right now.

So maybe going over there wasn't the best option.

What, then? What could be done to make this right? To make him look at her with those kind eyes, make him want to pray for her, with her, again. Make him care about her?

She picked up the phone. Enough moping alone. Enough trying to figure it out your-self, Kendra. Haven't you learned anything from this? Letting others know might be a good thing.

Dialing Tandy's number, she waited two rings until Tandy answered.

"I'm calling a scrapping night."

"About time. We're all going nuts. Are you okay? Why won't you talk to any of us? What happened?"

"It's . . . complicated."

"Of course it's complicated, Kendra. It's

life."

Kendra smiled for the first time in two days. "You mean it's *my* life."

"Your life, my life, Joy's life, Meg's life — they're all complicated. If they weren't, we wouldn't be living; we'd be existing. Now tell me what happened."

"You know, I'd rather do this only once. I'll see you tonight. Seven?"

Tandy sighed. "Yeah, seven. I'll call the others."

"Thanks, T."

"Uh-huh. You can thank me by telling me what's going on. Clay's worried sick about Darin."

"Why? Has he talked to Darin?" Her heartbeat kicked up at the possibility of getting news.

"Are you kidding me? He's practically moved in with him. Been over there for two days, hasn't been to the diner, I'm desperately trying to help out and keep things running while Clay sticks by Darin's side, but we're going to need to order food soon, and I have no idea how to do that."

"Has he said anything about how Darin's doing? What he's thinking?"

"These are guys. I'm lucky to hear what they had for dinner."

"Call him. Ask him questions. Find out if

345

Darin . . ." *What, forgives you? Loves you? Wants you back? Don't kid yourself.*

"Find out if he's okay."

"Kendra, his best friend has holed up in his apartment for two days and is showing no signs of leaving anytime soon. I think it's safe to say Darin is *not* okay. What *happened* with you two?"

"Too much to go into now. Call the sisters. I'll see you tonight."

Kendra hung up before Tandy could hear the tears in her voice. At least Darin had a friend to get him through this. He didn't need to be alone. Thank God for Clay.

And for the sisters. They'd help her figure this out. How many times had she listened to their problems over Momma's old scrapping table, offering up solutions and defenses for their crazy choices? They'd know what to do.

Four hours later Kendra bumped down the gravel drive to Daddy and Momma's house. Meg's van, Joy's Lexus, and Tandy's Beamer sat like sentinels to the side of the porch. She parked beside them, took a deep breath, and got out of the RAV4. *Please, God, let them know what to do.* The old porch stairs creaked beneath her weight as she hurried up them. *Please, please.*

She pushed through the heavy front door and went in search of the three women in the world who always had her back no matter what stupidity she exhibited. She found them in the kitchen, huddled over a batch of brownies.

"Hey, y'all. I hope you made at least three hours' worth."

"Momma's recipe was for two hours. I doubled it." Tandy cut her a square and offered it. "Ready to scrap?"

"Is a sheep ready for shearing?"

"Oh, come on. It's not going to be that bad." Meg pulled her along to the stairs. "Besides, everything looks better with chocolate and scrapping."

"Amen to that." Joy brought up the rear, toting the tray of brownies.

They trudged up the stairs to the scrapping studio. Instantly Kendra's heart lifted. No matter how much damage she'd done, this room reminded her that life went on.

"Okay, Ken," Tandy started, "you called the scrap night. Spill it."

And she did. She told them about meeting Harrison at the jazz club in Nashville, how it started off as just fun conversation and progressed to something more. How she excused it because it wasn't physical, then cut off contact when it got physical.

How he came back into her life and they set boundaries. How she hadn't heard from him since the accident. Hadn't even thought of him for a while until she sat down in that chair in Lorena's office.

Meg dropped her brownie. "He's married to *Lorena?*"

Kendra nodded, reliving the misery of that moment.

" 'Of all the gin joints in all the world . . .' " Meg quoted.

"Hey, are you graduating to movie quotes now?" Tandy stuffed a piece of chocolate in her mouth.

"Variety is the spice of life," Meg countered.

"So let me get this straight." Joy's eyes were serious on Kendra. "You befriended a married man, spent time alone with this married man, enjoyed conversations with him that — let's be honest — he should have been having with his wife. And he just dropped off the face of the earth?" She crossed her arms over her chest. "I'm not buying it."

"That's what happened." Kendra chewed brownie, feeling better now that the sisters were on the case.

Joy shook her head. "Fool me once, shame on you. Fool me twice, shame on me."

"What's that supposed to mean?"

"That means you lied to us the first time we asked if you were seeing someone other than Darin. And you're still lying. You expect us to believe Harrison just disappeared from your life?" She snapped her fingers. "*Poof,* like that?"

"I never understood why, either, Joy. But that's the truth."

"Um, I may have a little light to shed here." Tandy raised her hand. "He came to see you in the hospital."

"No, he didn't."

"Yes, he did."

"Tandy, I was out of it a lot in the hospital, but I'd remember if Harrison had come to visit."

"That's just it. You *were* out when he came. I was in the room."

"What?" Kendra threw her brownie back on the plate. "And you didn't tell me? What'd he say?"

"He told me not to tell you."

Kendra planted her hands on her hips. "Why?"

"Does it matter? He was trying to do the stand-up thing and end it."

"But you should have told me."

"What good would it have done? He said his good-byes that day. Your calling him up to prolong the good-bye or say it yourself wouldn't have accomplished anything other than keeping you in touch with him."

"That wasn't your call to make."

"Fine, get mad at me. But I only did what he asked me to do, and it *was* my call not to ignore that."

Kendra picked the brownie back up and chomped on it, fuming. Harrison had been to her hospital room? No wonder he didn't return her calls. He got his closure, his final good-bye. She was left wondering what she'd done to drive him away, whether the idea of her disfigurement rendered her unworthy of him.

And, all the while, it hadn't had anything to do with her.

"Okay," Joy ran a glue runner down a photo, "now we know why it ended. For whatever reason," she shot a look at Kendra, "ending it was good."

Kendra had to agree. If Harrison hadn't ended it that day, who's to say where they might have ended up? How far down that slippery slope they would have slid? Another kiss? Something more?

"Sorry, T."

Tandy walked over to Kendra and slung an arm around her. "No worries."

"I'm confused," Meg said.

"That's news." Kendra grinned.

"Ha ha, very funny. I thought you said you told Darin about Harrison."

"Not quite. I told him I'd been seeing another man and that it had ended. I didn't give him names, and I didn't tell him the man was married."

"Why not?"

"I didn't see a reason for it. Remember, Darin's first wife left him for another man. I thought if I shared that Harrison was married, it would only hurt Darin more."

"And make you run the risk of losing him," Joy said pointedly.

"Yeah, that, too."

"Wow, finding out that way. That must have been tough." Tandy shook her head.

"It was. For both of us." Kendra ached all over again at the memory.

"And he hasn't talked to you since?"

"No. I've called him over and over. Left umpteen messages, but nothing."

"Clay said he's hurting and trying to figure things out."

"You talked to Clay?"

"I called him after you and I hung up. He's a little mad at you right now."

"Darin or Clay?"

"Both."

Kendra slumped on her stool. "What am I

going to do?" She turned plaintive eyes to her sisters.

"Well, you're not going to give up; that's the first thing," Joy said.

"What we need is a plan." Tandy went to Momma's old desk and got a piece of paper and a pen.

For once Kendra thanked God for Tandy's insane commitment to planning. "Okay. Where do we start?"

"First, we figure out why he's mad."

"Duh," Meg said. "She cheated on him with a married man. I'd say he's mad about that."

"Yeah, but why? Because he didn't know and feels duped? Because he feels like he's reliving his past? Because he feels dumb for not suspecting? What exactly does Kendra need to apologize for?"

"I think it's because he feels like I'm his first wife all over again."

"Okay," Tandy scribbled on the page. "So you've got to show him how you're different from her. How this situation is different than his first marriage."

"And how do you propose I do that?"

"You already have, sort of." Meg cropped a picture. "You didn't leave him for the other guy, *and* you're trying to reconcile.

His ex didn't do either of those things, did she?"

"I don't think so."

"Good, then that's a start."

"But I've already done those things, and *he's still not talking to me.*"

"Wait, wait, we're just getting started here." Tandy nibbled her pencil.

Kendra took a deep breath. "Go ahead."

"What else is he mad about?"

"You mean there has to be more?"

"There doesn't have to be, but there probably is," Tandy guessed. "For him to still be talking about it two days later, I'll bet there's more."

"He could be wondering if she's lied about anything else," Meg offered, positioning the picture on her layout.

"Hey! I did *not* lie about anything else."

"I'm not saying you did. I'm saying he might wonder if you did. Shoot, he might even be questioning his ability to know if *anyone* is telling the truth. I know I would be."

"Ouch?"

"Well, goodness, Kendra, think about it. The man's first wife cheats on him, and he doesn't know until she tells him. Then you do close to the same thing, and he doesn't know until you tell him."

"He knew before she told him."

"He did?" Joy looked up from her photos.

"He said he did. He just didn't say anything for a while because he didn't want it to be true."

"You think he knew about you and Harrison before you told him?"

"He said he knew there was someone else. I'm almost certain, though, that he didn't know Harrison was married at that time."

"Okay, so we're back to him feeling duped."

Kendra nodded, and Tandy made a note on the paper.

"What we need here, then, is a plan for reminding him you're (a) not his ex," Tandy ticked off the points on her fingers, "and (b) not deceiving him anymore."

"How do I do that? I mean, both those things are true, but how do I make him see that?"

"Assuming, of course, that he wants to see it." Joy inked up a sponge.

"Again, two days of talking about it makes me think he's still invested in this relationship." Tandy laid her pencil down and picked up a photo.

"Gosh, I hope so." Kendra tilted her head back and stared at the ceiling. Could Darin be done with her? Finished? Sick of the whole situation?

"Kendra, quit worrying." Tandy put photos on top of each other in groupings.

"Get out of my head."

"I would if I could, but you're sitting over there brooding when we should be planning your comeback."

"I'm all ears."

"Okay, first you're going to need to grovel."

"Groveling. Check."

"And then beg."

"Begging I can do."

"And then plead."

"Pleading. Will do."

"Wow, you *are* serious about him." Meg slid a finished layout in a page protector. "The sassy, satisfied Kendra Sinclair is going to grovel, beg, and plead?" She raised her eyebrows. "Wish I could be a fly on the wall for that."

"No, you don't. It's going to get ugly, and the fewer witnesses around, the better." Kendra hopped off her stool to pace around the room. Too much nervous energy. "After I grovel, beg, and plead, what then? What if he looks at me and says, 'Thanks for your pride on a silver platter. You can go now'?"

"He's not going to do that to you." Tandy slid her photo groupings into envelopes.

"Stop being melodramatic."

"He could. It's a possibility we have to consider."

"We considered and discarded it. Moving on." Joy cut a length of ribbon and applied glue dots to either end. "Timing — how long do we give him before she does her I'm-so-sorry thing?"

"Clay will know." Kendra stopped pacing and turned to Tandy. "Ask him. Please? He'll tell you if Darin's ready to hear me out."

"I don't know, Ken. I asked him for details before, and he wouldn't give me anything. He knows I'm going straight to you with whatever he says."

"Then tell him I'm going to make things worse by showing up there before Darin is ready to see me. Tell him he's a bad friend if he *doesn't* tell me when things are right."

Tandy sighed. "I'm happy to try." She took out her cell phone and dialed again. "Sweetie, it's me. You with Darin?"

Kendra stopped by Joy's layout while Tandy talked with Clay. "That looks really good, Joy."

"Thanks. It's not the same as baby pictures, but I'll take what I've been given and be content for now."

"For now?" Kendra pulled herself out of

her own predicament long enough to take stock of the fresh worry lines on Joy's face. "Until when?"

Joy shrugged. "That's my problem. I think yours is a little more pressing tonight."

Kendra looked to Tandy's face, saw the sadness there, and quickly moved her eyes back to Joy's layout. "Only if I've got a shot at fixing things."

"Oh, you do. There's always the chance to say you are sorry. Always."

"Even if he doesn't want to hear it?"

Joy's blue eyes sharpened. "Even then."

The snap of Tandy's phone caused them all to stop what they were doing and focus on her.

"Well? What'd he say?" Kendra's heart felt as if it had paused in midbeat, then jumped into overdrive.

"He said to give it a few days."

"A few days? Is he kidding me? I'm dying here."

"But Darin's dying over there. And right now Clay says if you showed up on his doorstep Darin's likely to say things you'll both regret."

"I don't think those thoughts are going to magically go away in a few days."

"No, but his boil might just cool to a simmer." Tandy pushed her hair back and blew out a breath. "Look, you're the one who asked me to call Clay; and, let me tell you, I don't love being in between my sister and my fiancé. Why don't you just take Clay's advice and wait a few days?"

Because a few days stretched before her as an eternity? Because every part of her being wanted to rush to Darin's side and jump right into the begging and pleading mode? Because the idea of Darin in agony over what she'd done was more than she could bear?

Kendra trudged back to her stool and collapsed onto it. "Oh, all right. I'll give it until Monday. But then all bets are off, and I'm giving that man the best begging and pleading he's ever heard in his life."

"Provided you've talked to Lorena by then." Tandy shot a glance at her, then lowered her eyes to the table.

"Excuse me?"

"That's one of the things Darin's stuck on right now, according to Clay. He keeps wondering how you could befriend a woman whose husband you were dating."

"I didn't *know* he was her husband! I explained that to him."

Tandy nodded. "Yeah, he knows that, too. But I think you need to talk to Lorena before you go to Darin's."

"That makes sense." Meg's head tilted as she thought about it. "It would help you show that you're not like his ex, that you *do* care about the people you hurt, and that you *are* trying to do something about it."

"But wouldn't that just be heaping more hurt on her? I mean, look at what my confession did to Darin! Why would I do that to Lorena, too?"

"Put yourself in her place, Kendra." Joy's quiet voice calmed Kendra by a few degrees. "If you were married to Darin, and he went out and befriended another female, would you not want that woman to tell you the truth?"

"Well, yeah, but I'd prefer my husband tell me."

"Lorena's husband isn't talking." Meg held up her hand to stop Kendra's protest. "So far as we know, her husband hasn't told her anything about you. You have to assume he hasn't or that she's the world's best actress."

Kendra thought back to Lorena's bumbling sincerity, her open naiveté. "Definitely not that good an actress."

"There you go then. You have to tell her."

"I don't know, girls. It feels like I'm unloading my guilt onto her."

"It's not about you, Kendra. It's about

her. About admitting to her that you've wronged her."

Kendra sighed. Such a mess. A complete and utter mess. How had she gotten to this point?

An inch at a time, that's how.

"I'll think about it."

"But —"

And Kendra held up her hand this time. "That's as much as I can do right now. I'll think about it, do the right thing, and then go see Darin after the weekend."

If he opened the door.

Twenty-Two

The weekend dragged by with all the speed of honey from the comb. Kendra looked at the clock thirty times in an hour, sometimes more. It seemed Monday would never arrive, and she couldn't decide if that was a good thing or bad.

Sunday afternoon fell hot and humid on Stars Hill and the parishioners of Grace Church. Kendra walked out into the sunshine, her skin immediately damp with perspiration the second the light hit it.

Ugh. One last gasp of summer before the welcome cool of fall, according to the weatherman. Suffer through it today, and all would be better tomorrow with the coming of a cold front.

Kendra looked around for the sisters and saw them huddled beneath the shade of a giant elm. She sauntered over, determined to appear at ease though her heart was bound up in knots.

"Hey, Ken." Tandy waved. "Made any decisions about Lorena?"

"Shh." Kendra looked around but saw no churchgoers in hearing range. "Keep your voice down. Do you want the whole town talking about my business over Sunday lunch?"

"Sorry, sorry." Tandy ducked her head. "Wasn't thinking."

"Have you, though?" Meg's willowy beauty stood out among them. Even in all this heat and humidity, she looked dry and tired. "Decided what you're going to do?"

Kendra sighed. "I don't know, y'all. I just don't know."

"Ask Daddy."

"Are you kidding me? The less Daddy knows about this, the better."

"Oh, please." Tandy tucked a curl behind her ear. "He knows something's up, and he's going to corner you about it the first chance he gets anyway. Besides, he'd know more than any of us if you're supposed to let the spouse know."

"Fine then. But only because I'm desperate for somebody to tell me what to do here."

"Whatever gets you to talking is fine with us." Meg's chin came up, and she waved over Kendra's head.

Kendra turned to see Jamison and the kids coming down the church steps.

"Gotta run, y'all. Got a roast in the oven that's probably dry as the Sahara right now. Ken, when you talk to Daddy, tell him no more long sermons, you hear?"

"Yeah, I'll be sure to critique his sermon style right after I tell him what a conniving daughter he has."

Meg, by now halfway to the church, turned and began walking backward. "He already knew that." She twirled back around before Kendra could shoot her a death stare, and Kendra watched as she swung Savannah up in her arms.

Hmm, maybe not as tired as she looked, after all.

"Want me to stay for your talk with Daddy?"

"No." A slight breeze rustled the leaves in the old elm. "But thanks."

"Whatever you need."

"Even if it puts you between your fiancé and me?"

That crack had hurt more than Kendra liked to admit. Pretty soon, Tandy would *have* to put Clay first.

"Even if." Tandy hugged her, then headed for the parking lot.

Kendra stayed beneath the elm, watching

Daddy shake hands and nod as people told him stories about their week.

Such a good Daddy. Darin was like Daddy in some ways. Dependable, trustworthy, caring. What would he say when she told him about Harrison?

She almost ran for the RAV4 but stopped. No escaping this. Time to face the consequences of her own actions, the demons she allowed to drive her to this point.

She turned her feet toward Daddy and began walking. The crowd had cleared out now, people escaping into the air-conditioned comfort of their cars. On their way to lazy Sunday lunches under circling ceiling fans.

Daddy saw her coming and met her halfway down the steps. "I thought you'd run off with your sisters."

"Not today. You have plans this afternoon?"

"Not a thing." Daddy cocked his head to the side and looked at her. "Something on your mind?"

She nodded, not trusting herself to speak lest it all come tumbling out right here on the church steps.

"All right then, I'll meet you back at the house. Go on and see if you can't scare us up some lunch, hmm?"

"Thanks, Daddy."

Kendra went for the RAV4, no idea what would be coming out of her mouth in just a few minutes, but certain it was something Momma and Daddy never dreamed would cross their kitchen table.

Fifteen minutes later Kendra sat down and accepted Daddy's proffered hand. Bowing her head, she listened to him ask grace on the meal. The act comforted her, eased the tension in her shoulders slightly. No matter what, Daddy would always be here, saying grace over his meals.

"So you want to pretend we don't have things to talk about and do the small-talk thing for a while?"

Kendra choked on her sandwich, the only thing she'd been able to scrounge up in a hurry from the kitchen. "Guess not." She coughed and set her sandwich down. "It's like this . . ."

And she told him the whole story. Everything she'd told the sisters and even some stuff she may have left out. Daddy didn't take his eyes off her the whole time; and, though she was ready for it, even had her guard up to shield it, she never saw judgment enter his stare.

With every word another part of her let it

go. Released any part of attraction she still felt toward Harrison, surprising her even as it did so that the attraction was still there. But it was overshadowed by the enormity of the betrayal they'd perpetrated. Not just on Lorena, but on her family as well. And on each other.

"Well," Daddy said when she'd finished and filled her mouth with cold sweet tea, "you always did do things big."

"What?"

"Your mother and I never worried you'd do something we wouldn't know about and have to reap the consequences alone. We knew whatever you did would be on such a large scale that the whole town would know it by daybreak."

"Is the town talking?"

"Surprisingly enough, no. At least not to me. It doesn't matter anyway. What matters is that you've recognized the fault in what you've done and received forgiveness for it."

"I got forgiveness from God, yes. But I haven't talked to Darin yet."

"Why not?"

"The sisters think I should talk to Lorena first."

"Harrison's wife?"

Kendra nodded and hoped he'd tell her

what a ludicrous suggestion that was. Instead Daddy sat in silence while Kendra chewed her sandwich. He took a bite of his own, looking no longer at her but at some distant point on the white wall. His jaw worked the sandwich, and he washed it down with a long swig of tea.

"Hmm. I think they have a point there."

"You mean I *should* tell her? But isn't that heaping hurt on her to get rid of my own guilt?"

"That depends on your motivation for telling her. Would you be saying it to make yourself feel better?"

"No." Kendra thought about it for a second. "No. If I told her, it'd be because I think she needs to know. I think, in her position, I would want to know. I think she already knows; she just needs to be confirmed in it."

"Then tell her. The worst she can do is throw you out on your ear and yell at you."

"Blame me for breaking up her marriage."

"No, she may say that, but we both know that isn't true. All responsibility for this doesn't rest on your shoulders, daughter."

Kendra popped the last bit of turkey into her mouth. "You're sure I should tell her?"

"I'm sure at the end of the day it isn't my call."

"But you're advising me to tell her?"

Daddy rubbed his chin and thought for a minute. "I am."

Kendra pushed back from the table. "I need to go then. I've got a call to make." Completely forgetting her dirty dish, Kendra wandered out of the house and to her RAV4. She made it home on autopilot, only fully realizing she was home when she held the phone in her hand.

What's his home number? Mistresses and special friends only have cell phone numbers.

I'm such an idiot. She put the phone back in the cradle and went to her computer. Anywho.com called up the number in two seconds. Harrison and Lorena Hawkings. Franklin, Tennessee.

She scribbled down the number and returned to the living room.

Miss Kitty, sensing her mistress's unsettled state, hopped up onto the sofa and padded over to her lap. Purring, she bumped up against Kendra while Kendra dialed with a shaking finger.

"Hawkings Residence."

Her body froze at the sound of Harrison's deep voice.

Shoot, what now? "Hi, can I talk to your wife?" and pray he doesn't know it's me?

She slammed the phone down, staring as if it were a snake.

What now? Call back?

No, he'd just answer again.

Write a letter?

He could open the mail.

Go to her office tomorrow?

No, this definitely didn't qualify for workplace chatter.

Kendra sat down on the couch in a huff. *And I thought deciding to tell her was the hard part.*

She considered the situation from all angles, then gave a sad laugh. "How ironic is this, Miss Kitty? I'm trying to avoid the man and get around him to the very woman I helped him betray."

Miss Kitty meowed and Kendra rubbed her ears.

"There's a way to do this," Kendra reasoned aloud. "Should I be giving Harrison the chance to tell her before I do?"

Miss Kitty closed her eyes and purred as Kendra's nails dug into her fur.

"Hmm. That'd mean calling up Harrison on purpose. And given the way Darin's hurting right now, I don't think he'd cotton to me calling Harrison — no matter what reason I had."

Kendra looked over at the phone, then

snatched it up. She dialed Tandy's cell number and waited.

"Tandy Sinclair."

"Hey, it's me. I need a favor."

"Am I going to end up in jail?"

"No, but you may end up on the wrong side of Clay for a while."

"Kendra," Tandy's voice held a note of warning. "I told you I really don't like this position."

"Yeah, but you also said you'd help me make this right."

"That I did. Okay, what are we doing?"

"I talked to Daddy, and he says I should go ahead and tell Lorena."

"Good. So call her. You don't need me."

"I tried to call her. Harrison answered."

"Oh."

"Yeah, 'oh.' Now I've got to figure out a way to get to her without his knowing. Or I've got to call him and tell him I'm about to tell his wife."

"I feel like I'm in a Jerry Springer episode."

"Welcome to my world."

"We could drive up there. Then we might get the throwing chairs and screaming just like Jerry."

"I was thinking more along the lines of you calling and getting Lorena on the phone. He won't recognize your voice."

"Or, like you said, you could give him the chance to tell her. Might be better that way."

"Better for who? Do you see me telling Darin I talked to Harrison again?"

"Ooh, good point."

"Thanks. I'm trying not to do more damage than I already have."

"Wow, this is a mess."

Kendra slapped her hands on her thighs, startling Miss Kitty. "Well, yeah! That's what happens when you start having relationships with men sporting wedding bands."

"You should write a book about this."

"Tandy, focus."

"What? I am focused. There are probably lots of women out there who have had relationships with married men, didn't sleep with them, and excused it all away just because there was no sex. You should tell them about the kind of mess that happens."

"How about we just get me through this and talk about book deals later?"

Tandy sighed. "Yeah, you're right. Okay, so you want me to call and get her on the phone? Tell her to call you?"

"No, I want you to come over here, call her, get her on the phone, and hand the phone to me. Or I can come there. Which-ever."

"Why not just have her call you?"

"Because she might mention it to her husband on the way to the phone." Kendra tried not to sound as exasperated as she felt. Getting herself out of these murky waters was a whole lot harder than diving into them had been. Explaining every reason behind her actions to a litigator sister bent on having explanation for everything didn't help.

"Ooh, you're good at this."

"Tandy!"

"Sorry, sorry. You're right. I'll be over in a second."

"Thank you." Kendra set the phone down and laid back into the plump cushions. In a few minutes this part would be all over, and she could focus on begging her way back into Darin's life. Because, after all this, she had no idea what she'd do if he didn't let her back in.

Not that he had any reason at all to do so. Unless he was as lonely without her as she felt without him. Unless his world didn't spin as fast or as fun without her to tilt it for him. Unless he was happier with the silence her absence created.

Kendra absently gazed around the room,

then stopped on a picture of her and Darin in a red frame.

Starting again on the right side, she allowed her eyes to pan the room. Slowly.

How had she not noticed this?

She, a lover of color, lived in an environment decorated in shades of white. Her carpet served as a white cloud for her feet. Her walls reflected back Arctic white. Even her pillows were variations on white, accented with dove gray and pale gold. The entire room looked like an iceberg.

One big, frigid iceberg.

Except a slash of red encircling her smiling face beside Darin's.

Her conscious mind now embraced what her subconscious always knew: Darin Spenser represented the color in her life. His color was safe enough for her life even though she couldn't control it. Before, she could only pour color onto a canvas, either on an easel or on the canvas of her body in clothes and jewelry. Color she controlled.

But she couldn't control Darin.

Kendra shook her head, blinked, and looked around again. Yep, the whole thing lacked even a hint of color except that photograph and frame. She pushed off the couch and walked across the room, coming to a halt before the red frame.

Her own face, almost golden in the sun, laughed back at her. Darin's head tilted into hers, his eyes sparkling in the sunshine. His face crinkled into a grin. She gently lifted the frame and carried it back to the couch.

She was still holding it ten minutes later when a knock sounded on the door. Kendra kept her grip on the picture as she went to answer it. Tandy stood on the other side, and her eyes went to the frame in Kendra's hand.

"Okay, let's get this show on the road. What is that?"

Kendra held it up. "It's a picture of me and Darin." Her voice still held the awe of her discovery.

Tandy wrinkled her nose. "Oookay, and you've got a death grip on it. Why?"

"Come here." Kendra led Tandy into the living room and pulled her into its center. "Look around."

Tandy turned in a circle, then looked at Kendra. "It's a living room."

"No, dummy." She spun Tandy in a slow circle. "Look again."

Tandy did as instructed. She gave Kendra a worried look. "It's still a living room."

"Yeah, but what color do you see?"

"Oh, that's easy. You love —"

Tandy stopped and checked out the room.

"Wait, why isn't there any color in here?"

"Exactly."

"No, not exactly. I'm serious. You're a painter, for goodness' sakes. You love color. Why have I never noticed this?" Tandy kept looking around the room, trying to find a spot of color anywhere.

"I just saw it myself. When this was on the table over there." Kendra held up the picture.

Tandy took it from her, peering at the photo. "Oh."

"Yeah, oh."

"I can't believe I didn't notice this before. You've never had color in here?"

Kendra shook her head. "Nope. It's been this way since I first moved in."

Tandy's face softened. "Oh, Kendra."

"I know. I know. I finally allow a little color into my personal life, and look what I do — stomp all over it and leave it bleeding on the other side of town."

Tandy put her arm around her sister and pulled her to the sterile-looking couch. "Okay, we're going to fix this, though. Starting right now." She reached across Kendra and picked up the phone. "What's Lorena's number?"

Kendra told her, and Tandy dialed. Kendra picked up Kitty and petted her, keeping an eye on Tandy.

"Hello, is Lorena home, please?" Tandy shot Kendra a thumbs-up. "Thanks."

She handed the phone to Kendra. "He's going to get her."

Kendra swallowed, unable now to think of what she could say. What were the appropriate words for confessing to a wife that you've been with her husband? Emily Post didn't cover this.

"Lorena? Hi, it's Kendra."

"Oh, hi, Kendra. How are things in lovely Stars Hill? Are you feeling better?"

Kendra raised her eyes to Tandy, who nodded her encouragement. "They're okay. Listen, I need to tell you something. And I wish I didn't have to tell you this, but I do. It's about why I lost it in your office."

"Oh. Okay. Are you all right?"

Kendra grimaced. Here she was about to obliterate the woman's marriage, and Lorena asked if *she* was all right.

"I'm going to be, Lorena. The thing is, remember how you told me you thought your husband was cheating?"

"Oh, yes. I must have been wrong, though. Everything's been fine for the past couple of months." Lorena's voice was too bright. Fake.

"He isn't having sex with another

woman."

"That's what I said. I just thought something was happening that wasn't. My mistake. I'm so glad I didn't take your advice and accuse him, though."

"Well, wait. I don't *know* that he's not having sex." *Gosh, could you be any worse at this?* "The thing is, I didn't know Harrison Hawkings was your husband until I saw his picture in your office."

At Lorena's gasp, Kendra looked to Tandy. Tandy grabbed her hand and squeezed it in support.

"I see." Lorena's voice had become deathly still. "Are you having an affair with my husband, Kendra?"

"Not like you're probably thinking, and I haven't seen him in two months." Kendra rushed to set the record straight. "I spent a lot of time with him, though. I first met him this spring. At a jazz club when I was singing. I didn't know immediately he had a wife, but I didn't stop talking to him even after he told me. He kissed me. We kissed. Once. The rest of it was just conversation."

"I don't understand. You had conversations with my husband, and you're calling me for what reason?"

"Because they were conversations I shouldn't be having with a married man."

"So you're dumping your guilt onto my lap. Is that it?"

"No! No. That's not it at all." Kendra took a breath, and Tandy squeezed her hand harder. "Listen, I know this sounds weird; and, trust me, I thought long and hard about calling you. But at the end of the day, what I shared with your husband amounts to an emotional affair. And if I were in your shoes, I'd want to know. I especially thought you'd want to know that you weren't wrong in your suspicions."

Silence hummed over the phone line, and Kendra pressed her lips shut, willing herself to give Lorena the time to respond.

"I'm not sure what you want me to say." Lorena's clipped words sounded like shards of glass hitting stones. "I assume you've broken the news to Darin?"

"Yes. I told him that day in your office." Kendra wondered how Lorena could care about a client right now. Maybe she wanted to focus on something besides her own life. "We haven't spoken since, though not because I haven't tried. I'm still trying, actually."

"Darin is a good man. An honest man. I can't see him with a cheater."

Kendra closed her eyes against the pain. *Cheater. Just like Sylvia.*

Except Sylvia wouldn't be making this call. Sylvia would be running as fast as she could in the other direction right now. "You're right. He's having a hard time, and I can only pray that God will heal him."

"Oh, you're going to *pray*, are you?" Lorena's voice turned snide. "Mighty convenient. Break up someone's marriage and get forgiveness just like that."

"It's not like that, but I can see how you'd feel that way."

"Can you? Let me tell you what you can see, Kendra Sinclair. You can see your way out of my life *and* my husband's life. Don't you ever call here again, and if I find out you've been in touch with my husband, I'll make sure your little boyfriend never does business in this town again."

Kendra heard the click and jerked the phone away from her ear.

Tandy eased up on her grip. "What'd she say?"

"She threatened to kill Darin's ability to get real estate up there."

"Oh, please. She doesn't control the whole town."

Kendra set the phone down. "You'd be surprised. They're a pretty tight-knit community up there."

"But why would she punish Darin? He

didn't do anything here."

"I don't think she's rational right now. She's just trying to save her marriage. I'd be doing the same thing." Kendra leaned into the cushions. "Gosh, I'm exhausted. I feel like I've just painted a thousand canvases."

Tandy patted her hand, then got up and headed for the kitchen. "You need tea. With lots and lots of sugar."

"Tea? I've just confessed to Harrison's wife, and you're bringing me tea?"

"And chocolate."

"Well, now you're talking."

Later that night, after assuring Tandy for the one hundred and forty-second time that she was fine already, "just go see Clay before he calls here again looking for you," Kendra walked into her studio.

Despite Lorena's response, she knew that calling had been the right move. The dark cloud, hanging over her head for months, finally dissipated; and Kendra wanted to dance for joy at the cleanness inside.

I am not Sylvia. I do not have to be Sylvia. And I proved that today.

A grin spread across her face. No more worrying about repeating the mistakes of her birth mother. Kendra opened her mind to the idea of being, of becoming, the woman Momma and Daddy told her she could be in God's eyes.

The clean woman.

The free woman.

The purposeful woman.

She could be that now. No more Harrisons. No more anything that resembled the life she'd known her first eight years.

She could walk with her head high now — not because she had to take on the world and fight it every second but because she could relax in being herself. In the knowledge of her worth as a daughter of the King.

And her first step would be painting something colorful to hang in the living room.

Not in red. Not yet.

Maybe light blue — the color of fresh, clean skies.

Her footsteps were light as she crossed the studio and arranged an empty canvas onto the easel. She touched the button to activate the stereo and put in a CD of piano jazz. The happy notes lifted her spirits, and her hands began to move over the brushes and paints.

This painting, she had a feeling, would be different from anything else she had done. Because, right now, she could paint wonderful forgiveness.

She squeezed electric blues and shining yellows onto the color wheel, then chose a brush. Fixing her gaze on the canvas before her, she said, "Honesty," and began to paint.

Her fingers made small strokes at first, dabbing the color to block in her thoughts. With each new spot, each change of color from aquamarine waters to azulene skies, the image rose in increments before her. Celeste, azure, and cerulean alternated to give her vast sky its depth. Puffs of argent-colored clouds danced across the sky. Hyacinth undulated in the waves, with dots of crystal blue hanging in the air from children at play in the water.

Kendra laughed aloud as her hands danced above the canvas, dabbing titian and thistle together for sand, emerald and cobalt for tiny bathing suits, heather and indigo for blankets on the sand.

When she finished with a final flourish and smile, she stepped back and gazed upon a work she knew she hadn't been alone in creating.

Toddlers frolicked along the shoreline, tossing water into the air, their heads tossed back in laughter. Waves moved along the surface, creating smiles of water. Half-built sand castles stood precariously while their makers ran for more sand. In all their faces, in every single movement, lay honesty. Openness. Commitment to the moment at hand. No worries for the next. No plans for tomorrow. No excuses to make. No stories to create. Just the thought of enjoying the sun, the sand, and the sea.

She laid her paintbrush down and turned to look in the mirrors lining one wall. Shades of blue dotted her face where she'd swiped at her hair. They blended beautifully into the caramel of her skin and highlighted the new light in her eyes.

She tilted toward the mirror and saw, yep, the cerulean was in her hair as well. "That'll take forever to get out." But she didn't care. Not about paint in her hair. Not about anything. Nothing could take this lightness of being from her.

Leaving the room, she padded down her white-carpeted hallway and entered her white-walled bedroom. She crossed to her white-tiled bathroom and stepped into the shower, making sure a white terry towel hung at the ready.

All this whiteness could be fixed, she thought as she picked up her white bar of soap and sudsed up. She just needed more pictures of her and Darin in frames of red and blue and purple and yellow all over the house.

Which she would have as soon as she went over there and begged forgiveness.

The thought stopped her happy movements. What if he wouldn't talk to her? What if he said, "Thanks for the apology, but I'm moving on now"? What if he took all his color and never came back to her home? What then? Because, as wonderful as painting "Honesty" had been, she didn't want her home full of color from her own hand. No, this home's canvas needed painting by somebody else.

And that somebody was Darin Spenser.

Whether he knew it yet or not.

Twenty-Three

By Thursday Kendra decided waiting was designed by small-minded idiots bent on torturing the people who actually wanted to accomplish something.

She sloshed another bowl into the sink and scrubbed it with the dishrag. "Kitty, what are we waiting on? A sign in the clouds? A holy Post-It note floating down from God? Permission?"

Every day since the disastrous yet freeing phone call on Sunday afternoon, she'd asked Tandy if today was the day.

And every day Clay came back with the same answer.

Wait.

Kendra wondered if Clay would still be saying the same thing ten years from now.

"When I've died from loneliness in my little white apartment." The hot water felt good on her hands as she rinsed off the bowl. "You know what I think? I think it's time we went over there and started the healing process. What do you think, Kitty? You ready for your momma to go do some serious groveling?"

Kitty twined around her ankles, purring.

"Yeah, that's what I think." Kendra pulled her hands from the dishwater and dried them on a towel. Enough with the waiting. Clay meant well, but there would never be a perfect time for this.

Today, right now, was as good a time as any.

She marched through the apartment and snatched the keys off the table by the door. Pounding down the stairs, Kendra gave a fleeting thought to the possibility of failure, then tossed it off like yesterday's garbage.

The outcome didn't lie in her hands. Only her actions did.

She revved up the RAV4 and reversed down the driveway, mentally rehearsing her lines. *I'm sorry. I was dumb. I should have told you. I have no excuse. I'll do anything.*

I love you.

She swallowed hard. Maybe save that one for after he forgave her. Might not be good to drop that kind of bombshell in his lap.

The historic-reproduction streetlights on Lindell were just coming on as she drove down the street. Dusk, the magical time when the world looked foggy enough to be a dream, descended on Stars Hill. Kendra turned onto University and followed it to the highway. She took the next off-ramp and turned right toward Darin's.

Please, God, let him be at the apartment. Let him be ready to hear me.

Before her heart was ready, but after her mind had convinced her to ignore her heart, Kendra pulled into the parking lot of Darin's apartment complex. Rows of town-houses stood silent, observers of the falling night.

Kendra parked, stepped out of the car, and shivered despite the heat radiating from the black pavement. She stepped forward, faltered, and stepped forward again.

Now or never.

Crossing the distance to Darin's door was harder than running five miles in wet sand. She slogged through the wall of indecision, though, and arrived on his doorstep. Her finger pushed the doorbell, and she wondered how she'd made it the whole way from the car.

The door opened and there stood Darin.

"Hi," she offered.

He looked awful. A wrinkled Van Halen T-shirt and ratty blue jeans hung on his body like forgotten laundry. His jawline sported a stubble she guessed at being at least a week old. Behind him, she could see fast-food bags and wrappers all over the coffee table. No sign of the fastidious Darin Spenser she knew existed in the immediate vicinity.

"What do you want?"

She recoiled from the harsh tone. "I–I just wanted to talk to you. For a second."

"So talk."

Oh, God. Her soul cried its best refrain. "Can I come in?"

"I don't think you'll be here long enough for it."

She stared at him, trying to find the warm, humorous man she'd dated the past six months. The guy whose fingers raised goosebumps along her arm and whose kiss made color explode in her world. The warm, tender man who helped her after her accident, who listened to her stories and laughed in the right places.

He was there, she knew. Somewhere beneath this layer of protective anger.

"All right." She gulped. "I wanted to tell you I'm sorry."

Darin took his eyes off her and focused instead to a spot just above her head. She went on, needing him to hear her words.

"I'm sorry for not telling you about Harrison. For seeing him while we were to-gether." She rushed on, words tumbling faster than she could think them through. "For seeing him at all after I knew he was married. For not being the woman you deserve me to be. For doing anything to remind you of the hell your ex-wife brought you. For hurting you like this. For every-thing. I'm so sorry, Darin. For everything."

His jaw worked, and his fingers were white from his grip on the door frame. "That all?"

She shook her head. "No, it's not. I've got lots more. I can beg. I'd love the chance to beg, really. I need you to know how sorry I am and that I'm not your ex."

"Funny, you sure sound like her."

His words hit so hard she actually touched her face to see if he'd slapped her. "Darin, please. I can't undo it, but you have to know I would if I could. And I'll never do anything like this again. I've talked to his wife."

"You what?" Darin's eyes came to her. "What did you say?"

Could it be . . . ? Was this her saving grace? "I talked to Lorena. I told her."

"Why would you do that? What, there's not enough hurt going around, you thought you needed to spread some more?"

"No, of course not. She already suspected. You heard her that night at Joe's. I just told her what she already knew. I let her know she wasn't paranoid but that her husband wasn't sleeping with somebody else, only talking."

"Only talking." He nodded. "Yeah, that makes it okay."

"It doesn't make it okay. That's not what I'm saying." She stumbled to a halt and regrouped. "Darin, I'm sorry. For all of it. I'm sorry, and I'm asking you to forgive me."

He looked at her for a long moment. She held his eyes, hoping he'd see in hers how changed she had been these last few days. Trying to say with her gaze what her mouth had done so poorly.

"I forgive you, Kendra."

Hope blossomed in her heart, and she started to smile.

"But that doesn't mean I want you back."

He shut the door in her face and she blinked. *What just happened? He forgives me? Then why am I on this side of the door? He forgives me?*

She shook her head to clear it. Now what? Getting Darin's forgiveness but not his return to her life didn't seem possible. But that's exactly what he offered. It's the *only* thing he'd offered.

She looked at the door. Considered knocking. What could she say, though, that she hadn't already?

Maybe Clay knew Darin better than she did. Maybe she needed to wait.

Kendra turned and plodded back down the steps, trying to figure out her next move. He forgave her. Well, at least that was a step in the right direction. All she had to do now was remind him why they were good together. Why he couldn't live without her. Why his life would be wrong without her in it.

Kendra glanced back at Darin's windows, but the blinds were closed. Fine. If he wanted to stay closed off for a while longer, she'd let him. But sooner or later he'd have to come back out in the world. And when he did, she fully intended to be there.

She drove to the Sisters, Ink offices, not quite ready to return to her colorless apartment. Two buildings down the lights from Clay's spilled out into the street. Kendra turned her steps in their direction and walked.

Relief washed over her when she saw Daddy and Zelda sitting at a table by one of the windows. She hurried across College Street and into the diner.

Daddy looked up and waved a greeting. She waved back, weaving through the tables until she got to their booth.

Daddy stood and hugged her. "Hey, Ken. Tandy told me the call didn't go too well."

Kendra looked at Zelda. "*Daddy.* Perhaps we shouldn't blab my business to everybody within hearing distance?"

Zelda smiled and pursed her lips. "Your secret is more than safe with me, dear."

Kendra considered getting angry, but enough problems already existed in her life for her to borrow this one as well.

"Had dinner yet?" Daddy gestured to the booth. "We haven't ordered yet. You're welcome to join us."

"You sure?" The prospect of eating with Daddy, even if she had to talk to Zelda during the meal, sounded so much better than dinner alone.

"Sure he's sure." Zelda scooted to the far side of her seat. "Have a seat and tell us the latest."

Kendra gave in and plopped down beside the redhead. "Thanks. Not much to tell. Tandy told you Lorena balked. Darin just shut his door in my face. All around, I'd say things are going downhill and setting land-speed records in the process."

"Oh, honey. Darin won't forgive you?"

"No, he forgave me. He just doesn't want me."

"What kind of man doesn't want my daughter?" Daddy sat up straight. "I think I need to have me a talk with this boy."

"Now, Jack, don't go meddling in their business," Zelda said, and Kendra gratefully shut her mouth. "Kendra and Darin will figure this out on their own."

"Doesn't seem to me like they're doing too good a job of it so far, if he's shutting his door in her face."

"Jack, the man is hurting. There's no accounting for his actions right now, and you know that. Stop thinking with your daddy heart and go get us some Cokes." She shooed him out of the booth. "Go on now."

To Kendra's surprise, Daddy obediently left the booth and headed to the counter. "Wow, I'm impressed."

"With that?" Zelda waved her turquoise-ringed fingers in the air. "That's nothing. Wait until I'm ready to order." She grinned at Kendra, who reassessed the woman's hold on her daddy. "Don't go looking at me like that, now. I'm not the enemy. Your daddy needs a woman to help him out every now and then. He's been a bit lost since your momma went home to the Lord, and he likes me pretending to boss him here and there. But make no mistake, he does what he wants, when he wants, same as I suspect he always has."

"Man, you've really got his number." Kendra looked at her with approval. "Just how much time have you two been spending together?"

Zelda smiled and tilted toward her. "Enough for me to know your daddy is a fine man with a heart of gold."

"Well, shoot, you knew that in the first two minutes."

Zelda leaned back and laughed. "That I did, Kendra. That I did."

Daddy came back with their drinks, and Kendra took a long swig of her Diet Dr. Pepper.

"So if I'm not calling the boy and talking some sense into his head, tell me your grand plan for fixing this, Zel."

"I don't have one yet." Zelda cocked one eyebrow at Kendra. "But give me a few minutes."

"Take your time," Kendra returned. "I've got all night."

Friday morning's overcast sky was perfect for her mood, Kendra decided. Though a nice, loud thunderstorm would be even better.

She parked the RAV4 behind the Sisters, Ink offices and went inside. Her lime green watch showed eight, which gave her a whole two hours to work on membership issues until going over to Sarah's for her final fitting.

She booted up her computer and waited while e-mails poured in. "Shoot, I've got to start coming in here more often," she mumbled, watching the e-mail count hit triple digits. As Sisters, Ink grew, so did the demand on her to keep up. The Darin Debacle, as she'd taken to calling it in her mind, was not good for her work focus.

The counter finally crawled to a stop, and she moved the mouse to the top line. E-mail by e-mail, she kept up a steady rhythm. Input a new member. Send a welcome e-mail. Read a member's suggestion. E-mail Tandy with the idea. Read a member request. Decide if it merited discussion. Send to Tandy, Joy, and Meg for further review. Check the forums and discussion board stats for traffic. Approve pictures for the gallery.

By the time she looked at the clock, almost two hours had passed, and if she didn't leave right now, she'd be late for the fitting. She closed her in-box and dashed for the front door.

The sky outside hung heavy with pent-up rain, and she kept an eye on the incoming clouds while she stepped next door to the shop.

"Hi, Sarah. Tandy here?"

Sarah looked up from the register. "She's in the back with your sisters."

"I'm the last one?" Kendra picked up her pace. "Fabulous."

Sarah smiled her understanding and went back to a stack of receipts.

Kendra entered the dressing room to find Joy and Meg standing before the mirror in their pale gold dresses and Tandy sitting in the corner. "Hey, y'all. Sorry I'm late."

Meg looked even more like a goddess now, no puckers or folds of fabric anywhere. The hemline of her dress just brushed the floor as she turned. "You're not late. We're early. I couldn't wait to wear this dress again."

"Then I'm glad we found them," Tandy said.

"I think that's the first endorsement of a bridesmaid dress I've ever heard." Joy smoothed the front of her dress, though it already lay perfectly across her flat abdomen. "Though I'll agree, these dresses are beautiful."

"Are you kidding? This is the first time I've felt like a female since I had James."

"But that was six years ago!" Kendra's eyes widened. "Seriously?"

"Yep." Meg pivoted and preened in front of the mirror. "When you have kids, everything goes south, and that body you thought looked hideous in high school suddenly seems like perfection when compared to the stretch marks and sagging skin."

"You make pregnancy sound so awful," Joy said.

"No, it's not awful. What it does to your body, though," Meg patted her stomach, "is pretty awful."

"Meg, stop scaring the rest of us off parenthood." Tandy crossed her legs. "You just don't like that pretty soon you're going to have some grandkid competition. Admit it."

"Grandkid competition?" Kendra looked at Joy. "Are you . . . ?"

"No." Joy hung her head and smoothed her abdomen again. "Not yet. Still trying."

"You dope, I'm talking about me and Clay," Tandy said, and Kendra turned to her.

"You're planning on having kids that fast?"

Tandy shrugged. "I don't know. Maybe not right away, but in a year or so, yeah. I think Meg here would prefer we wait until her kids are married, though."

Meg shook her head. "Please. I think it's great you and Joy are going to have kids soon. I'm just saying, think long and hard before you go praying for stretch marks, heartburn, and labor pains."

Kendra went to her fitting room and put on her gold dress, leaving her sisters to bicker about parenthood. At the rate she was going, she'd be fifty before she walked down the aisle, much less considered pregnancy.

She donned the gold gown and went out to join Meg and Tandy. "Here we are, your chosen three. Still love this dress?"

Meg put her hands together over her heart. "Oh, please, Tandy. Say you love this dress."

Tandy grinned. "Of course I do. You all look gorgeous in them."

Kendra turned back to the mirror and raised her eyebrows. "You're sure? There's not a whole lot of color here."

Tandy stared at her knowingly. "Which would be a problem if this was your wedding, but I'm pretty happy with gold, thanks."

"Huh. The way my life is going, I can forget any plans for a wedding anytime in the foreseeable future."

"I'm sure Darin will take you back as soon as you talk to him." Joy stepped down off the dais.

"Are you now? Because it sure didn't feel like he was taking me back yesterday when he slammed his door in my face."

"What?"

She filled the sisters in on yesterday's dismal conversation at Darin's.

"Why did you go over there? Clay said Darin wasn't ready."

Kendra shrugged. "I couldn't sit around waiting anymore, Tandy. I had to *do* something."

"And your something involved ignoring the wisdom of Darin's best friend?"

"Look, I know now it was a bad idea, but I had to go find out for myself. I had to do what I could to let him know how sorry I am."

Meg jumped in, cutting off Tandy's retort. "What's your plan now?"

"I don't know. Wait, I guess. It's all I can do. He forgave me. He's just got to get to the point where we can start again."

"You don't have a plan?" Tandy came up out of her seat. "You went over there, knowing Clay said not to, hurt Darin a little more — and you don't have a plan?"

"Whoa, Tandy. Look, I told you. I had to make sure he knew I'm not his ex-wife. I'm not running away like she did. I'm not leaving him for someone else like she did. I should have called you first. I'm sorry. But I knew you'd try to talk me out of it, and I knew just as much that I had to go over there."

Tandy put her fists on her hips and stared Kendra down. "Did you stop to think how your actions might affect me? Or Clay? Or Clay's relationship to Darin?"

"I did. And I decided that the faster we can get past this, the easier it's going to be for all of us."

That stopped Tandy. She dropped her fists. "Oh."

Kendra came down from the dais and stood in front of Tandy. "I'm really grateful for you talking to Clay for me. I wasn't trying to go behind your back. Okay?"

"Yeah, okay. I just hate being in this position."

"And I hate that I've put you in this position. But eventually, Darin and I will figure things out."

"You sound pretty sure of that," Meg said.

"We have to," Kendra replied. "We just have to."

"Well, you're not going to move forward if you don't see him. How about coming to Heartland with Clay and me tonight?"

"I don't think Darin's going to be at Heartland, Tandy. He looked wrecked when

I saw him. A country dance hall is the last place he'd want to be."

Tandy whipped out her cell phone and punched buttons while grinning at Kendra. "Clay? I think we should bring Darin to Heartland tonight." She waited a beat. "I know, I know. But he can't stay holed up in his apartment forever. Tell him it's for his own good." She paused. "Good idea. I'll see you tonight, sweetie. Love you." She flipped the phone shut. "Darin will be at Heartland tonight. You coming?"

"You are the best sister in the world."

"Hey! Watch it there, sister." Meg protested.

"Okay, one of the *three* best sisters in the world."

That night Kendra looked at herself in her full-length mirror. Her spirals were conditioned to perfection, and her red and yellow skirt hid most of the scarring on her leg. The gloss she'd found in Sarah's shop earlier made her lips look plump, and her skin, for once, gleamed.

"Watch out, Darin Spenser." She sashayed over to the closet and pulled out her brown dancing boots.

She pranced out of the apartment and out to the RAV4, ready to do battle for Darin's heart. He'd loved her once. She saw it in his eyes, even if it didn't cross his lips. Tonight he'd hear it cross hers.

The lights of Heartland beamed their welcome to the world, and her tires crunched on the gravel of the parking lot. The moonlight bounced off the black paint of Darin's Barracuda, and her heart began thudding in her chest.

"Steady, girl," she whispered as she swung the car into a parking space. "You can do this."

On legs wobbly with nerves, she exited the RAV4 and walked to Heartland's door. Reaching for the knob, she noticed her hand was shaking and took a deep breath. "He's just a man." But the man she wanted for the rest of her life. The man whose love she'd killed with her actions. The man who fit so beautifully, so seamlessly into her life. He was *her* man.

She opened the door and stepped inside.

Boots pounded a steady rhythm on the hardwood. Skirts swirled and cowboy hats twirled as the dancers spun in time to the music. Kendra breathed a little easier, letting the comfort of the surroundings minister to her. Daddy and Zelda were at their customary table in the far corner, their heads bent low in conversation.

Kendra walked further in, looking around to find Darin. Or, for that matter, Tandy.

She squinted into the shadows where lightbulbs had burned out. Was that him? She couldn't tell since the Darin she knew would never slump like that. Darin always stood tall, easy in his own skin.

But as she stepped forward and he shifted, she could see that it was, indeed, Darin. Quickening her steps, ready to start this thing up again, she hurried across the room.

She was three tables away when a redhead walked up to his side, handed him a cup, and leaned into him.

Kendra stumbled, grabbing at the table beside her.

What was this? Her heart lurched while her mind scrambled to make sense of the scene. Darin with another woman?

The redhead flirted up at him, her body language clearly telegraphing the words Kendra couldn't hear pouring from her mouth. And Darin smiled back. Touched her shoulder. Drank from the cup she'd brought him.

They were here *together*.

How had this happened? *When* had this happened?

Not since yesterday. That couldn't be possible. The man Kendra talked to yesterday was about as far from being with a woman as she was from marital bliss. Who was that girl? She didn't look like anybody from Stars Hill, with her Six jeans and fake boots.

Kendra stood frozen to the spot, frantic to leave before he could see her but powerless to turn away.

When, finally, her feet began to obey her order to escape, she glanced back for a last look and caught Darin's eyes. They widened, then narrowed, and she felt a lead-like weight lodge in her heart. His arm came around the redhead and bent down to her level.

Kendra tore her gaze away, knowing if she saw Darin kiss that woman, she'd lose it right here in the middle of Heartland. She pushed through the crowded tables and fell through the door into the parking lot.

"Kendra?" Tandy's voice made her look up. "What's wrong? What's happened?"

Hot, jagged tears poured down her face, and Kendra sobbed. "Darin's here."

Tandy caught her arms and held her up. "I know. Clay talked him into coming. What's wrong?"

"He's here," she gasped, her heart breaking on the words, "with someone else."

"What?" Tandy looked over her shoulder at Clay. "Who is he with, Clay? You didn't

tell me anything about him bringing someone."

"And you didn't tell me Kendra would be
here."

"Clay Kelner! You *knew* about this?"
Outrage flooded Tandy's voice.

Kendra swiped at her nose, sniffing and
trying to make sense of things.

"Yeah, I knew. I told him it'd be a good
idea."

Kendra rounded on Clay. "You *what?*
What is *wrong* with you?"

"What's wrong with *me?* What's wrong
with *you?* Cheating on my best friend with
a married man?"

Kendra advanced on him and, before she
could stop herself, slapped him across the
face.

"Kendra!" Tandy rushed to Clay's side.

"What? You're going to tell me you're on
his side in this? Darin's in there with *another
woman* right now." She shook her head.
"Because your *idiot fiancé* doesn't *approve*
of me."

"Kendra, that's not what —"

"And why would I approve of you?" Clay
butted in. "You cheated on him with a married man!"

Kendra goaded him. "But that's not all, is
it? Go ahead, admit the rest. You don't think

I'm good enough for him."

Clay's angry look turned to one of confusion. "What?"

Kendra ignored him. "You think he can do better than a girl who grew up with men coming into her room every night, right? You want him with a good girl. One with no past and no regrets and no ability to hurt him, right?"

Clay had lost all anger now and was looking to Tandy for help. "No, I don't think that. What are you talking about?"

But Kendra was on a roll. "You hope that redhead is a perfect little virgin raised by the perfect little parents in the perfect white house with the perfect white fence. You want him with *her*." Kendra's voice broke on the word, and she moaned, a terrible, animal sound that scared her into silence.

She turned and stumbled toward her car, desperate to get out of there as fast as she could. Back to her clean apartment that reminded her how she'd escaped all that. How she didn't have to be that now.

She fumbled with her seat belt, missing the hole the first two times and biting back a swear. *Don't resort to Sylvia's language. You are not Sylvia. You are Kendra Sinclair, and you've been cleaned and redeemed.*

The passenger door opened, and Tandy

hopped into the passenger seat.

"Don't you need to go be with your *sweetie?*"

"I'll deal with him later. Right now, I'm with you." Tandy buckled her seat belt in one smooth action. "Drive or hand me the keys."

Kendra blinked, then rammed her own buckle home. "Fine."

She revved the engine, then spun gravel out of the parking lot.

TWENTY-FOUR

"Look, I know you're mad, but would you please find somewhere and park? I'd rather not end up dead on the side of a dark country road."

Kendra swerved the RAV4 into a small ditch, throwing herself and Tandy against their seat belts, and killed the motor. "Better?"

Tandy unbuckled herself and turned in her seat. "Much. Now tell me what that was back there?"

"That was your fiancé being a complete moron."

"Yeah, yeah, skip to the part where you think you're not good enough for Darin."

"*I* don't think that. Clay does." Kendra hit the steering wheel. "The moron."

"No, he doesn't." Tandy held up her hand. "No, he *doesn't*. He's mad that you hurt his best friend, and he's not ready to let you off the hook yet. But he does *not* hold your childhood against you."

"Why does he get a say in when I get off the hook? Who is he? Master of the universe?"

"No, he's Darin's best friend, and you'd do the same for me, so quit dodging the question."

Kendra rested her head on the steering wheel, the fight draining out of her as fast as it had come. "I don't think that. I used to think it, but I know it's dumb and not true. But knowing that and feeling like somebody else is thinking it are two different things."

"Why are you so mad at Clay?"

"Tandy," Kendra twisted her head to look at her sister, "he told Darin to date other women. You think I'm going to *thank* him for that?"

"Okay, you're right. That was stupid on his part, and don't think he's going to escape my wrath over it."

"Good. Nice to know you've still got my back."

"I do in this instance. But, Ken, it's going to get hard from here on in when you two disagree. When I'm his wife, I'm going to have to go home with him even when he does dumb things that hurt you."

"Sounds messed up to me."

"I didn't say I'd go home and be all sunshine and roses about it." Tandy grinned, and Kendra sat back in her seat. "It's just . . . hard. You and I, we've always had each other's backs, no matter who it was. Daddy, Meg, Joy, anybody. And I'm scared about how that's going to change once I'm Clay's wife."

"Tandy, I don't care if you're married with a dozen kids. I will always be your sister."

"And I'll always be yours, but when you and Clay go at it like this, I don't want you to hate me when I go home with him."

Kendra sighed and stared out the windshield at the dark sky. Stars scattered across it, tiny pinpricks of light. "This adult stuff stinks sometimes."

"Yeah, it does." Tandy leaned toward Kendra, resting her elbows on the console. "But being in love beats jump rope and curfews any day."

Kendra laughed. "I guess you're right about that."

"So we're okay?"

"Yeah, we're okay."

"Good, now let's figure this Darin thing out."

The laughter died in Kendra's throat. "I don't think there's anything left to figure out, Tandy. He's with somebody else. Let it go."

"Let it go? Are you kidding me? Not on your life. He's with that woman because my dumb fiancé told him it was a good idea. That's easily fixed."

"I don't think so. I can't imagine even looking at any man other than Darin. If he can go so far as to take another woman out . . ." Kendra hung her head. "I can't take it. I can't fight that."

"Kendra Sinclair! What's wrong with you? I've never known you to back down from a fight."

"I don't when the hill is worth dying on, Tandy."

"And Darin's not worth it? I thought you loved him. I thought you wanted to spend the rest of your life with him."

Kendra gazed back out at the stars. "When I was seeing Harrison, I knew Darin wouldn't like it if he found out. But I also knew we hadn't explicitly said we weren't seeing other people. I know that's a technicality, and I shouldn't have been with Harrison anyway because he was married, but still. Me seeing Harrison is a completely different thing from me throwing a man in Darin's face just to prove I could."

"And you think that's what he was doing

411

tonight?"

"You told Clay I was going to Heartland?"

"No, I just assumed he knew."

"He knew." Kendra nodded, eyes still on the sky. "He knew, and even if he didn't, Darin did. We've gone to Heartland every Friday night for, what, nearly six months? He knew I'd be there, and he wanted me to see him with her. That's cruel, Tandy." She turned and met Tandy's eyes. "It's purposefully mean. He brought that woman into my hometown and tossed her in my face like a shot glass of cheap whiskey. That's not a man I'm going to spend my life with. I can't." Kendra gripped the steering wheel.

"Kendra, don't give it all up because of one stupid thing he did."

"That wasn't just stupid, though, T. That was cruel."

"You're right." They sat in silence, listening to the cricket song outside.

Kendra sniffed and cranked the engine. "Guess I better get you back to your fiancé."

"I'm sure he's fine. You need some company tonight?"

Kendra thought about going home to her white walls and white couch. Right now it seemed like the perfect amount of quiet. "No, I'll be okay."

Tandy gazed at her a moment longer, and

412

Kendra let her expression confirm her words. The peace of a stark room without color or complication beckoned her.

"All right." Tandy sighed and gazed up at the stars. "But promise me if you need to talk, you'll call."

"I always do, sis."

The next week flew by in a flurry of wedding plans, and Kendra threw herself into her role as maid of honor. Never had she talked with so many cake decorators, florists, and musicians in her life. But talking with people prevented her from thinking about whom she *wouldn't* talk to anymore, so that was all right.

She scanned the wedding checklist and marked off "Confirm floral arrangements." Only a few more boxes to check, and this wedding would be planned, confirmed, and reconfirmed.

Looking out the window over the breakfast table, she saw Corinne Stewart out for her morning stroll and waved at the sweet lady. Corinne's hair nearly glowed in the early sunshine, her pink track suit looking like cotton candy.

Kendra sighed, turning away from the happy image of Corinne. Her own walk/jog that morning was riddled with indecision

413

about Darin. She pushed up from the chair and hit Play on the answering machine like she'd done fifty times last night.

"Kendra, hi, it's Darin." The message hummed along as she sat there. "I need to talk to you about, um, everything. Call me back, please."

The machine clicked and shut off.

"Everything? Including that redheaded vixen you were conniving with at Heartland?" She whirled away from the answering machine and went back to the breakfast table. "I don't think so, mister."

Her apartment had a little color in it now, at least. Two paintings from what she now called her "Dark Period" hung in the hallway, their pulsing reds reminding her of the night she'd painted them after dancing with Darin at Joe's.

Joe's. That's what she needed! Joe would let her come sing. Kendra hurried back to the phone and snatched it up, then headed for her computer. Anywho.com gave her the number and she dialed, hoping someone would pick up the phone this early at the jazz club.

"Joe's Jazz."

"Hi, Cassandra. It's Kendra Sinclair."

"Oh, hey, Kendra! How are you?"

"I'm good. Listen, I was wondering if you

414

might be in need of a singer tonight."

"As a matter of fact, we are. That's why I'm in here working the phones this early. We got a cancellation last night, and I'm trying to fill it. Why? Are you offering?"

"I am."

"Then I'm going to buy a lottery ticket because this is definitely my lucky day."

Kendra smiled. "Do you need a song list from me beforehand?"

"Oh, just bring one with you and be here about an hour before opening. I'll make sure Joe's down here to run through some stuff with you. You're cool with off-the-cuff?"

"I'm best at off-the-cuff."

"Great. Then we'll see you tonight at five."

"Thanks, Cassandra."

"No, thank *you.*"

Kendra hung up. Scrapbooking with the sisters hadn't helped; and when she'd tried to pour this onto a canvas, her brush had stayed frustratingly still. Maybe three hours at a microphone in a moody jazz club could help her let go of the sadness.

What had she been thinking?

Singing in Nashville to a roomful of strangers was one thing. But Joe's? Where she knew everybody? Where they knew her?

415

As Darin's girl? What *had* she been thinking?

She squared her shoulders before the mirror. "You were thinking that you're going to go insane if you don't work through this. You were thinking that it's time to let it go and get out of this rut. You were thinking," she turned and checked out her dress from the back, "that this dress doesn't belong in the back of your closet."

The purple dress from Sarah's clung to her frame in all the right places. It hugged her hips, a bit less now since she hadn't had an appetite the past couple of weeks, and draped gently over her legs. The surplice top did its job of pulling the eye past her waistline and up to her face.

Best of all, she felt like a pretty woman in this dress. And that had made the price tag easier to swallow.

She slid her feet into sling-backs and walked out the door to Joe's, determined to rid herself of this emotion in the next five hours in the only way she knew possible — slow jazz.

The sun beat down on her as she left the RAV4 and walked to the door of Joe's. Thank goodness it'd be down in an hour or so. Hard to feel bluesy with trickles of sweat snaking their way down your neck.

She opened the door and escaped into the air-conditioned ambience. Cassandra came from behind her maitre d' stand.

"Kendra." She held out her hands, and Kendra took them. "Thanks again for doing this. You've saved the evening."

"Oh, I don't know about that. You might want to wait until the end of the night to make that kind of judgment call."

"Nonsense." Cassandra walked with her through the lobby and to the piano on the club stage. "You're always wonderful."

"Thanks."

"Did you bring your song sheet?"

Kendra handed it over, and Cassandra gestured to the microphone. "All right. I'll get Joe."

Kendra couldn't help but remember the last time she'd been here. With Darin.

And Lorena.

She pushed the thought from her mind, then reconsidered and welcomed the rush of emotion into her being. She'd need that kind of melancholy for tonight. It's what she'd come to exorcise anyway.

"Hi, doll," Joe said, and Kendra startled at Harrison's pet name for her. "You ready to knock 'em dead tonight?"

"I'll do my best," she returned and went to stand behind the microphone.

Joe played the opening notes of "Lovin' Arms," and Kendra took a breath.

"If you could see me now, the one who said that she'd rather roam."

Kendra closed her eyes and let herself feel the words while she sang them from her soul.

"Just for a while, turn back the hands of time."

Darin's face, haggard and lost as he stood by his door, filled her mind.

"Looking back and longin' for the freedom of my chains."

Kendra poured herself into the song, knowing the desperation of the woman behind it. Hating the hurt even while she embraced it. Despising the pain between her and Darin. Abhorring her part in causing it.

She let the final *"I can almost feel your loving arms again"* fade into the silence and opened her eyes.

"Problems with Darin?"

Joe's knowing look rested on her, and she didn't try to deny it.

"Yeah."

Joe nodded and hit the opener to Kendra's next song.

Kendra closed her eyes again and gave into it, desperate to feel this fully so she could let it go.

Song after song, Joe played on and Kendra sang. She went through "Fool That I Am" and "All I Could Do Was Cry." She sampled some Patsy Cline, wondering aloud how she could have been so "Crazy" and not caring who heard her. Oblivious, really, to the people who filled the room. Hour after hour, the tears coated her throat with an emotion only fit for the blues and slow jazz.

She swayed to the soft music, holding the microphone, letting it anchor her to the here and now while her mind traveled back over the past six months with Darin. She remembered that first night on a blind date with Tandy and Clay when they had come to Joe's.

Her voice broke on *"Stormy weather, since my man and I ain't together."*

And still she sang on.

She felt his lips during that first kiss. Heard him whisper her name while they stood at her door.

And still she sang.

Watched him again while he supported Clay the day Tandy left for Orlando. Saw him laugh. Followed the line of his arm to his hand carelessly thrown over the steering wheel.

And still she sang.

Recalled the way his colorful shirts stretched cross his broad chest and the line of his neck when he bent to hear her.

How he held her hand when they prayed.

How his fingers moved on his guitar.

And still she sang.

The way he helped her after the accident, patiently by her side, up and down her steps.

The slump of his shoulders against the wall at Heartland.

Joe changed songs, and Kendra breathed into the microphone, *"I've got your picture that you gave to me."* She sang about a man who left her with letters and pictures but belonged to another woman, and it was all she could do to finish the song. To acknowledge aloud Darin's other woman.

She turned to Joe when the notes had died away, her throat raw, her eyes burning from unshed tears, and nodded for him to start the last song.

She didn't look at the crowd. Neither needed nor wanted to know who was there. These songs were her life. They were her. They were what she was left with after the wreckage of Darin.

And this one, well, it would always be with her.

"Sitting home alone, thinkin' about my past.

Wonderin' how I made it, and how long it's gonna last."

She let herself hope with the old lyrics for a man who would care for her. Not because she needed a keeper or a parent, but because she chose to be cared for. Because she needed someone she could care for and who would care for her.

"Some folks think you're happy when you wear your smile. What about your tribulations and all of your trials?"

She opened her eyes and looked out at the crowd. They watched her, the women's faces naked with like emotion. The men's hungry to hear her. She met their gazes, letting them see this need that burned in her.

"How I wish, oh, how I wish someone would care."

And then her eyes traveled to the corner of the room — and stopped cold.

Darin stood there, and unless this light played tricks on her, those were tears snaking down his cheeks.

She finished the song, then walked the three steps over to Joe and whispered in his ear. Joe nodded and put his hands back on the keyboard as Kendra stepped back to the mike.

"I want to thank y'all for listening to me tonight. You might have guessed that I've

421

lived a lot of these songs." The crowd murmured their appreciation, and she tilted her head. "I've just got one more, and then I'll let you all enjoy the sounds of Joe Frazier on the piano for a while."

She inclined her head to Joe, and he played.

There's somebody I'm longing to see.
I hope that he turns out to be
Someone to watch over me.

She didn't close her eyes this time but stared at Darin. He needed to see this. Needed to know what he had thrown away. What he had lashed out at. What he had tossed aside so he could get even. What he wouldn't listen to her say that day when she stood on his doorstep and begged.

She smiled.

Although he may not be the man
Some girls think of
As handsome . . .

Darin chuckled in the back, and she let herself enjoy that while she sang on about this man who carried the key to her heart. When she sang her desire for him to put on some speed, Darin began walking to the front of the room, and she struggled to breathe deeply enough to finish the song.

He took his time, weaving through a crowd that had completely stopped dancing to listen to this final song. By the time he reached the middle of the room, people began to notice this man making a beeline for the singer. They made room for him, watching the two of them as he shortened the distance between them.

Kendra didn't hide a thing. She let it all out, put everything on the line, and prayed it would be enough. While Joe played the last few notes, Darin took three easy strides and gathered her in his arms.

His eyes bore into hers, and his arms felt warm and safe around her. "I love you, Kendra Sinclair."

"Oh, Darin." The tears she'd held at bay through three hours of soulful blues spilled over. "I love you, too."

EPILOGUE

One week later

Kendra stood in the bride's chamber of Grace Church, one hand on her pale-gold-draped hip and the other firmly grasping a bouquet of gardenias and purple hyacinth.

"Tandy Sinclair, you're going to be late to your own wedding. Come on, quit fussing with that veil, and let's get this show on the road."

Tandy grinned at her and stood up from the dressing table. Her strapless white wedding gown encased her body like a glove as she walked over to Kendra. "You're just in a hurry to see your man."

Kendra rolled her eyes and wiggled her toes in her shoes. "I'm in a hurry to get these shoes off and have some fun."

"She's got a point there, T," Meg piped up. "These dresses are great, but the shoes are murder."

"Suck it up, sisters." Tandy tilted her chin

in the air and strode to the door. "Today's my wedding day."

"How that equates to poor shoe choice is anyone's guess," Joy muttered, falling into line behind them.

Kendra gathered Tandy's train in her hands. "Okay, sis, let's rock and roll."

Tandy opened the doors and walked through the foyer to the closed sanctuary entrance. Daddy came over to greet her, and Kendra saw him whisk a tear off his cheek.

"You look lovely, Tandy."

"Thanks, Daddy. I wish Momma could be here for this."

Daddy offered her his arm. "Me, too, darling."

Kendra heard the opener for "At Last" and stepped around Tandy. "Excuse me. That's my cue." She glanced back and winked at her sister. "I love you, T."

"Back at ya, sis." Tandy winked back, and Kendra stepped through the doors of Grace Church's sanctuary. It looked like every resident of Stars Hill packed the pews of the little country church.

Kendra let her gaze roam over them, then looked to the altar and saw Darin's eyes on her.

From the look on his face, he appreciated

Tandy's choice of dress. He beamed at her, and she grinned back. Who knew? Maybe the next time she walked this aisle, it would be to meet him at the end.

She slid her eyes a few feet over to Clay, who looked as nervous as a long-tailed cat in a roomful of rockers. Without a guitar in his hand, Clay didn't love being in front of a crowd. This must be really hard for him. Kendra gave him a sympathetic glance and, reaching the end of the aisle, turned left and took her place on the stage.

Meg was a few feet behind her, pale shoulders gleaming in the morning light that lit up the stained-glass windows. Joy followed along, her black hair shining in the sunshine as well.

When Joy had finished her last two steps, the music changed to a playful rendition of Vivaldi's "Spring," and in came James and Savannah. James walked like a little soldier, his tiny shoulders stiff, back ramrod straight, and eyes intent on the ring pillow in his chubby hands. Kendra stifled a giggle and watched as Savannah threw rose petals *at* people instead of onto the floor. By the time she'd reached the end of the aisle, the place was full of good-natured titters.

Then the time-honored notes of "The Wedding March" sounded, and the people rose as one, turning to behold the bride's entrance.

Kendra held her breath as the doors opened and Daddy and Tandy stepped through. Tandy radiated joy, her face glowing with happiness. Kendra risked a quick look to Darin and caught him watching her. He tilted his head toward Tandy and raised an eyebrow.

What does that mean?

Kendra trained her eyes back on her sister. Time enough later to find out.

She listened as Tandy pledged to love, honor, and cherish Clay for the rest of her life. She teared up when Clay pledged the same to her sister. Harrison and Lorena had done this once . . .

She shook her head. Her past mistakes would not mar the perfection of this day.

Reaching up to wipe away a tear, she again caught Darin looking at her. He smiled, and she knew he knew what she was thinking. She smiled back, then watched Tandy and Clay bow their heads while Daddy prayed over them.

"We ask Your blessings, Father, on this union of two of Your children. Let their days be long together and full of joy in You. Give them patience and peace, understanding and grace, as they reflect to the world a love

You created. In Your son's precious name, amen."

Daddy raised his head and addressed the congregation. "It is my pleasure to present to you, for the first time, Mr. and Mrs. Clay Kelner."

A cheer went up from the crowd as Clay kissed his new bride. Kendra laughed with joy, so very grateful that her sister had found this love.

Thirty minutes later, with shoes kicked into a corner and toes wiggling free, Kendra took a sip of fruity punch and tapped her knife to her glass.

The crowd hushed and Kendra stood, ready to make her maid-of-honor speech.

"Six months ago I welcomed my sister home and thanked God for her visit. A week after that, I prayed she'd be gone before she could fall back in love with this scoundrel."

She waited while the crowd laughed.

"But seeing them today, I'm amazed at the love two people can share." She looked at her sister. "You are a fabulous woman and an awesome sister to me, Tandy. We've seen each other through a whole lot of years and yearnings and fights and laughs. I don't know what kind of woman I would be if I didn't have you in my life the past two decades, but I do know this: I would have been a lesser person for it. Your love is a balm to my soul and a strength to my days."

She looked at Clay. "And I'm trusting you to take care of this lady I love. Watching you today, seeing that love in your eyes for her," she took a breath, "I'm grateful my sister is loved so much."

Clay nodded, then stood and hugged Kendra while the crowd clapped their approval. She sat back down and took a calming drink, battling back the lump in her throat.

Darin leaned over and put his hand on hers. "That was beautiful."

"Thanks."

"I know it's hard for you. Letting her go."

Kendra closed her eyes a moment, then opened them to meet his. "It is."

He stood and offered her his hand. "Come take a walk with me."

"Um, we're kind of in the middle of a brunch here?"

"I don't think they'll miss us for a few minutes. Come on. Just a short little walk."

She watched his eyes twinkle and pushed her chair back. Taking his hand, Kendra followed Darin out of the fellowship hall and into the church courtyard.

A breeze rustled the trees, and she took in their blazing golds and oranges. The deep tones contrasted with the whisper-soft blue of a new sky.

Darin motioned for her to sit on a bench, and she did. He sat beside her, and his eyes were so earnest, so completely focused on her, that she lost all interest in the trees.

"Kendra, I am so sorry for what I did to you."

She put her fingers over his mouth. "Shh. We've been over that. We both did dumb things. We're both sorry, and we're both going to let it go, right?"

He pulled her hand down from his mouth and held it. "Right."

"So no more talking about it. What's done is done. It's over."

He kissed her palm and said, "The thing is, we're both going to mess up again."

"Hey, I have no plans for further mistakes, mister."

He grinned. "Of course you don't. I don't either. Nobody plans to mess up. They just do. I'm going to say or do something that hurts you, and you're going to say or do something that hurts me." He shrugged. "That's part of living in this fallen world. We don't get it right all the time."

"Well, this sounds like a really rosy future. Thanks so much for setting the scene. Glad I could be a part of the ride. Should I get off now?"

"That's what I wanted to talk to you about. Whenever we do the next dumb thing, I want you to know that I'm not going anywhere. I'm not getting off this ride. Ever."

"What?" Her eyes opened wide, and her heart pounded in her ears. "What are you saying?"

In a daze she watched him slide off the bench and go down on one knee, crinkling the fallen leaves lying on the ground. Hope, so long dead in her life, rose up and cheered.

"I'm saying, I'm not ever leaving you. And I hope you're not ever leaving me, even when I do dumb, hurtful things. I'm saying . . . I'm asking . . . Kendra Diane Sinclair, will you marry me?"

Kendra looked full into this face that had dominated her thoughts and dreams and heart since the first day she laid eyes on it. She thought about the good times and the dark, dark times. She remembered his face the day he learned about Harrison. And then looked at it again today, so full of unconditional love, she felt she'd die from its purity.

Even if they spent the rest of their days fighting — which was unlikely, given the past few months — she'd rather be fighting with him than at peace with anyone else. No matter what, she wanted to be by his side, living their lives together, listening to jazz, laughing about nothing and talking about everything. Happiness didn't — couldn't — exist outside of this man's presence in her life.

That knowledge opened not just her heart but her lips. "Yes, Darin." She leaned down to him, drinking in the perfect artful beauty of this day. "Yes, I'll marry you."

His grin grew and he took her face in his hands, long fingers gently grasping her skin.

"I love you, Darin Spenser."

"I love you, future Mrs. Darin Spenser."

And Kendra melted into him, knowing it wouldn't be a perfect happily ever after, but it would be a *real* happily ever after. And that was even better.

ABOUT THE AUTHOR

Rebeca Seitz loves to read, write, scrapbook, and spend time with her girlfriends. She's also founder and president of Glass Road Public Relations, a thriving entertainment publicity firm. Seitz lives with her husband and son in southern Kentucky, where they are busily renovating their 109-year-old home to make way for their second child.